MW01103578

We Are Still Here

We Are Still Here

C.J. BEUHLER

thistledown press

Copyright © C.J. Beuhler, 2005
All rights reserved

All rights reserved. No part of this publication may be reproduced or transmitted in any form or by any means, graphic, electronic or mechanical, including photocopying, recording, or any information storage and retrieval system, without permission in writing from the publisher. Requests for photocopying of any part of this book shall be directed in writing to Access Copyright, 1 Yonge Street, Suite 1900, Toronto, Ontario, M5E 1E5.

Library and Archives Canada Cataloguing in Publication

Beuhler, C. J. (Chris J.)
We are still here / C.J. Beuhler.

ISBN 1-894345-81-9

1. Innu—Juvenile fiction. I. Title.

PS8603.E93W4 2005   C813'.6   C2005-904854-9

Cover and book design by Jackie Forrie
Author Photo by Kim and Val Bennett
Printed in Canada

Thistledown Press Ltd.
633 Main Street, Saskatoon, Saskatchewan, S7H 0J8
www.thistledown.sk.ca

 Canada Council   Conseil des Arts   Canadian   Patrimoine
for the Arts   du Canada   Heritage   canadien

Thistledown Press gratefully acknowledges the financial assistance of the Canada Council for the Arts, the Saskatchewan Arts Board, and the Government of Canada through the Book Publishing Industry Development Program for its publishing program.

ACKNOWLEDGEMENTS

I wish to give special thanks to Madelon Smid. She is solely responsible for introducing me to the world of creative writing. She has spent untold hours constructively reviewing my work and mentoring. In the process, she has managed to lead a confirmed technocrat into the richest world of all . . . the world of imagination.

Thanks also to John Lent, my editor, who showed me so many ways to refine *We Are Still Here*.

CONTENTS

This book is dedicated to my life partner, Gail

SPIRITS OF RAVEN

Raven watched the human below his tree with intensity. He knew he must not make a sound and risk discovery. These human-beasts were extremely powerful hunters. As he watched, he was also aware of his own reduced powers. He was a weak old bird. Sitting still made him ache to his core and his vision had begun to fail. One day soon, he would be passing his spirit and his essence on to some other beast, hopefully one of his family.

The human crouched in the caribou moss, with shiny objects that he alternately held and put down, but the purpose of this man's actions was beyond Raven's ability to comprehend. His mind began to wander and he drifted back through his many years to the time that had created the need in him to return to this tree every mating season. There had been a terrible storm, coming late in the cold season. Yes, and the great roaring noise in the sky . . . so loud it had shaken the tree in which he'd slept.

Raven remembered when he was young and that morning after the storm when the light began to return.

He recalled his exuberance at seeing the dawn as he shook the snow from his feathers and clucked to himself. That night's snowstorm had forced him to seek shelter in the lower branches of his perch. Here, the neighboring trees lessened the moaning wind, and the higher boughs sheltered him from the wet snow. Perhaps today the caribou he had been following would die and he could feed. It had been many days now, and he was feeling the energy sapped from his flesh. The chill of the late spring morning had begun to penetrate his heavy down feathers. He had to feed today, or he would soon become carrion for some other beast.

He filled his wings with the morning air and stepped from his perch, diving first to gain speed, then flapping his wings a few times to regain his height. He soared in ever-increasing circles seeking the caribou.

Suddenly, fear deepened the physical chill he was feeling. What did he see? That smell, sweet and pungent at the same time. No beast he knew had this scent. Raven hovered on the wind, his eyes filled with what he saw below. The trail of this beast was huge. It had knocked down trees in its path and gouged through the snow to the ground underneath, throwing the earth back onto the snow alongside its path. What was this? His entire being filled with fear. He considered plunging to the treetops below to seek the best refuge he could find. So large a bird he had never seen, but it lay unmoving. Was it dead? It seemed to be losing its life force onto the ground, but the colour was clear, and that smell, sweet, yet so strong it almost burned his nostrils. This was truly a strange beast.

His hunger was strong and this much food would sustain him and every scavenger nearby for many moons. He glided closer, maintaining his height in case he needed to dive quickly for a refuge below.

Then he saw the human slowly emerging from the broken side of the bird's belly. He had seen a few humans before in his years. They were beasts to avoid. They killed many other beasts, but unlike others, they covered themselves with the skins of their prey. Raven decided to be prudent and leave the area.

His hunger was very strong by the time Raven found the now dead caribou. He quickly looked around for other beasts coming to the carrion. Seeing none, he dove to the ground and feasted. After gorging himself, he flew to a low branch to rest and observe any activity around his find. As he rested, he could feel the strength and warmth from the dead animal's flesh course into his being. He thanked the spirit of the caribou for giving him life, many more days of life. He slept and dreamed, of giant birds that swooped down on roaring wings consuming every beast they encountered. He awoke in the darkness, and felt safe hidden in blackness. He shifted on his perch and fell back to sleep, a sound sleep that lasted until the return of the light.

At dawn, Raven stretched his wings into the morning breeze and slipped silently into the air. The snow was melting now, but the huge path behind the giant bird was still plain to see. The bird was dead. It had not moved. He glided in for a closer look and saw the human on the ground just ahead of the bird. The human was moving with great difficulty, one leg strangely bound and not bending as he stumbled along. Raven decided it would be a long time before he would attempt to feed here. He wanted to keep his distance from the strange killing powers of humans.

As he watched, he saw the human move to the side of the dead bird, where he began removing some of the hide. To his surprise, the hide appeared hard and retained its shape after it was removed. This was indeed no ordinary beast. Raven would probably be unable to penetrate such a heavy hide. The caribou would be his best bet this spring. The human began to drag the piece of hide back to where he had emerged from the bird's belly. He re-entered the belly only to emerge a few moments later with his paws full of strange things. The bad leg was becoming red with the human's life force.

Had the human killed this huge bird and brought it to the ground? Raven was so terrified at the thought that he forgot to feel the air in his wings and almost stumbled out of his controlled flight. A quick flap of his wings and he regained his speed, but then he saw the man's face turn upward. *He will surely kill me now*, he thought. He folded his wings to his sides and instantly entered a dive.

The air began coursing through his feathers as he approached a speed he had never before dared to attempt. He dove behind the nearby hill and when out of sight, began to break his fall. He managed to summon enough strength to extend his wings into the screeching air and slow his descent, then he flew level and slowed further as he fought to regain his composure. His fear was not enough, however, to stay his natural curiosity. A short while later, he returned, soaring over the downed bird, but at a height greater than he had flown before.

The human was now on the water, sitting in the upturned piece of the bird's skin. A beautiful fish was in the skin beside him. The human took something shiny from his side, began removing pieces of the fish and eating it. Something else was shiny and much smaller, the golden colour of the sun. It glinted as the human worked on the fish and Raven began to covet this beautiful item for his nest.

Day after day, for two moons, Raven soared and watched as the human caught fish, then one day he was on the water again, but there were no fish. The human did not move, but seemed to stare up into the sky. The bad leg was dark brown now and as he approached, Raven sensed the odour of putrid flesh. Raven decided to be more cautious than usual since this was a human. He was unsure just how powerful a spirit these beasts possessed.

As the season progressed, it became clear that this human had no more powerful spirits than Raven, so Raven slowly became bolder, finally approaching closely, even feeding and attempting to acquire his shiny talisman.

Dawn arrived without a breath of air. As the sun's fire rose into the sky, its heat began to infuse everything it touched with warmth. A gentle mist began to rise from the water of the little lake and the water reflected the trees and sand in a perfect inverted picture of its shoreline.

Raven floated soundlessly in the sky above, skillfully moving from thermal to thermal as they rose from the land. Below him in the little boat, a few flies buzzed around, but they were fewer than in the past. Raven glided to the edge of the up-turned skin, flared and perched. A few tiny ripples, generated by his landing, rolled away across the water. He cocked his head to the side, looking down onto his coveted prize.

Day after day, he had returned, but it had eluded him. He hopped down into the boat and ambled toward the golden ring, rocking his body haltingly from side to side with each step. He grasped his coveted prize, jerked and twisted with all his might. The bones parted and fell to the bottom with a clatter. Raven leapt into the air with his prize and flew to his nest, where he gave the ring a place of honour among his trinkets.

He was convinced that such a striking object would attract a desirable mate. He happily spent the next few days finishing his nest and seeking a mate to show his prize. He spent most of his time now in the air, voicing his best male call and listening for a response. When it came, it was from below in a thicket about two miles from his nest. He circled slowly, his heart beating much harder than his physical efforts demanded. He uttered the coaxing call, hoping to bring her into the air where he could see her in flight. Nothing . . . no response, no motion in the thicket. *Perhaps she does not see me*, he thought. He made his most aerobatic wingover and sideslipped rapidly down toward the bush, repeating his coaxing call.

Then she was airborne, rising toward him, her flight feathers reflecting the sun's fire. He knew instantly she must be his mate. He dove and joined her climb, beginning the aerial dance of courtship unique to ravens. He would fly so close to her as to disrupt the airflow over her wings. The instant she bobbled, he would place his wing below hers, touching it ever so lightly to restore her flight. Then he would move above her, uttering loving chortles and feigning a descent onto her back.

At first, she dropped away instantly when he moved over her. He persisted. Eventually, she responded by flaring her tail-feathers, slowing her flight to the point of loosing the lift over her wings. Many more times, she would regain her speed at the last moment and resume controlled flight . . . teasing him. At last, she allowed herself to lose flight speed and they tumbled joyously toward the earth, he holding to her gently with his claws and beak.

They separated as they approached the ground, each regaining flight speed. He called to her, "Follow me," as he turned toward his nest. He regained altitude, circling regularly to ensure that she remained with him. At last, they were over his nest, about 100 feet above. She looked down and her eye caught the glint of golden light from the ring. She descended immediately to the nest and began to hide the beautiful trinket in the soft down at the bottom of the nest. His proposal had been accepted!

Thereafter, they were inseparable, flying and feeding together, strengthening their bond. At night, she would enter the nest to sleep and he would perch in the branches above her, standing guard. As the warm weather strengthened, she deposited two beautiful eggs in the nest. From this time on, he flew alone again, bringing food to her.

One dull, cloudy morning, she clucked to him, awakening him on his perch. He hopped down to see her rise from the nest, revealing two chicks. His work now began in earnest. He haunted the bears as they fished the streams, stealing every morsel he could for his brood. This was the season of plenty. He had to ensure their health and growth. The chicks grew quickly and he and his mate gained strength and vitality throughout the season.

In mid-summer, he was gathering fish from a recent bear-kill when he heard the sound that drives fear into every raven's heart. The arch enemy, Eagle, was screeching his victory call. With a sinking heart, he flew toward the sound, toward his nest.

Nothing remained in the tree. The nest was in tatters. His mate and chicks lay on the ground below. Immediately, he dove at the eagle, crying his defiance. The huge bird perched in a nearby tree with a shard of black-feathered flesh hanging from his beak. Raven dove, climbed, and cawed at the top of his lungs, his loss burning anger into his flesh and energizing him. Finally, Eagle tried to escape, and Raven went on the attack. Being a much smaller bird, he easily out-maneuvered his opponent. With each pass, he wrenched another feather from a wing, the tail, anywhere he could grab. Eagle began to labour to remain aloft, and Raven redoubled his efforts.

Exhausted, Eagle sank to the ground. Raven gave his best victory call, even though his heart was at its lowest ebb. The eagle would be unable to fly until his flight feathers grew back. This is the most vulnerable time for an eagle. This late in the season, he might well starve to death before flight returned to him. Raven vowed to stay and watch, vowed to bring every morsel he ate into the view of this eagle, to chase and harass him at every opportunity. He would see this enemy dead.

His mate had steadfastly remained on her nest, attempting to defend her brood. One pass had plucked her from the nest, breaking a wing and deeply wounding her back. Eagle had dropped her to the ground and left her to suffer while he plucked the chicks from the nest, then dropped them beside her. At his leisure, he descended and killed them, then tore them open, more in vengeance than to satisfy any hunger. After this, he had risen to a nearby tree to give his victory screech.

Raven returned to the site of his nest. Over the next days, he began to consume his mate and chicks. While eating, he tried to bring their spirits into his own, but they were not here. Eagle had taken them. He fashioned a rough nest of twigs and transported their bones, one by one, to the nest where they would remain for him to visit. He searched for the ring, but could not locate it. This was the talisman that had brought her to him, and he wanted to retrieve it for her, but could not. Heavy-hearted, he flew to a nearby tree to spend the night.

Raven remained in the area for two full moons, daily visiting his nest and daily harassing Eagle. It was weakening, and Raven took every opportunity to dive and pluck yet another feather, risking his life with each attack. After the second moon, he found Eagle dead at the base of a tree. He dropped to the ground and gorged himself on the finest parts of the bird, taking its spirit into him and regaining the spirits of his mate and chicks. Now this eagle's spirit too would spend its eternity in the heart of Raven.

Season after season Raven trekked back to his nest to relive memories of his brood. The area had suffered a dying of the trees, from the tiny pests that infest all of nature from time to time. For this reason, he now lived many days away, where the feeding was still plentiful. As he aged, Raven found the trek increasingly difficult, his aging wings and poorer flight feathers sapping his strength a little more each time he came. The nest and bones had long-ago disappeared. Though he looked every year, the ring remained elusive. He sat perched in his old tree, now a rotting spur into the sky. He slept and dreamed of his home so long ago.

He woke to the roar of another hard-skinned bird. As he watched from his perch, it landed on the water, then it floated, spluttering, its nose whirling, to the centre of the lake. It stopped there and two humans emerged from its belly to stand on the two boats upon which the bird floated. They looked down into the water at the old boat lying on the bottom, the boat where Raven had gained his prize talisman.

They re-entered the bird's belly, and it spluttered into life and the nose whirled. It moved slowly to the shore, where again it stopped. The humans emerged and began taking many strange bundles from the bird. One human remained on shore with the bundles, raised his paw into the air and waved it side to side. The bird coughed yet again, and moved out onto the lake. Around and around it went on the water, roaring louder than the waterfalls in the mountains, then it rose into the air, its roar subsiding to an ominous rumble. Much faster than any bird Raven knew, it flew from sight.

Raven turned his attention to the human who remained, and who opened the bundles and scattered things around on the shore. The human made a large brightly skinned, overturned nest, then moved the other bundles inside. After a time, he approached Raven's tree with two shiny objects in his paws and a bundle on his back. The old raven watched the human below his tree with intensity. The human had not looked up, so he must not make a sound and risk discovery. These human-beasts were extremely powerful hunters.

As he watched, he sensed a strong spirit. This was a spirit made up of many generations of the beasts and humans in this being's history. Like himself, this was a powerful being of nature, in harmony with the land and sky and waters. His interest grew and his fear began to subside. He was calmed by this man's respectful actions and by the strange droning sounds he created with his voice.

The human took the shiny objects, joined them with a flexible stem and pointed one of them at the caribou moss. To Raven's astonishment caribou moss appeared on the upwards extended leaf of the second shiny object. It was so enlarged as to reveal the minuscule blossoms on the stems of the plant. This was indeed powerful magic. This human could create many things, Raven sensed. Warming rays of sunlight shone down on them, making the moss on the leaf turn white and almost disappear. The human turned as if to retrieve something else from his bundle when he froze in mid-motion.

As Raven watched, the human bowed to the ground, reached out and produced the greatest magic of all — the treasured ring!

The old raven cawed raucously from the tree above. His fear evaporated. He had spied the one remaining thing in his life that he needed to re-connect his spirit to his brood, to the human who had given him life force those many days . . . the treasured ring. He stumbled from his perch and flapped to the ground in a frenzy of wings beating, uttering his loudest alarm call. He flopped to the ground not far from the human, turned his eye to him and glared fixedly into the man's eyes. He ruffled his feathers to appear as large and fierce as possible, but his efforts seemed only to emphasize his great age.

The human seemed duly alarmed by his cacophonous arrival, so much so that they both remained in their relative positions for what seemed a long time. Slowly, the human reached out with the ring in his up-turned paw. Raven remained motionless a few seconds longer, then slowly stepped forward, turning from side to side and clucking softly.

The human remained motionless. Encouraged, the old raven reached slowly into the man's paw and gently took the ring. He held it tenderly in his beak, absorbing the last of the spirits he needed. His life was now complete; he had re-connected with the spirits of the ring. Tenderly, Raven placed the ring back into the man's paw.

The human spoke in Inuktitut to the old raven, "Go now, Raven. May your spirit soar always. You will be known to humans as Iniktuk."

The old raven stumbled into the air and flew haltingly to his tree. Having completed his final contact with all of his spirits, he was at peace with the world. The remaining spirits in the talisman needed this human to connect them with their home.

Man's Encounter with Raven

A tortured screaming croak came from the tree above him. Startled, Hinoch looked up to see a bedraggled old raven literally tumbling to the ground. It managed a landing of sorts, then fixed him with the eye of many souls. Hinoch recognized he was in the presence of a Great Spirit of nature. He sat respectfully awaiting Raven's next action. His mind was racing. *Of course! The ring! Ravens are notorious in their attraction to shiny things. It may have been his courting talisman when he had been a young bird.*

He extended his hand and slowly opened it, revealing the ring. Instantly, Raven's focus moved to the ring and after a short while, he began to approach with the uncertain weaving action ravens have when caught between their fears and their desires. Gently, the bird picked the ring out of his hand and held it. Hinoch could sense he was re-connecting with old memories and spirits attached to that talisman. Then tenderly, Raven returned the ring to his hand.

This raven is now at peace, I see it in his eyes, he thought. Hinoch spoke in Inuktitut to the old raven, "Go now, Raven, may your spirit soar always. You will be known to humans as Iniktuk."

The old bird flew to a nearby tree and perched. Hinoch felt he had been dismissed and that he would not see the old bird again. Somewhat flustered, he returned to his original activity.

On this particular spring morning, he had found a beautifully lit patch of caribou moss. Fiddleheads were poking their first tentative fronds into the light, ready for picking nearby. There would be a feast in his camp tonight! He had his digital camera set up with the extreme close-up lens attached. He was monitoring the quality of the colour and the lighting through the data link from the camera to his notebook computer. Caribou moss was one of the prettiest plants in Labrador. At this degree of magnification, it looked like something from another world, alien yet beautiful. To appreciate the intricacies of the plant; however, an extreme close-up was necessary.

As he worked, he began to sing an old chant to nature his father had taught him as a child. When he was alone in the outdoors, he always liked the sound of this old song. While he sang, Hinoch snapped the photos, then began to pack his equipment up to return to his campsite. He wanted to transfer these photos to a CD before his batteries began to fail.

His attention returned to the ring. It was coated with the decay of many years of plants, half buried in the soil as it had been. It was strange how he had glimpsed the golden reflection in the moss as he turned to get his light meter. He rubbed the ring vigorously in his shirt to remove some of the dirt. It came up quite nicely, and he began to examine it. As he was doing this he noticed that the inside bore an inscription. He read, "Forever . . . Dianne."

The photograph completely forgotten, he sat back onto the moss-covered ground and contemplated his find. How could this ring have come to lie here, 80 miles inland from the Labrador coastal community of Cartwright? To whom did the ring belong and how long ago had it been lost?

A haunting chill ran through Hinoch's body. His instincts told him this could not be a happy story, even if the owner had merely lost the ring while on a hunting trip. With the sensitivity of a native of this land, he knew that a dramatic series of events belonged to the history of this find. "There are many spirits attached to this ring," he said, sensing the power of its past. All these thoughts came to him gradually as he sat in the sun, time passing without notice. The lowering sun and cooling of the breeze brought him back to the moment.

Hinoch returned to his camp, transferred the photos to CD, ate and climbed into his sleeping bag, determined to get an early start in the morning. He would leave this tree to its spirits and begin an organized search of the area. Sleep came easily as it always did when he was on the land, the sleep of a baby untouched by the cares of the world.

The next morning dawned with a stiff breeze from the north. Hinoch studied the topographical map of the area, hoping to identify a landmark that he could use as a benchmark for his search. He determined that the hill four miles west would be visible for some ten miles in any direction. He decided to begin his search pattern from this promontory.

To his surprise, as he passed the old snag, Iniktuk watched him intently from the top-most branch. He was not one hundred feet past the tree when the old bird flew past and perched a few hundred feet ahead of him. This occurred repeatedly as he made his way to the hill. He was being led. Did this old raven understand what he was doing? As he approached the hill, he noticed the bird was more to his north and west, over an area of newer scrub growth and thickets.

I will climb the hill, set the trip start on my Global Positioning System, then start searching where Raven is waiting. That way I will have accurate coordinates to eliminate repeating the ground I cover. Once I am down in that thicket, it will be very slow going indeed.

Iniktuk circled slowly in the sky to the northwest of the hill, and then descended, landing on a tall pine at the edge of the undergrowth. The old raven must be tired, he thought to himself. I wonder if he will wait to see if I follow him?

The view from the top of the hill was so expansively beautiful that Hinoch paused, absorbing it. There is not a camera made that can capture this feeling, he thought. I am always amazed at the rolling expanse of hills shading from blue to hazy shadows in the distance. This type of vista is far too immense for any glass lens to capture. Hinoch set his hand-held GPS to his present coordinates, then set the record feature to track his movements through the bush below.

The sun was gaining height in the sky and the bush became warm, with a fog of blackflies swarming in the hazy rays. Hinoch took some oil, infused with juniper and pine tar, from his pack and rubbed it onto his exposed skin. Best way to avoid being bitten by a blood sucker is to smell like a tree! He chuckled to himself, remembering his father showing him how to make the potion. It had saved him from many an unpleasant day in the wilderness.

There was plenty of sign in the area from caribou. They were moving inland to avoid the pressure of hunting from the settlements along the coast, but the grazing was harder here too and many starved in bad winters. Hinoch's people were suffering too, finding it increasingly difficult to hunt enough game to get them through the winters. Hunters came from the cities every year and took many trophies, leaving the valuable meat to rot where it fell.

Nature will give freely to those who are not greedy, he thought. Maybe someday the people from the city will learn that they do not need to hoard things of false value and destroy everything they encounter. Take only what you need and leave the rest. It will multiply and ensure your tomorrows.

He had travelled forty yards through the bush when he again felt the presence of the old raven, but he could not see him through the dense undergrowth. He stopped and listened. "Caw, Caw, Caw," Iniktuk called to him from his right, deeper in the undergrowth. He chastised himself, Here is a twentieth century man following an old bird through the wilderness! It is a good thing my university friends are not here to see me now!

The bush became a thicket, so dense he had to begin cutting a path with his machete. His progress became measurable in inches.

"Caw, Caw, Caw."

"All right, All right, it is easy for you, you do not have to slug it out down here in the bugs and trees," he puffed aloud as he struggled to make headway. He heard a soft chortle and looked up to see the old bird circling slowly overhead with that fixed intense gaze focused down onto him. "It is my turn to rest, Iniktuk . . . lunch time!"

The old bird clucked sharply and flew fifty feet or so ahead, then disappeared into the bush below. "Caw, Caw, Caw!"

"Okay, Okay, I am coming, but I expect you to have the table set for two!" He continued on, hacking his way through the bush. With a "Thunk," his blade struck hard, sinking into rotting wood then ringing against metal. "The plane!" Hinoch was sweating and breathless, but climbed up onto the hulk of the old bomber.

From his vantage atop the old war-bird, he could see the hill, not 500 yards away. He set the new coordinates into his GPS as the destination point.

"I am less than two hundred yards from my camp! I certainly came here by the round-about route!" His mood became more somber as he surveyed the site. This feels like a final resting place, he thought.

The crash had wrought severe damage, but the immensely strong airframe of the old Mosquito had remained largely intact. Even the flight deck had survived the impact, but the bent control column told the story of heavy contact between the pilot and the instrument panel. He could see now by the growth of bush over the plane that it would have been unlikely that he would ever have found it alone, from land, or in the air.

"He was probably badly injured," Hinoch wondered aloud. "I wonder if he lived for any time. Maybe he built that old kayak at the bottom of the lake."

His thoughts were all but confirmed when he looked at the right side engine, then the left. The cowling had been removed, not torn from the right engine and what he had seen at the bottom of the lake resembled the remaining cowling. "Probably was him," he mused.

Were there not usually two crew members on these? he asked himself. He began to look around for signs of someone else around the site. He stopped and looked up again toward the hill, then to the west. He thought he saw Iniktuk flying into the distance.

A stout, weathered stake in the ground just ahead of the nose of the plane looked like a possibility for a gravesite, so he climbed down from the fuselage for a closer look. The ground had sunk in front of the stake and rocks bordered the depression. The stake was a tree stump about three inchès thick that someone had chopped down using a small blade. He kneeled beside the site and spoke softly, filled with respect for this unfortunate soul.

"I think I can assume you were the first to die here. May your spirit live on in peace."

Hinoch moved to the side of the fuselage, clearing the brush away from the wreck to allow him a better look at the entire plane. As he came to the rear quarter of the fuselage, he could make out the faded letters "KTL." The letters had a faded Roundel located between the "K" and the "T." Later, alongside the nose, he found a faint picture of a scantily clad girl with the name above it "Katie-Lee." He spent the next two hours taking digital photos to document the crash site. He took as many shots of the airframe as possible, as well as of the moniker and the call letters with the Roundel. He even photographed the serial number on the exposed engine and the interior of the cockpit.

He decided he was going to spend the night. Rather than risk missing some important detail through hurrying, he would sleep here, then go over the site again thoroughly the next day. He gathered some cedar boughs and spread them to form a thick mat inside the fuselage. This would serve nicely as a makeshift bed. He ate some of his dry rations and very soon was asleep.

✦✦✦

Patter, patter, patter. The soft sound of a light rain on the fuselage slowly brought Hinoch to a state of awareness. Before he opened his eyes, he remembered where he was from the strong, sweet smell of cedar encapsulating him in the confined space of the airplane. He got up, chewed some dry rations and donned his rain suit before stepping outside. In the murky sky above, he saw a young raven, circling around him, watching his every move.

Hinoch completed his documentation of the crash site and was now eager to return to his computer so he could transfer his pictures to a CD-ROM. This way, he would have a more permanent record of his find. He struck out for his campsite using the hill as a visual reference point and his GPS to home in on the coordinates he had placed there when he set up camp. Once out of the heavy bush, it took only another minute to reach his campsite.

He looked back on his route. The plane was completely hidden, yet so close. He could see now that this new growth had sprung up from the swath cut by the aircraft as it skidded to its present resting place. He went into his tent and transposed the coordinates of the wreck site carefully to his map.

Hinoch spread his dingy out onto the beach, then retrieved the pump. He inserted the spigot of the pump into the valve, first wetting the spigot to ease its insertion. The rubber of the pump and the flapper valve wheezed rhythmically as he worked to inflate the small craft. When it was ready, he pushed it into the water of the little lake and stepped aboard. Soon after, he had a beautiful Brown Trout in the boat with him and was about to return to shore when he heard the raven in the sky above him. He looked up, then down and shivered as he saw, some thirty feet below, the other cowling of the plane. It was a crude approximation of a kayak. In the shell, he saw bones . . . human bones. In a rush of realization, he felt linked to the spirits he was encountering. Emotionally chilled, he paddled to shore.

The trout sizzled over the stove's intense little flame and the smell of freshly cooked fish quickly awakened his youthful appetite.

Ahh, fresh trout and fiddleheads for lunch. Life could not be better, he thought to himself. Unless a vision of beauty were to walk out of the woods about now. "An unlikely thought," he chuckled aloud.

He finished his meal and sat back to relax for the afternoon.

His thoughts returned to the kayak in the lake. It took a little time to make that boat, so the survivor must have been reasonably healthy, at least for awhile. Once he began catching fish, his prospects would have improved greatly, so what finally finished him? Did an injury become infected? Did the bugs suck him dry, or just drive him mad, so that he sank the boat to get away from them? These black-flies have driven many a person to madness. His thoughts raced on through the afternoon as he rested in his camp. Toward evening, he noticed that the old snag now had a roughly built nest in its highest branches. The young raven seemed to be feeding on something in that nest.

Day after tomorrow, the plane will return, weather permitting, so I had better be ready to load up by that morning. I wonder if I should go back to the site and take something as physical proof of what I have found? He thought better of that idea, No, that does not seem right somehow, I will leave that decision to the Air Force Museum, since that will likely be the object of my first inquiry for information on this flight.

Again, he spent a leisurely day, enjoying the stark beauty of Labrador in spring. This was his home, the place he knew he belonged. He was as much at ease here as city people in their living rooms. He made some beautiful photographs, even capturing a shot of the young raven who seemed so intent upon following his activities.

The Single Otter arrived as planned, skimming to a stop at the shoreline, the propeller making its last revolution as the pontoons touched the beach. They gathered up his gear and loaded it into the plane, chatting about the success of the trip, but Hinoch kept his spiritual revelations to himself. They taxied out onto the lake, circled to gain airspeed and ripple the surface of the water to free the floats. After take-off, they flew directly to the crash site and circled over it. Hinoch could see it clearly, now that he had cleared the bush away, but he doubted if he would have spotted it otherwise.

The flight to Nain was smooth and uneventful. Although somewhat pre-occupied, Hinoch thoroughly enjoyed the company of the pilot and the vistas of Labrador below them. He knew he would spend his next days absorbed in the search for information about this old warplane. The urge to solve the mystery was building rapidly.

QUEST

The dial-up line to the Internet was slow the next morning, but he managed to find the website for the Royal Canadian Air Force Museum in Ottawa. He composed an e-mail detailing his find, including a few photos showing the aircraft identification symbols. Signing off, he hoped that they would have some information for him soon. He wanted to resolve the growing need within himself to return the ring to its rightful home.

Three days later, Hinoch woke to a strange sound on the roof of his home. *"Ssssssh, tick"*, pause, *"Ssssssh, tick."* He pulled his curtains and looked out into the lane.

Fresh snow, this will kill many insect pests, coming this late in spring . . . good!

"Sssssh, tick."

"What *is* that?" Hinoch puzzled. He jumped into his clothes and mukluks and stepped outside. His metal roof had three streaks where the snow had slipped off the roof and a young female raven perched on its peak. As he watched, she stepped from the peak and slid down the roof, *"Sssssssssh, tick."* Her claws made the tick as they slid off the edge, where, wings now outstretched; she glided to her perch atop a nearby pole.

She was having a grand old time in the snow, playing like a child on a hillside. It was impossible for Hinoch to ignore the sense that this was the second bird he had met three days ago at his camp near the plane wreck. He felt the conviction rising within that this bird was directly related to the old raven he had encountered so memorably just days ago. He smiled at her, fencing playfully with her beak on the light standard and scrambling to remain perched on the slippery street light.

"Enjoy your day my friend, tonight will be very cold," he predicted. In Inuktitut he spoke to her, "I will call you Tuk." He turned, feeling the chill air now through his shirtsleeves.

Hinoch had a playful nature as well, so while eating his breakfast he prepared a cord with some dried caribou jerky tied to one end. Later that morning he went out and tied it about six inches below his clothesline, turned and went immediately inside. At his window, he sat down to watch the fun. Before long, the inquisitive raven was balancing on the clothesline, trying to reach the tasty morsel suspended below. It took her only a few minutes to abandon attempts to reach down and remain perched. She simply hung by one claw, holding the tasty morsel in the other, feeding contentedly. In no time, she had eaten every bit. Then, she simply dropped while extending her wings. Two powerful flaps and she righted herself, then flew to her perch, congratulating herself with a sound that Hinoch interpreted as happy chuckles.

Hinoch went to his computer and loaded his photo-editing program. He felt somehow disconnected from the nature photos he had taken. He reviewed them peremptorily and edited some of them for contrast and lighting; then printed them. These images became subject guides for his drawings, to which he added his artistic interpretation. Hinoch used parchment and artists' pencil for his work.

The prints made from his originals were gaining worldwide renown, commanding handsome prices. *National Geographic* had selected some of his photos in the past; he was hoping for an assignment from them in the future. He felt at ease selling signed prints of his drawings, but he drew the line at the mass-produced, unsigned prints that some artists called their bread and butter. He looked at the computer printed pictures, but none of them spoke to him. He returned to the computer, still needing a photo that could inspire him.

He found himself looking at the photos of the old Mosquito bomber. He focused on the photo taken on that hazy, rainy morning. As he stared, he began to sing his Nature Song. Effortlessly, his mind drifted into a meditative state. Was it just the weather of that morning, or something more? Something was drawing him to this image.

The printed picture was disappointing; it did not possess the same nuances of light and shade necessary for the effect he wanted to create in his drawing. Hinoch returned to the computer, adjusting the light and grain-iness of the photo to see if he could enhance the effect. Finally, with a second printout, he had something he felt in his mind worthy of interpretation. He turned to his easel with the picture in hand. This would be a new subject. He usually avoided drawing man-made things; they seemed so bereft of feeling. This one was different though, compelling him. He clipped it to the side of the easel.

With minimal reference to the photo, Hinoch drew an accurate representation of the aircraft and the surrounding bush. Consciously freeing his spirit, he started to draw the trees and the mist over the plane. Hours went by. Exhausted, Hinoch sat back to look at his work from a less detailed perspective. It would be an interesting picture, he thought, but it still needed something. He decided to stop for the day.

This routine repeated itself for four days, days consumed entirely with his undivided efforts to interpret this image correctly.

The morning of the last day, he awoke to two children laughing and playing outside his home. They were throwing snowballs, each emitting piercing squeals whenever one hit home. Hinoch watched them for awhile until they saw him looking out at them. Immediately, they dropped their hands full of snow and ran to his door.

Without knocking, or asking permission they bounded in, tracking snow across his linoleum floor, slipping and sliding on its shiny surface. They piled onto the bed with him, laughing and squirming in a true fit of giddy happiness.

"Morning 'Noch," one finally mumbled as they quieted themselves.

"Good morning, Monty, Dick. You seem to be enjoying the morning."

"The snow's too cold for good snowballs. They fall apart in a cloud of powder when they are flying through the air. You only get a snow-wash when they hit."

"Good thing you boys wash now and then," Hinoch joked with them.

"We wash with seal oil, water's no good," they replied. "You're cold all the time if you wash with water!"

"Would you like some toast? I have Partridge berry jam."

The boys smiled broadly at this prospect, so Hinoch bade them remove their sealskin parkas and boots. Then he gave them a rag to wipe up the floor. He donned his sweat suit and began making the toast and setting the table. The boys had moved to the window and were giggling at something they saw. This was their second home, maybe their favorite home, judging by the time they spent here. Hinoch suspected their parents abused them quite frequently.

"What's going on out there . . . another snowball fight?"

"No, a silly blackbird."

"That is a raven. Blackbirds are much smaller and they live further south. What is it doing?"

"Turning the street lights on."

Hinoch went to the window and looked outside. Sure enough, Tuk had roosted on a streetlight, sitting on the electric eye. Sensing darkness, the photocell had activated the light. "She was not born with a foolish mind. She is warming herself. She is truly a cunning spirit, cunning far beyond her years."

"'Noch, why do you always call animals spirits?" Monty asked.

"My father has taught me that each animal has a spirit, but that some have collected the wisdom of many spirits and are very powerful. This bird is just such a being."

"How do animals collect spirits?" Dick sprawled on the floor, sliding his feet back and forth on the slick linoleum.

"First, they are sensitive enough to be aware of another animal's spirit, then as they eat that animal, they consciously invite that animal's spirit to continue living within them." Hinoch made the motions of a comforting embrace, trying to defuse their concerns.

"What if they don't?"

"Then the dead animal's spirit floats free and is lost in nature." Hinoch raised his hands, palms upward, his eyes darting around the room.

"What happens to you when you take in a spirit?" With a thump, Monty joined Dick on the floor.

"You gain the wisdom of nature that spirit possesses. This way, you understand the workings of the world you live in better. If you take in the spirit of a hunter, you gain those skills, either to hunt better yourself, or to survive if you are hunted."

"Do you eat dead people?" Monty asked, apparent disgust in his voice.

"No Monty, we transfer our spirits to each other when we are still alive through our teachings, our songs and with the brotherhood ceremony."

"What's that?" Dick interjected, rolling onto his stomach, hands under his chin. He was settling in for a good story.

"Two people who have become close may share their spirits by composing a song of brotherhood. Whenever they sing the song, their spirits are together."

There was a short silence as the boys absorbed this idea, then Monty asked, "Are there evil spirits?"

"No, only spirits following their own dictates of nature. City-man is the only one who perceives evil in the world."

Both boys showed their naïve concern. Dick blurted, "Why do they do that?" They were engrossed now, concentration written on their young faces.

"Because they do not understand. They see something happen that is different from what they think should occur, so they call it wrong . . . evil."

Monty played with a thread hanging from the sleeve of his shirt, finally wrapping it around his finger and pulling it, leaving a frayed cuff.

"How many spirits have you eaten?" he asked, still focusing on his cannibalistic impression.

"Many. I invite the spirit of all flesh I consume to join my spirit."

"Can we do that too?" Dick blurted, sensing an adventure.

"If you are willing to learn how to become aware of the spirit and accept it into your life."

The boys fell silent; toast was ready and their young appetites had assumed precedence over conversation. Later, Monty asked, "Do toast and jam have spirits?"

"Yes, when the wheat was alive in the field and the partridge berries were on the plant."

"Where are they now?" Monty asked, stirring a crust of bread into a smear of jam near the edge of his plate.

"Most likely, they died without an aware spirit nearby, so they are floating around in nature."

Dick, always the hunter, asked, "Can you catch a free spirit?"

"Yes, if they attached it to something important in their lives, it can reside there until someone becomes aware of it and invites it into their own spirit."

"Can you do magic?"

"No, Monty, magic is a city man's tricks and deception."

The boys slipped away from the table and began to gather their parkas and mukluks.

"Thanks for toast 'Noch, see ya!" They pulled on their mukluks and bounded out the door, parkas in hand, flapping wildly behind them.

I need to think! Hinoch pulled his jacket over his head and stepped outside. He looked around his village, tucked in the protection of the valley, against the shoreline of the bay. It was a collection of poorly built shanties and shacks. The two best buildings were his metal-roofed, one-room cabin and the General Store perched at the head of the concrete dock.

Twice a year, the ferry came with heavy provisions, then the mail and light freight came Monday and Friday on the old "Lab Air" Single Otter from Goose Bay. That was it. Other than the odd snowmobile snarling its way through the gaps between buildings and children playing, the sea breeze was the only constant sound.

Hinoch scanned the village he valued so much as a sanctuary, filled with his people, people he understood.

My father insists on living in the north, hunting, fishing and gathering wild plants in season. He wants the same life for me, but our people here in Nain would all lose the Inuit ways if I went back to the wilderness. I remember the impoverished life of our people then: alcohol, drugs and despair everywhere. The best thing I can do is to spend my winters with my father and mother, help them and learn the ways of our people. I wish it was easier to travel to them year round, but the valley my parents live in is impassable, except when the snow is deep. They are getting too old to be out there alone, but they refuse to give up their connection to the land. My father has told me many times he would prefer to starve on the land than live in one of these missionary villages. I have offered many times to fly in provisions, but he refuses to accept them saying, "I will not become dependent upon anything that nature does not provide me directly."

Hinoch remembered them, as they were when he was a child. He had grown to ten years with them, then he had become sick with infection from a black-fly bite. They had brought him to Nain in a dangerous trip by rowboat to see the nurse. He recovered quickly, but his life changed forever.

Hinoch vividly recalled how the nurse had enlisted the help of the RCMP Special Constable. She had been determined he would stay with his uncle here in Nain and attend school. Hinoch remembered his loving old uncle and how he had learned to love school. Hinoch had been a brilliant student, eventually earning a full scholarship for Laval University in Montreal. How his life had changed then.

Hinoch shrugged off his thoughts, turned and strolled back inside. He removed his mukluks and returned to his sketch. Was it his fertile imagination, or truly a trick of light? He stood before his easel, transfixed. There, enhanced in the morning light, was the faint image of a young man's face. Dark recesses in the trees became the pupils of the eyes. The curve of the bushes below outlined his lips and chin.

Hinoch sat back on his stool, mesmerized by what he had unconsciously created. Maybe not all city people had impoverished spirits.

His thoughts flowed at random at first, then began to gel. *Unfortunately, all I have to go on are the barest of facts and the sense that the old raven was indeed, a Great Spirit. I am certain he possessed the spirits of those airmen. It seems to me that Tuk harbours a greater spirit than a young bird like her would normally possess. I can only assume I have encountered two Torngaks . . . so close together in time. My father taught me that spirits are handed down from one generation to the next. Yes, the old raven's spirits have been transferred — the handing on of a spiritual legacy.*

I am amazed by these events and my responsiveness to them. My own spirit feels much more powerful. I am becoming a shaman. My father's teachings and the quality of my encounters in nature have reached the point where I am now confident I can take my place as a leader and a shaman.

I know my father is pleased in his heart that I have always taken his teachings seriously. He is pleased and confident I will use his wisdom to help my people. I must keep them focused on the traditional meaning of life. I am anxious to return to my father's cabin this winter. I have many experiences to share and I know, many more teachings to master.

The drawing was now so familiar to Hinoch he saw the young man's face as an integral part of the picture. He knew there was a higher purpose to this drawing, and he decided others needed to see it. At his computer, Hinoch e-mailed his agent in Montreal.

Lucien delighted at the prospect of another work from Hinoch, especially when he heard that it would be a departure from his usual type of work. He immediately arranged the transportation of the original. Once duplicated, he planned to return it and the prints by airfreight for Hinoch's authentication.

Hinoch appreciated that Lucien was a successful agent. He knew Lucien extended himself for each client, ensuring their work penetrated the market as completely as their talent and its medium allowed. Lucien had great plans for Hinoch's works.

From the beginning, Hinoch's works had haunted him. They had a simple beauty that had attracted his critical eye immediately, but he knew he would have a tough time dealing with Hinoch's aversion to the idea of marketing his name and personality. Lucien had sensed the powerful feelings that Hinoch was able to project through his drawings. He knew Hinoch could become a household word if he were willing to become a marketed personality. He also knew that he would have a difficult task persuading him to pursue that kind of career.

Hinoch had roomed with Lucien in Montreal while they attended Laval University. Perhaps wisely, perhaps by sheer chance, the matron of the dormitory had placed the two shy, socially awkward boys together. Lucien came from wealth and lacked nothing in a material sense, yet he was shy and reclusive. Hinoch had only a few clothes and his precious copy of *Oliver Twist*.

In a short period of time, they had formed a communication less dependent upon language than upon actions and expressions. Lucien spoke broken English, with huge gaps in his vocabulary; Hinoch spoke like the textbooks he had studied. Their mutual feelings of inadequacy had bound them together in an alliance against the pressures they felt on campus. They had become close friends, enjoying a bond that they never felt the need to question. Their feelings for one another had formed quickly, born of their need for the support of a kindred spirit.

Hinoch remembered clearly the day they had composed their song of brotherhood. Lucien had told him years later that he sang the song as he worked. He claimed it helped him concentrate.

Hinoch was eager to have the original drawing back in his possession. He very rarely sold an original for the simple reason that he could not part with them. He strolled out of his house toward the general store. He needed some eggs and flour, but most importantly, he wanted to check his mail. He was impatiently awaiting a response from the Aircraft Museum in Ottawa, somehow anticipating great excitement on their behalf. He opened his mailbox and immediately saw the monogrammed envelope. *The letter is here!* He pulled it from his other mail and opened it on the spot. He read.

Dear Sir:
We very much appreciate learning of your discovery of the Mosquito bomber "KTL." It is indeed fortunate that your discovery arrived at the time it did. Until very recently, records of these ferry-flights were classified "Top Secret," since at the time, the Mosquito was truly a revolutionary example of aviation technology.
The aircraft you have discovered flew from Winnipeg, Manitoba, to Goose Bay, Labrador, on May 22, 1942. The following day, it departed for Iceland and was assumed lost at sea sometime later.
As for your request for information on the flight crew, it is not our policy to release classified information to persons not directly related to the lost airmen. We do this out of respect for the families. We will attempt, however, to contact the family. If successful, and the family is receptive, we will relay your information.
As for the aircraft, we will place it on our list of located wrecks. It is hoped that, at some time in the future, funds will come available for its recovery and restoration.
Thank you again for contacting us with your information.
Sincerely,
WO T. McDonald, CD

Hinoch believed this avenue of investigation would produce nothing more. His previous experience with government offices did not encourage him to expect them to make any significant effort on his behalf. They were not even interested in seeing the plane, and it had taken sixty years for them to open the flight information to the public. At that rate of disclosure, he would be with his own family's spirits long before they found the aviators' families.

The copies of the Mosquito drawing arrived on the next flight from Labrador City and Goose Bay. As usual, Lucien had boxed them up like a precious piece of glassware. He always packed the prints tightly between two sheets of plywood with the edges heavily padded; it seemed virtually impossible for them to incur damage. Indeed, a print had never arrived from Lucien that was creased, or bent. Hinoch made a practice of saving the box for the return of the authenticated and signed prints.

Back in his house, he first removed the original, then one by one, he removed and inspected the prints. The reproduction was flawless. As in the original, if you looked long and hard enough, the face of the young airman would form in the mist. Hinoch sat back in his chair and mused over the pictures like a father dreaming of the future of his children. His dreams were not of success and fame, but of the prints finding homes with kindred spirits who would appreciate them, see the faint face of the airman, and honour his spirit.

"The name . . . what is this drawing's name?" Hinoch droned aloud the old nature song taught to him by his father. He rocked in the chair, closed his eyes and sang. He drifted away and returned in his mind to his dinghy on the lake. His mind looked down into the water at the kayak on the bottom, then it floated over the trees to the old aircraft. The face was hovering in the mist over the old aircraft. The lips were moving, mouthing, "We are still here!"

Hinoch rocked slowly, his eyes slid open as his vision rose into his conscious mind. *These spirits are far from their families. They want to be with them. This ring has begun its journey as a talisman for the family. I have nothing that belongs to the other man, yet I sense his spirit somehow joined the owner of this ring. I hope the families have maintained contact.*

We are still here! Number1. Hinoch. He signed the first print, then set it on his easel. After a few moments he said, "Yes, that is your name." He immediately went to work titling, numbering and signing the rest of the prints. This done, he re-packed them for the return flight to Montreal the next day. He carried the box to the General Store and pre-paid its shipment.

He felt that he could relax. These last few hours he'd felt an uncommon sense of urgency. His stomach was tight, his throat ached, but he pushed himself on, working feverishly. These feelings were strange to Hinoch and he was glad that they were subsiding.

Hinoch settled down to his computer.

Dear Lucien,
I have signed and authenticated all of the prints. They will depart on the morning flight. You should receive them tomorrow evening. Could you send some of the prints to a gallery in Winnipeg and give them some publicity there? I received a letter from the Air Force museum in Ottawa saying that the airmen on this plane were based there. Who knows, someone might recognize the old plane and contact us. Please make sure you put my bio on the backs and frame them with the old barn-board wood.
Thanks,
Hinoch.

It was admittedly a thin thread, but he had faith Lucien would understand.

Hinoch was becoming obsessed by the ring. He could not leave it in his home; he felt he was abandoning something, or someone. Eventually, he wore it around his neck on a strong leather thong. Even there, he was constantly aware of it, as if it were influencing him subtly.

Two days later, the phone rang . . . an unusual occurrence in his home. He picked up the receiver. "Hello."

"*Bonjour, mon ami*! I received the prints last night; you were unusually prompt this time." His caller paused a moment then observed, "You're anxious about this one *n'est-ce pas?*"

"It was a great experience to find this old plane, Lucien. It has been lost for so long in the woods. I seemed to make a connection with it and identify with the people on board. It would be nice if the families knew where they were."

"Yes, it must be difficult for a family when one of them just disappears like that. Like a story with no ending. Anyway, there's a nice gallery in the Old Forks District of Winnipeg that'll be happy to receive some of your work. I've also submitted a news release for all the cities where the prints will be placed. You're getting pretty famous down here!"

"Maybe you could write a new biography for this one. One with enough information to allow someone to trace me back to your office. If it's someone from the family, you could tell them how to contact me."

"You don't have much to go on *mon ami*; don't be too disappointed if this produces nothing."

"I know, Lucien, but I cannot think of another way."

"I can. Come down here. We'll get you on videotape. You can tell the whole story. Then we'll release the tape to as many programs as possible."

Hinoch was becoming tense; he could feel himself tighten. "You're right, I know, but let's try it this way first."

"Listen, *mon ami*, you can't release the prints then talk about them later — they'll be old news. If you want the best chance for the picture to reach the right people, do it now, on TV."

"You're right, as usual Lucien, but no, I can't face that right now. Things I must deal with here are too important."

"You won't get another chance, *mon ami*, old news is nothing!"

"Thank you for your counsel, Lucien, but I cannot, not now."

"Okay. I had to try!"

"It is wise counsel, Lucien, I do appreciate you advising me, but I cannot."

"I understand. Better than you think, *mon ami*. Anyway, goodbye for now."

His stomach was in turmoil, churning on his anxiety. His throat ached as though he would not be able to swallow.

Hinoch had managed to avoid most contact with the modern world to this point. He panicked every time he contemplated dealing alone with the media, but it went deeper than that. Since attending Laval, he loathed the uncaring ways of city people, instinctively fearing their ways would impoverish his spirit. *You fool, you are worse now than when you went to Montreal for University. You are again anticipating things that will not happen!*

His abject feelings of abandonment as a child flooded back into his memory. As a young adult, he had known absolutely nothing of his new environment in Montreal. The people were so independent in their ways as to make them appear alien and cold to him.

He went to the back of the room where he kept his cleaning oils. He stripped and began to oil his body. The droning melody and simple, rhythmic Inuit phrases of his Nature Song calmed him as he worked over his muscular, compact body. He centred his thoughts on himself and his task. He toweled down and dressed, then washed out his towel in homemade soap. He felt better, more in control of his feelings as he focused on the task ahead.

As he thought more about his mission, his old confidence returned. He'd been given an important task. He must not let his own childhood fears impede his efforts.

"Remember, you survived then. You will be all right this time as well," he said, reassuring himself.

He went to his computer and composed an e-mail to Lucien.

My friend, I have reconsidered. I will come to Montreal if you can arrange an interview. Thanks, Hinoch.

A few moments later, his phone rang. He picked up. His voice was still tense and sounded gruff, "Hello."

"Hello again, *mon ami*! When is the next flight out of Nain?"

"Tomorrow morning."

"Okay, I'll have a ticket to Montreal waiting for you in Goose Bay. You'll probably get in here about eleven. I'll talk to my friend Ruti and see what she says. She is CBC's anchor for native interviews. We'll use my studio for the taping, then I'll submit it to all the morning news and art oriented shows. With any luck we'll be on the air before the end of the week."

"Thank you my friend, you always make me feel important."

"You are, my friend, you don't realize how influential your name is becoming in the art world."

"That is thanks to you, Lucien. See you tomorrow."

"*A bientot!*"

Hinoch hung up, his mouth so dry that his lips were sticking to his teeth. He truly feared his quest for the families of these airmen could mean the end of his comfortable, quiet existence in Nain.

He closed his eyes and envisioned himself looking out onto the placid waters of a misty lake. His father's image came to him, reminding him a Torngak had given him this quest, reminding him to use the lessons of his ancestors as his guide. He told himself he would complete it. As his body relaxed, he felt himself infused with calm. He assured his inner child that with the help of his ancestors, he could make this appearance and remain in control of his life.

The morning dawned clear and warm. Hinoch packed enough clothes for the next few days in his only piece of luggage, a military surplus duffel bag. After breakfast, well before the flight's arrival time, he walked down to the pier to wait for the floatplane.

He gloried in the beauty of the bay, its smooth waters stretching out into the islands in the distance, spreading its shores into the expanse of the Labrador Sea. Seagulls circled lazily overhead, searching the waters for the first sign of a school of herring. At the first rising ripple on the surface, they reeled and dove into the waters, turning the scene into a splashing, screeching melee. Seconds later it would be over, the fish would dive out of reach and the gulls would take to the air yet again to search for the next opportunity.

He was part of this cycle of life; Hinoch reveled in the certainty of it. In Montreal, he had pined for this proximity to nature. Today, he still childishly feared the loss of this delicate communion should he be absent for too long.

Faintly at first, the drone of the Beaver's engine began to impose itself on the natural sounds of the morning. Hinoch turned to see a dart of light reflect from the still distant aircraft. Gradually, the sound intensified as it positioned for an approach over the water. It turned smoothly and with reduced power, began to settle to the water, the wings leveled as it slowed to final approach speed. Just before the floats touched the water, the engine roared, giving the power necessary to keep the plane from flipping over as the floats sliced into the liquid below.

The plane taxied smoothly toward the dock. The engine wheezed to a halt and the pilot climbed down onto the float as the plane coasted. He grabbed a line and stepped onto the pier as it neared, then eased the plane to a halt. He tied the line and greeted his passenger.

"Hi Hinoch. So you're travelling with us today are you?"

"Yes, Tom, I'm going to Montreal. My tickets will be in Goose Bay."

"Okay, hop aboard and make yourself comfortable; I'll go up and collect the mail."

He reached into the back and grabbed the Nain mailbag, then walked up to the General Store. A few minutes later, he returned with a small bag of mail. He climbed into the plane, dropped the bag in the back, then secured the side door. Returning to his seat, he said, "It's a beautiful morning up there. The dawn was a real sight to behold!"

"Wonderful!" Hinoch replied, "I love a good view of the land from up there."

As they spoke, the plane slowly drifted away from the dock. Tom was quickly completing his pre-start checks as he chatted. He opened the throttle, adjusted the mixture and applied power to both magnetos, then selected the starter.

The crackling, popping explosions from the engine's stubby exhaust burst into the silence, assaulting his senses. The airframe vibrated, warm air gushed from a vent somewhere near his feet as he hunted for a truant strap for his seatbelt. The snarling exhaust blanketed any other sounds, even Tom's voice, telling him where to look for it.

Satisfied with the post-start checks, Tom advanced the power smoothly and turned the plane toward open water. Gradually it gained speed, but the smooth water was reluctant to release its hold on the floats. Tom rocked the control column forward and back a few times, causing the plane to level, then pitch up onto the backs of the floats. Suddenly the plane rose onto the steps in the floats and gained speed rapidly. Seconds later, they were in the air. Tom reduced the power and the plane settled into a comfortable rhythm, gliding smoothly in the air.

The trip went well. In Goose Bay, Hinoch transferred to a Boeing 737 for the flight to Montreal. He did not enjoy flying in this plane nearly as well as the little bush planes. It flew too high, making any details below indistinct and seemingly unreal.

Lucien met him at the arrival gate in Montreal.

"At last, my friend, I have you here in Montreal. This will be a memorable event for both of us."

"I sincerely hope it will be a *good* memory," Hinoch replied.

"It will, Hinoch, I will see to that. Don't worry, I am a master at these news releases and this one will be a triumph for both of us." Let's get your luggage and return to my place. "The limousine is waiting."

The trip to Lucien's penthouse apartment was brief and filled with Lucien's enthusiasm over having his friend at his side again after so many years. It seemed only a few minutes had elapsed when the limousine pulled into the underground garage of the apartment building.

"Just a short ride in the elevator now and we'll be home."

Hinoch's ears began to pop as they did when he was in a climbing airplane. "How many floors up to your apartment? Will we need oxygen?" he joked.

"Ahh, good, you're starting to feel better. We always did enjoy ourselves *n'est-ce pas?* Remember the late night snacks we had with food that we smuggled to our room?"

"Yes, Lucien, we did have a lot of fun together."

The doors of the elevator slid open and they entered directly into the great room of Lucien's apartment. Hinoch took in the grandeur and scale of this place. An expanse of windows gave the apartment morning sunlight and a glorious view of the cityscape. The north wall was completely mirrored with a full stock of liquor and wine, flanked by a bar of dark marble with elevated burgundy-leather armchairs. This main area was a huge room designed for entertaining crowds of people on opening nights for his many showings. Three large conversation pits were lined with sumptuous, built-in leather seating. A central fireplace with a funnel-shaped metal chimney provided the only appealing feature to Hinoch's eye. To the south, there was a small stage, complete with a professional sound system and to the west, hallways led to private living and sleeping areas. Everything was bright, shiny and boldly coloured.

It was a city person's dream, but he was already pining for his home. The great room was professionally decorated, but to Hinoch's eye, it lacked the warmth of a home.

"Come, sit down. Can I get anything for you?"

"I haven't had a lot to eat since I agreed to this madness, but you've relaxed me and I *would* like a snack of something."

"Let me guess, some scallops baked on a bed of spinach, some herbs sprinkled over it and a little rice. How does that sound?"

"Wonderful, but it is ten o'clock, where will we get something like that?"

Lucien went to his intercom, placed the order then went to his bar. "Let's see, how about a nice Californian Chardonnay?"

"Sounds good. You have your own kitchen staff?"

"Yes, and hot and cold running maids as well. You are helping to move me into the world of movers and shakers. I love it!"

"You understand, this is a single-purpose trip. I do this interview, then I return to Nain. My sole reason for being here is to maximize the chances of finding someone in the family of one of those airmen."

"Sure, Hinoch. You've got your reasons, I've got mine, but sometimes you make it difficult for me."

"I know, and I appreciate your loyalty. I consider myself fortunate to have such a worldly and wise friend that I can rely upon and trust."

"We're brothers, *mon ami*. We weren't born of the same mother and father, but we became brothers in that infernal residence at the university. Remember the little song you composed for us?"

"Yes I do, Lucien, it is our brotherhood song. That infernal residence, as you call it, was a place of frightening and strange wonders to me — running water, flush toilets and soft beds. I had never seen those things!"

"Yes, and through your eyes I learned to appreciate what I've got. To this day, I make a point of reminding myself how you had to learn what all those things were, and how to use them. Your wonder opened my eyes!"

A bell rang and Lucien said, "Come in Carla."

A middle-aged woman entered wearing a chef's hat and whites. She was carrying a thermador, which she placed on the bar. She removed the lid to reveal two plates of freshly baked scallops. The odours permeated the room and Hinoch's appetite immediately freshened.

"Enjoy, gentlemen," she said turning and leaving the room.

Lucien said, "Thank-you Carla, this looks delicious!" She nodded as the door closed.

"Come on, Hinoch. *Bon appetit!*" Lucien poured a glass of wine for each of them and sat at the bar, wasting no time digging in. Hinoch joined him, eating more quickly than he should, but his stomach had been denied too long. Conversation died as they consumed the delicacies.

As they pushed back, Hinoch stifled a yawn. Lucien got the message. "You're tired. Let's pick up again in the morning. Ruti and I'll work with you tomorrow morning to help you prepare your comments. I'll call you at seven, okay?"

"Sounds great, and now, if you will just show me my bed."

"This way."

Hinoch followed as he led him to his room. It was huge and opulent. The bed looked like something out of an English lord's manor. Mildly amused by all the trimmings, Hinoch secretly wondered whether this brash opulence was what his friend truly wanted.

"See you at seven, Lucien. Thanks for everything."

"Good night, *mon ami*, sleep tight!"

"Good night."

~~~~~

Hinoch stirred only when Lucien poked his head through the door, "Wake up, Hinoch. We have a busy day ahead of us. Get dressed and meet me downstairs in thirty minutes."

"Yes, thirty minutes, thank you, Lucien," Hinoch replied.

He got up, bathed in his oils, then dressed in his favorite shirt and slacks. Twenty minutes later, he entered the dining room. Lucien was playing the tape of a celebration of the hunt that Hinoch had recorded in Nain almost five years ago. The muffled drums beat a steady rhythm as the people sang a primordial sounding chant.

The women added a haunting rhythmic counterpoint to the song with their throat singing.

"I play this in my gallery whenever I'm promoting native art. It always sets the mood. Think it'll work for the interview?"

Hinoch felt a slight twinge of guilt. He had exploited his own people by giving this tape to Lucien, knowing he would use it for commercial benefit. It was done though, so he said, "You are the expert in public relations, I defer to your wisdom. I'm glad it is helpful to you."

"Did you sleep well?"

"Amazingly well, considering the fact that I was full of rich scallops and wine."

"My mother always used to say, when you're nervous, keep your stomach busy and it'll help to calm you. I don't know how true that is, but I like to eat, so it's a good excuse!"

"I never question the wisdom of my Elders, and I too like to eat," Hinoch chuckled.

A few moments later, the intercom buzzed and Lucien answered. "Yes?"

"Hello, this is Ruti, how are you Lucien?"

"I'm fine, no, I'm excellent, my best friend in the whole world is here. You're right on time, Ruti . . . come on up." Lucien activated the main door and watched the video monitor as she entered. He opened the door on the penthouse elevator as she approached. Moments later the door opened and a petite young lady with deep, dark brown eyes, long, braided black hair and a contagious smile stepped into the room. Lucien ushered her in and bade her sit.

"Hinoch, I would like you to meet Ruti, Ruti, Hinoch."

"Hello, Ruti, good to meet you." Hinoch instantly found himself responding to this woman on a spiritual level. He saw in her dark brown eyes a well of many souls. His instincts were fully alert as he began to perceive the depth of her person.

"Hello Hinoch, I am impressed that you have travelled all the way from Labrador to help market this drawing of yours."

"No, Ruti, I am here to begin my search for the families of the spirits I found at the crash site."

Ruti's eyes narrowed and Hinoch could feel them searching his soul for truth. Seemingly satisfied, she offered her hand and said, "I will do what ever I can to help you."

"Thank you, Ruti."

Lucien had observed this subliminal level of communication as it occurred and concluded that Ruti and Hinoch would prove to be a creatively exciting pair. "Well, I can see that you're going to get along well," Lucien interjected, "Can we start to plan the interview? We've got two hours before we have to leave."

They moved to the smallest conversation pit and sat near a large coffee table. Lucien hovered while Ruti and Hinoch discussed the story. As he listened to their discussion, he was aware they were communicating on many levels, not unusual for artists, but this interaction had something more complex, spiritual, at the core. His marketing instinct told him that a powerful piece was about to be created.

From time to time, Lucien suggested an adjustment to the direction of the dialogue to involve the average person in the audience, but in the main, he decided to accept the natural flow of the story line. He wanted to preserve the almost transcendental level of their communication rather than risk making the piece too pedestrian, destroying its powerful overtones.

They worked for nearly two hours, Ruti making notes and preparing her lead-in to the interview and Hinoch providing the details of the story.

Lucien clapped his hands almost feeling he was breaking a spell. "Its time to go, let's break a leg!" he said.

Hinoch looked at him incredulously.

"It's just a saying! It means good luck, okay?"

Hinoch smiled, a quizzical grin of acceptance that did not mean he understood. They gathered their notes and walked to the elevator, then rode down to the garage where the limousine was waiting.

In less than twenty minutes, the long black Lincoln pulled into the garage under the building where Lucien's offices were located. They entered the building and Lucien led the way to the recording studio where the camera and sound crews awaited.

Lucien spent the next few minutes familiarizing Hinoch and Ruti with the layout of the studio and the interview podium. He briefed the camera and sound crews, then took a seat nearby.

"Okay, Hinoch, now it's up to you and Ruti. Good luck!"

The lights came up and Ruti began with a smile that could melt the coldest heart.

"Good morning, and welcome to 'In touch.' I am Ruti Kayakjuak, your host and this is Hinoch Shiwack. Good morning Hinoch."

"Good morning Ruti."

"Hinoch is a rising star in the art world. He is a native Inuit from Nain, in Labrador. Over the last ten years, he has produced a series of haunting, beautiful interpretations of the flora and fauna of Labrador. It is clear to anyone who stops to appreciate his work that it possesses a level of communication that goes far beyond the visual aspect of charcoal on paper. This is what attracts his patrons and his fans. His interpretations of nature have appeared in the major art galleries of North America. If you linger over his works, you find yourself drawn to something other than the physical representation of the subject to a . . . dare I say . . . more spiritual plane." She turned her eyes to him. They asked the question she spoke aloud for the audience, "How do you accomplish this Hinoch?"

"Nature is full of spirits. I attempt to make the world more aware of their presence." Hinoch replied.

"Judging from the acclaim your work has received, you have been successful in your aim," she assured him as she turned to the camera. "Hinoch is a native, born and raised on the coast of Labrador. He is the son of Abel Shiwack, an Inuit shaman. He is the spiritual leader for his community and he strives to carry on the tradition of perpetuating the spiritual legacy of the Inu.

He has readily accepted this role, because he tells me, he has felt the growth in himself as he learned and he can see how this spiritual influence has added sensitivity to his art. Hinoch insists that his art is the tangible expression of the spirit world he encounters every day. His art is his attempt to show how important the spirits are to our everyday lives."

She turned to Hinoch and asked, "When did you learn that your art conveyed such a spiritual undertone?"

"My father saw my drawings as a child and instructed me to sing my Nature Song whenever I draw. Almost immediately after I began this practice, the pictures became full of life and spirit."

"What is your Nature Song?"

"Every Inuit child is given a song composed by their parents. It is their own special song that unites the family's spirits and makes us human beings."

"Human beings. Isn't that the translation of the word Inuit?"

"Yes, it is alternately translated as our People, or Human Beings."

"Just a little more background. This spring, Hinoch travelled up the Eagle River to the site of an old WW II plane wreck. He wanted to chronicle some of the intrusions modern man has made into this unforgiving land, and the prices paid. Though he knew the general location, he had yet to find the old wreck, buried deep in the underbrush, near a small lake."

She turned to him again; their eyes locked, "How did you know of the general area of the crash site?"

"The elders spoke of encountering it while out on their trap lines. One of the pilots who brings the mail to our village had seen a strange looking kayak at the bottom of a little lake. He had been forced down on the lake once to make repairs and had noticed a strange looking boat lying on the bottom in about thirty feet of water. One day, he was partaking in a discussion with the elders when the old plane was mentioned, along with the location. He recognized the description of the little lake and mentioned the sunken boat."

"And what was your involvement at this point?"

"Inu curiosity . . . possibly one of our strongest traits. I have always had a strong interest in stories of this kind and wanted to find the old plane. When I heard of the pilot's find, I concluded the location was better defined than I had previously believed. I felt it might be possible to locate the plane quite easily."

"So, you flew to the lake with him. What did you find?"

"Many things. One of my first finds was this old wedding ring." Hinoch withdrew the ring from under his shirt. "I was photographing some caribou moss when the sun's light glanced from it, attracting my attention. It is engraved, but I would like to keep that private for now. It will help me to truly know the person claiming it, if we meet."

"You expect to find the family of this long-lost airman?"

"I have been tasked by the spirits of these men to do my utmost to locate the families and allow their spirits to be reunited."

"How do you know this?"

"I encountered a Torngak, a powerful spirit in the form of an old raven. My people revere ravens as totems, the visible form of a Torngak. This raven led me to the crash site. It is unlikely I would have found it otherwise; it was so heavily overgrown. The spirits of these humans were in this old raven. When he died, they were handed on to a young raven and will continue to be handed down through her offspring until they are returned to their true home. This young raven now accompanies me every day around my home, waiting for me to have success."

"This is a fascinating story, but I'm sure it is totally unbelievable for our audience!"

"I think they understand it in slightly different terms perhaps, but they can see it clearly if they think about it for awhile. Christianity teaches that our bodies are of this earth and to the earth they will return, but our spirits are of God and will endure forever. The Inu support this belief entirely, but rather than envision an abstract concept such as heaven, they believe that our spirits remain here with us. In the Inuit view of life and death, the spirits can be passed on from one to the other. In their eyes, this is the mechanism by which successive generations become better people, possessing the accumulated wisdom of their elders.

If our people are attentive in the care of their spirits, they acquire a great deal of knowledge from them of the world in which we live. People who have inherited many spirits become powerful spirits themselves, capable of great things for their people."

"But what of the ravens?"

"They are the embodiments of spirits that could not be transferred directly, because the deceased passed on while isolated from the family. Ravens seek out ways and means of returning the spirits they carry to their proper place with the family."

"So the spirit is passed on when the family is present at the death?"

"Yes."

"Can others from outside the family accept a spirit?"

"Yes, if they are song-brothers. Inuit people do not work with people outside the family, so if they want to work with someone from outside, they adopt them. A ceremony is performed wherein songs of brotherhood are composed and sung, thus binding the outsider to the family. Song brothers can transfer spirits."

"Fascinating. So you found this aircraft, photographed it and then what happened?"

"I returned to Nain and went to work interpreting my photos as drawings. The photo of the aircraft took precedence in my consciousness, to the point that I could not satisfy myself with my customary photos of nature. I felt possessed by the haunting feelings I took with me from the crash site. This ring became so important to me that I could not leave it unattended, thus it is around my neck always. I drew this picture in five days and until it was finished, I did not fully understand what I had drawn."

"Some people say there is more to this picture than what we see at first glance."

"Yes, there is something else. I believe that I can see the face of one of the lost airmen in the mist over the plane."

"Have others seen it?"

"Yes, I am surprised at how many people see it clearly. It seems to be most prominent when the picture is lit from above and to the right."

"Can we do that now?" Ruti asked the crew behind the cameras. A few moments passed, then the lights dimmed, except for the lights on the right side of the set. The camera zoomed in on the picture and slowly the image seemed to materialize, until it was so plain that those viewing it could not imagine how they had not seen it before.

The set was silent for a few seconds, then Ruti whispered, "I have never seen anything so amazing!" Slowly the lights returned to their original settings and the face faded from view. The cameras pulled back to focus on Hinoch and Ruti.

Seeing her emotion, Hinoch spoke first, "Your response is very close to mine the first time I saw him."

"I find it amazing that you drew this person's image without knowing what you were creating!" She was silent for a few seconds. Hinoch offered no response.

WE ARE STILL HERE

She paused to compose herself a little, then in a softened tone asked, "So, you are promoting this drawing now." She smiled, wiping her eye with her forefinger, "Judging by its impact on me, it should be a raging success for you!"

"There are only one hundred prints for sale. My primary objective in marketing this picture is to locate the families, to help them return the spirits of their loved ones to their homes."

"I certainly hope this interview helps you."

"That is my prayer."

"So, as you have seen, the remarkable discovery of this wrecked airplane has produced a haunting work of art and a quest for Hinoch, a quest to find the families of the airmen who perished in the wilderness so many years past. If you have any information that could lead us to these people, please contact our studios at the number showing now on the bottom of your screen."

"Thank you, Hinoch for this fascinating story. I hope you find the people you seek!"

"Thank you, Ruti."

"Good night everyone!"

The cameras faded to black and the soundman slowly brought up the sound of muffled drums and chanting provided by Lucien.

Lucien stepped onto the podium and took Hinoch's hand.

"That's a great interview, *mon ami*. I just hope it's well received by the public. We may have missed the mark totally and we may have opened a floodgate of demand for more information about this lost plane. We'll soon see."

As they moved to leave the studio, each member of the crew shook Hinoch's hand and wished him luck. It was apparent that his message had reached them loud and clear.

They returned to the penthouse in relative silence as the car glided through the streets. Abruptly, the interior darkened as they pulled into the garage. They climbed out and rode up to the penthouse. After a short time, Ruti said her goodbyes, leaving Lucien and Hinoch to relax. Hinoch was tired, but felt serene, free of the tension he had been expecting.

"Thank you for convincing me to do this, Lucien. You are wise beyond your years."

"I hope we've all achieved our objectives, *mon ami*. I hope you find your lost families and I hope the prints receive the attention they deserve." He rose and went to the bar. "Would you care for something?"

"Yes, please . . . more of that Chardonnay. It was delicious."

Lucien ordered more scallops and opened a bottle. They sipped wine and dined in relative silence, then Hinoch began to sing their brotherhood song. Lucien joined in wistfully, tears coming to his eyes as he voiced the familiar old sounds not sung in unison with Hinoch for so many years. At the conclusion, they sat in silence honouring their years as brothers in spirit.

Lucien finally spoke, "Thank you, brother, thank you for coming and for being who you are. You don't know how much, or how often I miss you!"

"I miss you also, but I simply sing our song and your spirit returns to me."

"I'm going to sing it more often in future," Lucien said softly.

A STRANGER ARRIVES

Hinoch's flight home went smoothly, just an obligatory transfer to the Single Otter in Goose Bay. In the evening, as they approached Nain, Tom observed that a blanket of fog was rolling in off the ocean. "I'd better make this quick, or I'll be spending the night here!"

"After we land, just taxi up to the dock and I'll get out on the float and hop off."

"Okay, could you grab the mail bag on the way out? The outgoing mail will have to wait until Friday."

Tom set the plane down on the glassy water and taxied to the pier. Hinoch hopped onto the dock and waved as Tom turned back out to sea and gunned the throttle. The plane bounced across its own waves and became airborne a few moments later. Tom turned and flew over the pier, rocking the wings in reply to Hinoch's wave.

Hinoch entered the General Store and unlocked his post-office box. A monogrammed envelope caught his eye. He pulled it out and saw that it was another letter from the aircraft museum. He opened it and read:

Dear Mr. Hinoch,
We have exhausted our information in our search for the families of the aircraft. Since we cannot locate them, we have decided that there is no harm in you having our information of their last locations.

Flight Lieutenant Curtis Parker of 444 Ferry Squadron piloted the aircraft. His Navigator was Flight Sergeant Paul Hanson.

Flight Sergeant Hanson was unmarried and lived in single quarters at Canadian Forces Base Winnipeg. Flight Lieutenant Parker was married to Mrs. Dianne Parker of 441 Moorgate Street, Winnipeg, Manitoba. After the presumed death of her husband, Mrs. Parker vacated these military married accommodations. Unfortunately, we have no forwarding address, since it seems she eventually re-married, thus abrogating her right to a survivor's pension.

We regret that you will be unable to complete your mission, Mr. Hinoch, but this type of outcome is common in these situations.

Thank you again for corresponding with us.

Sincerely,

WO T. McDonald, CD"

"What is it Hinoch, bad news?"

Hinoch turned to greet Monty.

"Just disappointing, Monty. The government cannot trace the families of the people who died in that old plane crash."

"Too bad, now they're gonna be stuck out there forever."

"Possibly, but there is still a chance we may find them."

Hinoch retrieved the rest of his mail and left the store, turning toward his home. Monty accompanied him until he saw other children at play.

"'Bye 'Noch, see ya!"

"So long Monty, enjoy your day."

As Hinoch entered his home, the phone was ringing. He picked it up immediately.

"Hello?"

"Hinoch, *mon frere*, your interview was aired this afternoon and it is a great success; the drawings have already started to sell!"

"Has anyone contacted you about the pilot, or the navigator?"

"No-one yet, but I'm sure this was the most effective way of informing them. They might have to deal with the information first, then decide whether they want to revisit their loss, or consider it all in the past and done. Every family deals with grief in its own way. Some want to mourn in private; while others want everyone to join in and support them. You'll just have to be patient while they decide; that's assuming they even saw the interview."

"Thank you, my brother, I will remember that."

"It was good to see you again, Hinoch, I've taken to heart what you said about coming to Nain. As soon as I can arrange my affairs so that I can work from there, I'll come and visit."

"I fear your work would cloud the effect of being here. Couldn't you just take a holiday?"

"We'll see. You take care, *mon frere*."

"I will, Lucien. Thanks for calling."

For the first time in his adult life, Hinoch felt unbearably impatient. Somehow, he'd expected the response from the family to be immediate, but Lucien was right . . . they would need time.

Hinoch knew winter would be settling in early. The summer had blended almost imperceptibly into a short autumn, followed by killing frosts and heavy fogs that had rolled in and lasted most of the day. The land was cooling rapidly and the warm ocean was blanketing the coast with the comparative warmth of its waters.

He was already preparing for the seal hunt, which would be followed by his annual trek into the wilderness northwest of Nain to visit his parents. He looked forward to the trip this year. He had so much to communicate with his father. He'd learned and seen a great deal this year, not the least of which was the prominent place the spirits had assumed in his life. Since his father had taught him how to sense their presence and adopt them, his eyes had opened up to them, and even the world in which he lived with an amazing, brilliant clarity. He was, he knew, going back to his father having progressed farther into the life of a shaman.

He'd begun to exercise his dogs, a beautiful team of white samoyeds he'd bartered from an old white trapper who lived not far from his father. They were larger dogs than the customary huskies and malamutes, which meant that when in condition, they could pull tremendous loads. Their chief disadvantage was a rapid loss of endurance if food ran out on the trail. Unlike the huskies, they would rapidly decline in strength, forcing the distance covered each day to dwindle.

This was a serious deficiency if things went badly, so Hinoch spent the early winter every year provisioning his tilts, or caches, with frozen seal meat from the hunt. In this way, if food ran short, he could make for the line of tilts, spaced about seven miles apart, to provision his dogs for the last leg of the trail home. The tilts were simple one-room log huts spaced so he could easily reach the next one, even in the worst weather. The seal meat hung well up in a tree in a pail to protect it from scavengers.

Inside, a small wood-burning stove made from a five-gallon pail would keep him warm at night.

His father's tilt line extended south from his home. The first of these tilts Hinoch would reach was located at the opening to Abel's valley on the north side of Saglek Bay. His provisions would provide the same insurance policy at the north end of the trail.

Hinoch was collecting provisions for his father: rifle shells, flour, salt, a new ulu, a machete. The list was long, but he reveled in the details of completing it, so anxious he was to begin his trek north. The preparations helped him to wait patiently for the weather and ice conditions to be right.

Tuk watched these preparations with rapt attention. Hinoch enjoyed her companionship and often left scraps of food for her, or played games with her. The people of the village took almost reverent notice of this relationship, saying Hinoch's spirits were growing powerful to be honoured with the counsel of a Torngak.

The fifth of December dawned crisp, cold and clear, in brilliant sunshine. Hinoch stirred and winced as he rolled over only to receive a blinding ray of sunshine in his eyes. He shaded them with his hand then rose to survey the transformation of the village by the first winter snows. The previous snows had been fitful and heavy with moisture, often melting partially during the heat of the day. By contrast, this snow covered the landscape with diamonds that floated around the village in sparkling wisps on the slightest breeze.

Winter was finally here. The ice had been forming on the bay for nearly a month now. The recent cold temperatures would have consolidated and hardened it and this snow would insulate it against any future warming periods. Hinoch began his final preparations. Soon the ice would be thick enough to venture far from shore. He hoped some seals would come in close this year so he could kill a few early in the season. These he would use to replenish his oil supply, provide fresh seal meat to fatten his dogs, and new skins for repairs to his *komatik*. Hinoch had built his sled in the traditional way, using strips of hide for cords. The structure, of wood and dried sealskin, was strong, yet flexible enough to withstand the uneven terrain he would encounter on the trail.

It was a busy time for Hinoch, but welcome because it brought him back to his roots, to what he'd been born to do. To his surprise, the following day, an unscheduled Single Otter arrived. It landed on the ice and taxied to shore, then spluttered into stillness. Hinoch went down to the plane to see if the pilot needed assistance. As he arrived, he saw a young woman climbing down from the plane. Her blonde hair was hanging out of the front of her parka hood. She wore clothes of the latest technology for severe climates, brightly coloured and loose-fitting.

"Hello there," he shouted.

She turned and waved, then began to walk toward him. She had the walk of a person accustomed to being outdoors. She placed her feet firmly on the ground and walked briskly. As she came closer, Hinoch could see she was a strong woman of his height, maybe a bit taller, with a ruddy, friendly face. As she removed her mitt, he noticed her hands were no strangers to hard work. She reached out and took his hand in an uncharacteristically firm grip.

"Hi. My name's Joanna."

"I am Hinoch. I am pleased to make your acquaintance. Welcome to Nain!"

Joanna looked at him strangely, surprised at his formality. After a slightly uncomfortable pause, she replied, "Thanks, Hinoch, I didn't get the impression from Lucien that you'd be this easy to find. Something about the seal hunt."

"He is right, I plan to depart tomorrow." Hinoch's throat began to ache. "How is it you know Lucien?"

"My mother saw your interview on *In Touch*, and wondered immediately if the plane you found was my grandfather's. She contacted my grandmother with the information and verified that the call-letters on the plane were a match. Granny had just one photo of the plane and fortunately, we could make out the letters on the side of the fuselage."

He could not believe his ears. "Could you tell me your grandmother's name?"

"Dianne Parker-Hanson."

"That's a coincidence; the navigator's surname was Hanson."

"Granny and the Hanson's were like one big extended family. In fact, two years after the crash, Granny married Paul's older brother, Carl."

Hinoch reached his hand out to her and beckoned her to follow. "Come, let's have some tea and you can tell me about your family." She moved to his side as he turned and walked up the hill to his cabin.

Caw, Caw, Caw.

"It seems my friend is anxious to meet you. She has accompanied me since I left the site of the crash. Tuk has become a part of every day life for me."

"You said in your interview that you believe the spirits of Curtis and Paul are waiting to be re-united with us?"

"Yes, Joanna. I believe this raven is the visible form of your grandfather and his friend's spirits."

"A raven? How can that be?"

"Ravens are special beings of nature. We believe many of them are the custodians of lost spirits. We call them Torngaks. She is a wild bird, but she is bound to the spirits she has inherited until they are properly re-united with your family. Here, squat down, close your eyes, concentrate on the memory of your grandfather and ask her in your thoughts to share their spirits."

"What?" She looked at him, incredulous, but decided to comply. "Oh, okay . . . like this?" As she squatted down, she made an effort to concentrate on her grandfather. She reminded herself of the countless stories she had heard of him. His image was given form thanks to the one picture she had seen of him, the one sitting on her grandmother's night table. After a few moments, Tuk extended her wings and floated down to the ground, the air whispering softly through her flight feathers.

"Slowly extend your hand, Joanna, and open your eyes." Joanna moved slowly and the bird observed her as her eyes opened. Tuk turned her head and with her eye fixed a tender gaze upon her. Tuk chortled to her as she ambled toward her, until she was resting against her hand with her breast. Then, slowly she brushed her hand with her beak, as though looking for something.

"What is it doing?" she asked softly.

"I believe she is looking for this," Hinoch replied. He began to sing his Nature Song softly as he reached into his shirt, folding his fingers around the ring. He felt a powerful surge of awareness, his mind's eye seeing two nebulous men in the place of the young raven. He withdrew the ring, still enclosed in his hand, and lifted the thong over his head. Bending down, he placed his hand upon Joanna's, then opened his fingers allowing the ring to drop into her hand. Tuk reached into her hand and picked the ring up gently, lovingly. After a moment, Tuk returned the ring to her hand, but did not move away. She leaned against her hand a few moments longer, gazing into her eyes, then moved a short distance away before returning to her perch atop the streetlight.

"That's incredible, but what's so special about this ring?" she asked.

"Look inside at the inscription."

She squinted, turning the ring into the sunlight until the engraving came into view. She clenched her jaw, and her cheeks drained of colour. She remained motionless awhile, then she whispered, "His ring!" She choked the words out, looking over the small gold ring as though it were the most important discovery of her life. "This is incredible. It's like closing a chapter of my grandmother's life that until now has been an open wound. She'll be ever so grateful to you, sir!"

"I am grateful to *you*, Joanna. That ring has weighed heavily on me since I found it. Its spirits are anxious to be at peace. What has just transpired here is similar to what happened to me in the wilderness with an old raven that I believe was Tuk's father."

Joanna rose slowly, her gaze fixed on her clenched hand.

"Mother said your picture was amazing. The face in the mist looked uncannily like an old locket photo she has of her father. Now this is just . . . well, it's incredible. How did you find it?" She was regaining her colour, but her emotion still showed plainly in her eyes and her shaking hands.

"Strictly by chance. I was taking some pictures of caribou moss and caught a glimpse of it as I moved around." Hinoch play-acted his movements, trying to clarify his words. She seemed to appreciate his efforts.

"I've spent some time with the natives of this country because I fly in and out of the north of Quebec and Manitoba. They have a wisdom, a timeless calm, which people from my home could never begin to understand, but I've never heard of anything like this before.

"I want to believe this is all true because my grand-mother is not well. I hope this won't be too much for her to bear. I'm going to return this ring to her and try to explain your beliefs about the spirits, but she'll have to decide what she wants to do."

"That is all anyone can do. I wish you success." Hinoch was silent for a moment, then asked, "Would you like that tea I promised you? Maybe something to eat?"

"That would be nice, Hinoch, and I'd like to hear some of the details of your discovery of the crash site."

Hinoch led her into his cabin and began to prepare a meal of poached salmon and rice. Joanna sat at the table as they talked, and took in the details of this simple, yet comfortable home.

Within moments, she spotted the picture. "There it is," she exclaimed, "is this the original?"

"Yes. It is yours also."

She turned back to him, surprised, "I couldn't take the original. Don't you have a print I could buy?"

"No, but even if I did, I believe the original belongs to your grandmother."

Joanna hesitated, silently coming to the conclusion it would be rude to continue protesting his generosity.

"Thank you. You've done so much for us already, how can we ever repay you?"

"Knowing that these spirits may soon be at peace is my reward."

"You said you wanted to go hunting tomorrow. Would it help if I took you up this afternoon to reconnoiter the ice from the air?"

"That would be wonderful. We should have enough light left after lunch for a good long flight."

They enjoyed their lunch and then headed back to the airplane. It was in excellent condition. The aircraft registration, emblazoned on the sides and wings, was 'CF-MPY.'

"I know this plane," Hinoch said to her. "This is the old RCMP plane from Goose Bay. My father's friend, Vince, used to fly her. He would fly in to visit my father's cabin in the winters. We enjoyed some good times together and I remember him often saying that Danny, the maintenance engineer, was meticulous. It will be wonderful to go up in it one more time."

"I bought this plane two years ago after I finished my commercial pilot's license." She patted the fuselage. "It had been retired from the RCMP when they got the new Twin Otters. It was flying with a little feeder line out of Port MacNeil when I found it."

"So you have followed in your grandfather's footsteps. You do him a great honour."

Joanna was surprised by his assessment of her motivations to fly; she had never considered her grandfather's influence. "It's more like it's in my blood. I just can't think of anything else I would rather be doing."

Hinoch turned to the east and scanned the bay, "It is going to be foggy soon; perhaps we should cancel the trip so that you can start back before it arrives."

Joanna remarked, "It doesn't look too bad yet; does it move in fairly quickly here?"

Hinoch sniffed the air. "Yes, as soon as the sea breeze begins, it rolls in very quickly. I can smell the ocean now."

"Okay, let's cancel it until tomorrow morning then. I've set aside at least four days for this trip and I'm prepared to spend longer if necessary." She looked down and shuffled some snow into a little pile with her feet. "This information is very important to my grandmother. She wants to know as much as possible about what you know of the events surrounding the crash."

"I'll be pleased to tell you all I know. It's going to be cold tonight. Will your plane start tomorrow?" Hinoch pointed to MPY.

Joanna smiled confidently, "I've got a tent to put over the engine and a heater. It'll take about two hours before it's ready to start."

"It sounds to me like you are well prepared for flying in the arctic."

"I had the best of instructors. I can probably fix just about any problem on that plane that doesn't need major replacement parts."

"That's good, because this country isn't known for giving many second chances."

She looked at him then, realizing for the first time he understood his world, but loved it anyway. "You're right there, you have to be careful and you sometimes need to act instinctively, no time to think it through. It can be pretty demanding when the weather's bad."

It was Hinoch's turn to look down and shuffle some snow, deciding whether to dare invite a woman into his home. He decided it was safe enough; it would not be a disaster if she said no. "I have a comfortable cot in my cabin that you're welcome to use."

"That's okay," she was about to decline, knowing there was only one single bed in the small one-room home. Then she decided to take the chance. "I've got an air mattress here that works great for camping. If you have a space on the floor I'll be just fine." She reached into the cargo bay and pulled out a duffel bag. "I've got lots of questions for you, so if you don't mind I'll just camp on your floor."

Hinoch began to feel self-conscious. He'd never spent a night in the company of a woman. He was not tense, or even nervous, but he wanted this woman to feel comfortable. He felt he already had strong contact with her through her grandfather's spirit.

Wisps of fog were drifting in on the freshening sea breeze, confirming Hinoch's forecast. Joanna felt comforted by his intimate knowledge of his surroundings. He offered to carry her duffel bag, but she demurred saying, "Don't spoil me, Hinoch, I don't want to get soft. You need your strength out here sometimes."

Hinoch smiled at her and for the first time, he looked into her blue eyes. Like a deer first sighting a hunter, he froze, caught up in her returned gaze. It took too long, it seemed to him, to think of something to say, something to break the spell.

"You have the eyes of a person with a strong and independent spirit. I can see that your grandfather lives on through you."

"Thanks, Hinoch. I've never seen him, but the family's stories have always fascinated me."

They spent the entire evening discussing not only Hinoch's discoveries at the crash site, but also his interpretations of the spirits he encountered there. Joanna proved a very open-minded woman. She took an immediate and genuine interest in the Inuit philosophy of life and nature, asking questions and sometimes dwelling a long time on Hinoch's responses.

"So you believe that this old raven was a . . . Torn . . . ?" she asked.

"Torngak, a powerful spirit in his own right before he encountered your grandfather."

" . . . and then he took in grandfather's spirit when he died?"

"Yes."

She cradled her face in her cupped hands, elbows on her knees, "So now you believe this raven that spends most of her time with you has inherited the spirits from the old raven and she's waiting to pass them back to my family. That sounds so wonderfully hopeful. I pray it's true!"

"When I go to visit my father, Abel Shiwack, I'll ask him to teach me the rites of transfer of the soul. Then I will be able to help you and the raven to complete our quest. I would suggest that when you return to Winnipeg, you explain this to your grandmother and your family. In spring, I will have returned to Nain and we can go to the crash site to re-unite the spirits. I feel that there, our feelings will be strongest and for that reason, the spirits will be the most potent."

"Good grief!" Joanna exclaimed, "It's three AM. We'd better get some sleep."

Hinoch agreed and went to his cot. "Good night, Joanna. Sleep well."

"No problem. I'm exhausted!"

Hinoch self-consciously turned his back to her as she prepared to climb into her bed.

"Let me know when I can turn around," he said somewhat sheepishly.

Joanna smiled, *Just as I thought, a perfect gentleman.* A few moments later she teased, "Okay, you can turn around now." Hinoch turned to see her warmly tucked into bed. "My turn to look the other way," she said, rolling over so her back was turned. Hinoch changed into his sweat pants, the only approximation of pajamas he owned, and climbed into bed. "Sleep well," he said.

"You too," she replied. Then she began to chuckle. "I feel like a little girl on a sleep-over, kind of shy and silly, you know?"

"I'm not accustomed to entertaining overnight guests either, but I must say I'm thoroughly enjoying the experience."

"Me too, Hinoch . . . me too . . . g'night."

"Goodnight."

~~~

Hinoch rose quietly from his bed before dawn and began making breakfast. Before long, the aromas alerted Joanna. She stretched and then said to Hinoch, "Do I smell smoked fish?"

"I thought I'd try to show you some Inuit cuisine. We very often eat fish for breakfast."

She dressed while he worked at the small cook-stove that also served as the heater. She padded up behind him in her stocking feet and looked over his shoulder. "Wonderful, I love fresh fish and . . . what are these?"

"Fiddleheads, they are the first shoots of the ferns you often see in the woods. I pick them in spring and freeze them for use throughout the year. They have a wonderful peppery flavor that wakes up the taste buds in the morning."

She looked around the room again. It was a bright, warm place with wood-plank walls and basic furnishings: kitchen chairs and table, the cot, a small freezer sitting next to the kitchen counter and the enamel bowl used for a sink. A woven carpet was the central feature of the floor, thick and comfortable, softening the effect of the bright linoleum. It was basic, but charming, made comfortable by Hinoch's artwork and his obvious happiness in this place.

Less than one hour later, Hinoch and Joanna were struggling to drape the heavy heating tent over the engine of the old Single Otter. The stove was in place under the tent. Joanna finished filling the stove with kerosene then wiped it clean. When she was certain there was no kerosene where it should not be, she lit the stove. Within minutes, the little enclosure was comfortably warm.

"I'll have to check from time to time to make sure the ice isn't melting under the stove. Don't want to taxi into a pile of mush. The skis'd freeze to it and then we'd have to chip them out. It's about minus twenty, so about an hour should be fine."

Hinoch was impressed. "You certainly seem at home in this environment. Your instructor must have been excellent."

"He was a good bush pilot. They're the ones who live long enough to retire from it. For as long as I can remember, I've wanted to fly in the North, so I looked around until I found someone who could teach me. He wasn't much on instrument flying, though, so I got that at flying school in Winnipeg."

"It sounds to me like you've been studying for a considerable length of time."

"Um-hmm. And I loved every minute of it. I feel lucky I had the freedom to do what I love full-time."

"Flying would not be my chosen path in life. I simply want to be a good leader for my people and carry on our traditions."

"Well, that's important, too, Hinoch. From what I've seen in my short stay, you've created an oasis of sanity here. Most native communities I see are the worst slums on the planet. You may not be ready for it, but your interview has created a stir down south. People are going to find you when they're ready and you'll be able to help them change their lives. You're probably going to end up being a famous person. You're well educated in the ways of the world, but you have the guts to insist on living your traditional life. You've conquered both ways of life, but you chose the old ways. That speaks volumes to people lost in the material world out there. Your interview with Ruti has planted a seed. Believe me, it's going to take root and grow."

Hinoch looked at her in fear, "I am afraid that we will be overrun by the outside world if what you say happens. That may prove to be the last blow to an already delicate environment."

"If it comes to that, you'll have to leave, like the Pied Piper, taking them with you to protect what's here."

"That's what I fear the most, being forced to return to a life out there!"

She grinned, looking at his forlorn face, "It's not so bad really. You've just got to stay focused on your dreams."

"I hope it never comes to that," Hinoch replied.

"Let's see if it's ready to go yet." Joanna reached up under the tent with her bare hand to feel the engine. "Feels pretty good, we'll give it a few minutes more while I do the checklist."

Hinoch and Joanna completed the external inspection of the aircraft then climbed into the frozen interior of the old plane. Hinoch smiled, remembering his first trip in it as he entered the cargo bay, the snow under his mukluks squeaking loudly on the frozen metal of the floor. He entered the cockpit, and recognized the worn paint on the controls and the hard seats as a place where he had spent many happy hours with his old friend Vince.

Joanna went about her checklist efficiently, quickly showing Hinoch how attuned she was to this environment. Her concentration was complete, yet not forced or uncomfortable. He could see she had internalized the location of every control so well she could find each one unerringly even in the pitch dark of an arctic night.

"We're ready to light the fires!" she announced as she rose from her seat. "Let's get the tent off and cool the stove down."

Hinoch followed her and began opening the tent as she extinguished the stove. "By the time we get this tent rolled up, the stove'll be cool enough to stow away," she said.

Within moments, they were in the cockpit, where Joanna opened the throttle, adjusted the mixture and applied power to both magnetos. She pushed the primer twice, then selected the starter. The rising whine of the starter was an old memory of Hinoch's — a precursor to good times. The propeller had not made one revolution before a cylinder fired, belching blue-grey smoke out the exhaust. Others followed in rapid succession and the engine was running with the coughing, spluttering crackle so typical of the Pratt and Whitney radial.

The gyroscope hummed as it came up to speed and the other indicators all moved into the normal range. Satisfied with the post-start checks, Joanna eased the throttle forward, then switched from one to the other magneto, noting the RPM drop. The plane vibrated madly with the strain of the cold-running engine against its mounts. She advanced the throttle to taxi onto the ice. Nothing happened. The plane had frozen to the snow. Undeterred, Joanna increased the power and rapidly moved the flight controls, causing the air from the propeller to push on the plane in one direction, then the other. The plane began to rock, then there was a dull snap as the skis broke free. The plane almost leapt forward.

She immediately reduced the power and the plane settled into a comfortable rhythm, gliding smoothly over the snow. Joanna smoothly advanced the power now and the old plane increased speed, then the tail rose into the air. Seconds later, she eased the stick back and they were airborne. As she reduced power, the propeller became visible again as a blur travelling across their field of vision. The old plane shed the thrashing, straining feeling of a few seconds back and became a smooth, seemingly effortless man-made bird.

She was an excellent pilot. Her hands on the controls seemed to sense every slight change in the airflow over the flight surfaces. She kept the plane in trim the way a champion sailor trims the sails of his racing yacht. They looked at each other and smiled. He could see the happiness in her soul.

They began to scan the ice, which now extended unbroken for nearly three miles from shore. Near the edge, Hinoch saw what he was seeking.

"There . . . to the left, breathing holes!"

Joanna strained to see, but could not pick them out. "You should be flying this thing. You must have the eyes of a hawk!"

"No, I have the eyes of Raven; he guides me in this world."

Joanna turned and studied his face. She could see in his eyes how intimately he identified with this place. "Whatever," she replied, "they're a lot better than mine!"

She began a gradual turn to the left. As they flew east from the ice over the water among the outlying islands, she pointed out seals she could see swimming. As they crossed back over the ice, she reduced altitude so she could see the breathing holes, faintly stained by the fish the seals had brought out onto the ice.

"Tomorrow, we will hunt seals," Hinoch announced.

They flew up and down the shoreline for awhile, exploring the various inlets and bays. They were all frozen now and the seals were dotted up and down the coast.

After an hour, she turned the plane back toward Nain. As they approached the village, she reduced power and Hinoch could feel the plane begin to sink toward the ice below. She applied power from time to time to keep the spark plugs from fouling on the rich fuel mixture. About five hundred yards from the village, the skis skimmed the surface. Joanna gradually pulled back on the stick. The old plane settled smoothly and glided on the snow.

She taxied the plane to the shoreline, turned it back out to the ice and then switched off the ignition. The propeller slowly lost momentum, the cylinders chuffed into the exhaust pipe and finally all was silent except for the whining of the gyroscope. Joanna switched off the power and it began to slow almost imperceptibly. It would continue to spin for a considerable time after they had left the plane. Hinoch felt the cold begin to penetrate the cockpit.

"Thank you, Joanna, it was great revisiting this old friend. It is a definite advantage to be able to spot the seals from the air before venturing out. Now I know where they are, and where the bad ice is located. Shall we go and get ready?"

Hinoch visited along the way with the people. In his wake, the village became a vibrant, active community. Dogs began jumping and yelping, children ran about in excitement, men wrestled with sled harnesses and gathered up their rifles. Final preparations for the hunt became a melee of frantic activity. Hinoch had been much more proactive. His sled was ready and was equipped with everything he would need. His rifle had been cleaned and stored in the shed, so it did not sweat when brought from a warm room and freeze with condensation. Hinoch's dogs were calm by comparison, although it was apparent they were looking forward to the first excursion of the season.

Hinoch and Joanna spent the evening quietly.

THE HUNT

The next morning, the neighbours' dogs were in an uproar, frenzied at the prospect of some activity. Hinoch's dogs by contrast sat calmly as he fit them with their harnesses, even waiting patiently as he prepared what would likely be their last meal of fish until next spring. The rich, fatty seal meat would sustain them during the cold season ahead.

Joanna observed these activities with the interest of a novice, seeing someone perform complex tasks in matter-of-fact fashion. She remarked on the ease with which Hinoch managed these massive dogs, to which he replied, "They too have done this many times; they understand what is necessary and are eager to be part of the hunt."

"The other dogs look anxious, too, but they're raising hell about it. I feel as if I could handle your dogs, but those monsters terrify me!"

"These dogs would respond to you in time, if you worked with them patiently." Hinoch could see Joanna was beginning to feel out of place. He wanted her to enjoy the day. He wanted her to join in the day's activities and share the simple joys they held. "Here. You can start by taking this food to them. Give each dog two pieces. Before you place the meat in front of them command them in a firm voice to sit, then to stay."

She did this for each of the eight huge dogs. They obeyed her without question and took the meat only after she had placed it in the snow before them.

"What about this pup?" she asked.

"He is my next Alpha male. I call him Alut. Next year, he will be my lead dog. Give him a small portion."

"That's incredible! I'm sure I'd be counting my fingers and toes if I were feeding those dogs over there, but these fellows are perfectly civilized!"

"They are my companions, so I treat them accordingly. Those dogs do not enjoy the same closeness to their masters. They are largely wild. Keep your distance from them, even from my dogs when I am not nearby. You will know when they have accepted you."

"It is getting dark," he continued. "Let's get lots of sleep tonight. Tomorrow will be long and demanding."

Without thinking, Hinoch took her hand as they walked slowly to his cabin. She almost jumped at his touch, but did not resist. Once inside, he asked, "Let me see your sunglasses. I want to make sure they will be dark enough for the snow. I wouldn't want you to become snow-blind."

"I bought 'em special for the winter glare. It can get pretty harsh up there. I've been told you can weld with them."

"That's good. I use welder's goggles myself. They do not fog up and you can be outside all day without strain. I think we are ready. Let's get a good night's sleep."

Joanna smiled, feeling a bit awkward about another night, but said nothing.

Hinoch stoked the fire while Joanna undressed and crawled under the covers.

Before dawn, Hinoch was up and preparing breakfast. Joanna tried to ignore the activity, but the smells were too enticing. She roused herself, dressed and started to set the table.

"There is ice fog this morning. If it doesn't clear, the women will have to beat the drums and throat-sing for our return trip."

"You mean you'll follow the sound of their singing?"

"That is the traditional way. I'll also bring my hand-held GPS."

Her laugh burst from her, spraying the remnants of her last mouthful of tea. "The thoroughly modern man!" she added, teasing.

He grinned, "Just prepared. I like to make use of the best things from both of our worlds."

"As you said earlier, this part of the world isn't known for giving second chances."

They ate breakfast, then prepared for the day. Outside, Hinoch's dogs were anxiously pacing. Hinoch pulled the harness out of the shed, hooked it to the *komatik*, then instructed Joanna to open the dog kennel.

Joanna tripped the latch. They leaped at the door. It flew open sending her sliding on her rear across the lane way.

"Wow, talk about eager!" she laughed as she dusted herself off. The dogs were at the shed in an instant, but Hinoch turned and held his hand out, palm down. The dogs moved to the side he indicated and lay down quietly.

He beckoned to the first dog and called her by name. She trotted to him and sat in front of him. He clipped her harness to the sled, then beckoned to the second female. Within minutes, the team was harnessed and ready to go.

"I noticed you put all the girls at the back of the train. Isn't that discrimination?"

"No, it's just reducing the number of distractions."

Joanna roared with laughter. "So do I have to follow behind you?"

"No, you can ride in the *komatik*. It will be good exercise for the dogs."

"Oh, goody, now I'm ballast! Okay, where do I sit?"

Hinoch felt a little awkward at her reaction, but undeterred, he opened the back of the covering over the *komatik* and patted a roll of sealskins. "Here, sit on this. You will probably start to get cool, so do not sit too long. Here are your snowshoes. A little walk now and then will warm you up."

The dawn was about to break as Hinoch mushed his dogs and they pulled out onto the ice. They pulled steadily and quietly, Hinoch standing on one runner, then the other, pushing with his free leg. A few other teams were following, but they were soon far behind.

In a remarkably short time, they were nearing the outer edge of the good ice, where Hinoch turned the team north. Some time later, he stopped and bade Joanna to don her snowshoes. The dogs lay quietly in the snow. In this early light, they almost disappeared into the white background, except for their black noses and eyes.

Hinoch took out his rifle and handed a second weapon to Joanna. "I will show you your good shots. Try to wait until they are completely out of the water, or they may slide back down the hole and be lost. Also, keep an eye open for polar bears. They sometimes like to share in the hunt."

Joanna's eyes widened, but she said nothing. She had never seen a polar bear up close, but she knew them to be the only beast in the arctic that feared no other. Her attention to her surroundings became more acute.

Hinoch led her to a knoll of ice, pushed up by the pressure of wind some time before. They crouched behind the knoll and scanned the horizon. Through the mist, they could barely make out the dark line of the water's edge. Slowly, Hinoch raised his rifle, aimed, then fired. The silence shattered with the abrupt crack of the report. Joanna looked at him blankly, "Doesn't gunfire scare them off?"

He smiled, "That is our first seal."

"You're kidding! Where?"

"Use your scope and I will line you up on him."

She peered through the scope and was amazed to see a blotch of red growing on the ice about four hundred yards away. As she stared, she could make out the faint shape of the seal.

"That's an incredible shot, Hinoch!" "I still can't see him without my scope."

"Scan about fifty yards to the left, another one is coming up." "I will back you up in case you miss."

Slowly, she scanned to the left. Then she saw the head of a seal bobbing up and down through the ice. *Wait . . . wait,* she coached herself, consciously controlling her breathing now. On the third bob, the seal seemed to squirt out onto the ice, then crawl a few feet before coming to rest. She exhaled slowly, placing the scope's cross hairs on top of the seal's chest. She squeezed the trigger gently. The report surprised her, the trigger was so sensitive, but the rest of the experience was far from delicate. The 7mm magnum shell drove the butt of the rifle into her shoulder and the scope hit her sharply above the eyebrow. She felt her flesh jump from the impact and her shoulder instantly informed her that it had not enjoyed the experience. Her glasses were askew, so she adjusted them, and looked through the scope again to see the seal thrashing on the ice in its death-throes. It was then she felt the warm blood trickling down onto her eyelid.

"I got him!" she whispered, turning to Hinoch.

"Yes, that was a good shot, but it looks as though the seal was not the only one to suffer from it. It appears you didn't pull the rifle butt into your shoulder firmly enough." He removed his mitt and licked his thumb, then wiped her brow. He repeated this a few times and Joanna felt a strange elation flow through her. She wondered if it was her imagination, but her senses all seemed to become much sharper and she was tingling from head to toe.

"You've got a nasty little nick there. Here put some snow on it." He reached down and cleaned up the small cut above her eyebrow with a handful of snow. In a few moments the bleeding had stopped.

"That is a Ruger sniper's rifle with an extended barrel and 7mm Magnum shells. It requires a firm hand."

"Thanks for the warning!" she retorted. "I'll remember that!"

He smiled, then turned toward the open water. In a few moments, he had taken another seal.

"Why do you talk like a text book?" Joanna asked, teasing.

Hinoch replied in his usual deadpan fashion, "I spoke only Inuit with my parents, until I was ten years old. When I was brought to Nain for medical treatment, the Public Health Nurse forced me to stay and live with my uncle. I was taken to school, where I began to learn English, the language of instruction. The younger children, with whom I was placed, teased me in Inuit that I could not learn because I was stupid."

"Children can be more cruel than adults can ever imagine," Joanna added.

"The teasing probably helped me. I was determined to prove them wrong, so I studied hard and learned from the books I was given. When I went on to university, I was shy because the environment was so foreign. My roommate, Lucien, had also learned English as a second language. He understood that aspect of my experience. He helped me adjust to the modern environment and we became life-long friends. He is now my agent and business partner."

"Well, I think it's refreshing to hear someone speak proper English. I suppose I should smarten up a bit."

Later in the morning, Hinoch began gutting and cleaning the seals, skinning them out, then tying the chunks of meat back into the skins. The fog persisted, absorbing all detail beyond two hundred yards, leaving only indistinct shapes out to four hundred yards, where everything dissolved into sunlit whiteness. Hinoch looked up toward the sun. It was a bright white dot surrounded by a halo of wondrous colours. As he cleaned the seals, he sang his Nature Song, his hands and arms covered in blood. He rewarded his dogs with the vital organs. By early afternoon, the seals loaded onto the *komatik*, they were on their way back to Nain.

As they rounded the point into the bay, Hinoch heard a snowmobile. It would approach, then move away, move to one side, then to the other. Joanna was snowshoeing alongside and Hinoch remarked, "Sounds as if someone is playing on the ice. I hope they know . . . " he trailed off, listening intently. Silence.

"Get in!" he shouted to Joanna. She jumped aboard, her snowshoes splayed across the sled as he urged the dogs ahead at full speed. Just as abruptly, a few moments later, he called his team to a halt. Hinoch saw that the ice here was slushy and darker in colour.

"Bad ice. They were not paying attention."

He grabbed a polypropylene rope from the *komatik* and attached one end to the frame, then called to his team to turn the sled around. He dropped the loop to the ice and tied the free end up high around his chest.

"Go to the lead dog and stay there. If I go through the ice, urge the dogs to come to you and walk backwards ahead of them. Do not allow them to run!"

"What's wrong, Hinoch? Do you think someone has gone through the ice?"

"Exactly. We don't have much time."

With that, Hinoch spun around and ran off trailing the rope behind him. Joanna stared into the fog, but only thought she could make out his indefinite shape moving toward a dark spot on the ice.

She heard the splash and knew instantly that Hinoch was now in the water also. She called to the dogs and they rose in unison, leaning heavily into the traces of the loaded *komatik*. Nothing. The runners had frozen to the ice!

She thought of her plane.

If I can get them to pull to one side, then the other, maybe they can rock this thing loose.

She ran to one side urging the dogs to pull. Her mind filled with prayer, *Please, do this for me, your master is depending on us!*

The lead dogs turned toward her and pulled mightily. The ice snapped under the runners and the *komatik* jerked ahead. The line to Hinoch drew taut. She stayed ahead of the dogs walking backwards until she heard, "Okay, stop!"

She held her hand out to the dogs palm down. They obeyed instantly, lying down on the ice. "Stay!" she commanded.

She exulted in her feelings. She was handling the dogs as though they were her own. Her inner voice was telling her what to do and she was able to perform these unfamiliar tasks as if they were everyday demands. Her face was flushed with emotion. She was both happy that she was able to help and filled with concern for Hinoch. She picked up the rope and ran following it to the far end, where she found Hinoch giving artificial respiration to a boy of about ten years. The lad spluttered then began to vomit seawater and breathe.

"Caw, Caw, Caw!" Hinoch turned instantly to see his raven beyond the jagged hole in the ice. She was flapping her wings enough to rise from the ice, then abruptly, she landed again on the same spot.

"There were two . . . Monty!" Hinoch rasped as he dragged his now freezing, waterlogged parka up from the ice. He drew his heavy ice knife and cut the line, then ran around the hole to the spot where Tuk waited. She did not flee, but remained close by as he worked feverishly, sending chunks of ice flying up with each powerful blow. Joanna ran to the team and called them to follow her. She led them a respectful distance from the hole then calmly re-tied Hinoch's safety line.

Suddenly he plunged his arm into the water and pulled another boy from the hole.

"Monty!" he screamed, his voice breaking into a soprano pitch. He held his fingers to the boy's neck, searching for a pulse. He trembled from the cold and from his growing anxiety. Could he bring him back? There was no discernible pulse.

His mind was bordering on panic. *How long has it been? If I can revive him, will there be brain damage?*

Within seconds, he began performing CPR on Monty's still form.

"Come back, Monty. Come back!" He worked steadily for nearly three minutes before Monty showed signs of life. Hinoch pulled the now breathing boy to him and wept. The bond with this boy had grown over recent years without either fully realizing its strength. Hinoch's heart was pounding from his exertions, but it was tearing apart at the thought of how close he had come to losing Monty.

"Come on, Hinoch" Joanna called from the sled, "Let's get them home where we can warm them up and treat them. Before we know it, you'll all have hypothermia!"

Hinoch staggered to his feet and dragged Monty along the ice like the seals they had just killed. He was feeling the sharp pains of the cold water now and his breath burned in his throat. He loaded Monty into the sled. His muscles screamed for relief from the searing pain. Each movement now required tearing his flesh loose from the grip of the freezing water in his parka.

He ran to Dick, feeling that his own consciousness was beginning to wane. The field of his vision was darkening at the edges to the point at which he felt he was looking through a black tunnel. He wrestled with himself to retrieve Dick who needed help breaking free of the ice in his sodden parka. They were indeed all in immediate danger.

Joanna was still dry and was unquestionably in the best condition. She helped Hinoch with his snowshoes, then ordered him, "Walk as long as you can. It will help to warm you."

Together, they loaded Dick and Monty into the *komatik* and wrapped both boys in the dry sealskins. She then grabbed the handles of the *komatik* and in her most commanding voice yelled, "Mush!"

The dogs rose and pulled. The loaded sled groaned, then began to glide over the snow. Hinoch trotted alongside, and looked at her with total amazement in his eyes, then turned away and called to the dogs to encourage them. Tuk circled slowly in the fog ahead.

~~~~

Monty and Dick recovered quickly from their misadventures, but became strangely subdued. The people were rendering the seal oil and cutting up the meat, which they froze for the winter. Hinoch was busy with the dogs, hauling the freshly frozen meat out to his tilt line.

Joanna encountered Dick and Monty near the General Store the day after the hunt and inquired how they were feeling.

"Fine," was all that Monty seemed willing to offer.

"You don't sound very fine. What's troubling you?"

"We're both having bad dreams," he replied flatly.

"About what?"

"We were in the water, then we saw Hinoch's raven. She was telling us that help was on the way and that we would be all right."

"You mean when you were in the water, you dreamed of Tuk?"

"Yes. We think she saved us and we want Hinoch to tell us how to thank her."

"Well then, be happy, I'm sure he'll be glad to show you how to thank her as soon as he returns and then the bad dreams will go away."

The boys brightened at this prospect and ran off smiling.

Joanna had packed and was ready to leave, but she hated leaving before Hinoch returned. As she was pondering her problem, she made tea, thinly sliced some smoked salmon and warmed some biscuits for lunch.

The door opened and Hinoch entered. "Just what I wanted! It is nice to come home and have my lunch waiting!"

"Hi!" She beamed. "Don't get too used to it. I've got a wilderness camp to rotate people in and out of this week. Even if the weather cooperates, it'll take me at least three days of steady flying. You wouldn't believe what these guys haul with them."

"When do you leave?"

"Tomorrow morning, early. I've refueled the plane and paid for the fuel at the General Store. They say they'll forward it to Lab Air for me. I don't want to annoy the competition!"

"Do not worry. They would never have missed it. I cannot say the same about you; I am already becoming accustomed to you being here."

"Me too, Hinoch, I'm amazed at how quickly I'm growing an attachment to — this place."

She placed the food on the table and they ate in silence. She was hoping for some kind of indication from Hinoch that he felt something for her. They hardly knew each other, yet she felt drawn to him by a force she couldn't define. Neither of them could think of the next thing to say, so they sat quietly, looking into each other's eyes with self-conscious glances.

His eyes told the story. Joanna was feeling the beginnings of a close bond, but he seemed unable to express anything . . . if he even felt it. *One day, perhaps,* she thought to herself, *but not now.*

Hinoch went to the cupboard and pulled out a bottle of Demerara rum.

"I keep this for the times when I am really cold and need a quick warm up. It is not that cold outside, but I feel as though I need a warm-up anyway." He poured two glasses of the deep brown liquid and sat down across from her. "Good luck, Joanna, may your travels bring you safely back."

He raised the glass and she followed suit. They touched the rims together, then drank the contents in one gulp. Watery-eyed, they sat back in their chairs in silence.

Next morning Hinoch accompanied her down to the plane, where he helped her drape the heavy tent over the engine. He made tea on the kerosene stove as they waited. They sat in the tent together, sipping the tea and trying to make conversation.

"The boys were a bit down yesterday. They said they were dreaming of Tuk when they were under the water. She was apparently telling them that help was on the way. Now they want you to show them how to thank her properly."

"Thank you, Joanna; I think it is time they started to learn how to honour the spirits around them."

"Damn!" she blurted, "I feel like I'm running away from home, or something. I feel like this is my home now, and yet it isn't."

"It's because you have a strong family link to this area. When you have spoken to your grandmother, you can return and we can resolve those feelings."

"It's more than that, Hinoch. Our adventure on the ice brought out something in me I never had to call upon before. I feel I wouldn't have been able to respond so well if you hadn't been there. It felt like you were guiding me without actually speaking to me."

"Again, we communicate well because of the family links we have. My family is now linked to yours spiritually. You have experienced the wisdom of my family working through your spirit."

"How could that happen?"

"When you cut your eye, I took the opportunity to share our spirits. I was amazed at how quickly you were able to use the wisdom of my family to gain full control of the dogs. I hope you will not be angry with me."

Joanna felt herself flush with a strange joy — a revelation, an indication that her burgeoning feelings for Hinoch may be shared.

"Angry? No Hinoch, to the contrary, I'm kind of flattered."

"Good, then I will await your return in spring."

"I'll be back as soon as I hear you've returned from up north. You're right, I don't understand a lot of things about this yet, but I'm sure you'll be able to answer my questions one day."

"You are a wonderful woman, Joanna, possessed of courage and kindness. Thank you for coming to Nain."

They finished tea and she reached up into the engine cowling to assess the time remaining before she could start.

"By the time I'm finished the pre-flight checks it should be warm enough."

Hinoch accompanied her as she walked around the exterior, then extinguished the stove and began rolling up the tent as she completed the in-cockpit checks. He stowed the tent and the now cooled stove in the cargo bay and secured the door. He walked around to her side of the cockpit and gave her the universal thumbs up. "Everything is secure out here," he said. "Have a safe trip and we will see you after I get back from my father's cabin."

She returned the thumbs up and said, "You bet!" She motioned him to step back, then started the engine. Within minutes, she had taxied out onto the ice and the plane was gliding across the snow, leaving a trail of ice fog in its wake. It lifted gracefully into the air, then turned and flew over him, wings rocking. He waved back until the plane was a speck in the distant valley.

He turned to walk back to his cabin and saw Monty and Dick standing forlornly at the head of the dock.

"What is wrong, boys?"

Monty replied, "I bin dreamin' 'bout Tuk since we fell through the ice."

"You owe your life to her, Monty. I had no idea you were under the ice until she alerted me."

"I know. Can you show us how to thank her?"

"Of course. Come with me." The boys turned to walk with him and he placed a hand on each boy's shoulder. "The first thing you will have to learn is that ravens are not simply big blackbirds. Their role on earth is to be the visible form of spirits separated from their families. Tuk is the visible form of her own family's spirits and of the two airmen who were killed in that crash I went to see last spring."

"She's got a lot of spirits in her then?" Dick inquired.

"Yes. Who knows how many wise spirits she harbours. That means she earns our respect. That is the first thing we need to show her."

"How?"

"We will go and sit quietly near her perch, close our eyes and think as hard as we can to picture ourselves as ravens soaring above the village. She will see our thoughts if we try hard enough, and respond in some way. That will be our clue that she is with us in spirit. That is when you can thank her in your thoughts."

"Sounds kinda boring to me . . . don't think it'll work," Monty said.

"If you think positively and your dream is strong enough, it will work, and you will find the result anything but boring. First, you must be willing to try. If you start with the idea that it will not work, you will be correct, but if you start with the belief that it *will* work, you will be correct."

"So, it's up to me?"

"Exactly, Monty. Our success as Inuit depends upon our attitude. Come now, sit down here and get comfortable. See, she is over there, already watching us. Now close your eyes and imagine yourselves as young ravens standing on the edge of your nest. You are about to fly for the first time. Spread your wings. Step off into the air now, feel the air in your wings as you descend, going faster, faster, now flap twice with all your strength. You are floating on the air. Look below at the treetops, then around you off into the distance. You see another raven coming toward you. It is Tuk."

He continued in a soft, chanting tone. "She joins you, showing you how to float on the air rising from the ground in the sun's heat. Now you are becoming tired, your wings are feeling heavy and you want to return to your nest to rest. She turns and leads you home. She slows, flaps her wings gently and settles onto the nest. You imitate her movements and make your first landings. Fold your wings to your side, and thank her for the lesson. Tell her you will never forget what you have learned. Now slowly open your eyes and sit quietly a few more minutes."

As they opened their eyes, Hinoch was sitting in front of them. On his shoulder, Tuk was roosting comfortably, looking intently at the boys. She clucked softly to them and ruffled her wings. The feathers on the cape of her neck stood out momentarily, then settled back. To the boys' amazement, she then hopped into the air and landed on Monty's shoulder. She pecked him on the nose as he turned to look at her, then hopped to Dick's shoulder, repeating the peck as he stared, eyes wide. Immediately, she was gone, floating back to her perch on the lamp standard.

"She has told you that you are welcome. Now, would you like some tea and toast?"

The boys smiled, still slightly overcome by their experience. They quietly got up to follow Hinoch into his cabin. Monty asked, "Hinoch, can we have songs of our own?"

"Of course, we'll make them up after we have tea."

Hinoch began loading the *komatik* for the journey to Abel Shiwack's cabin. The day was perfect, clear and crisp with a light breeze. The temperature was about minus forty. He was elated by the prospect of seeing his parents again. He had an added incentive this year, in that he felt ready to complete his journey into the life of a shaman. Every year he joyfully faced this journey to the wilderness northeast of Hebron, some one hundred and seventy-five miles. He was happy in spite of the dangers. The terrain was mountainous along the shoreline, with many sheltered inlets and bays. Hinoch had placed a line of nine tilts some fifty miles along the coastline expressly for this annual trek.

Springtime was often stormy. On his return trip, if the weather blew in, seven miles would be a good day. The tilts could well make the difference. The dogs would be tired and the seal meat on the *komatik* would be running low. If all went well, he could complete the trip in ten days; if not, it could take two weeks, or it could take forever.

Hinoch had the typical Inuit attitude toward such realities. His philosophy centred upon the present and the demands it made. Worry was not a common pastime for him, nor for any of his people.

He often told his people, "Make your best effort to succeed at whatever is at hand. If, in the future, it does not work out, worrying about it will have made no difference to the outcome. Reality, here, is everywhere you look. There are animals and fish in abundance to eat and clothe ourselves. Reality also is that we can die any day seeking that sustenance."

Hinoch understood his people dealt with every hardship with open eyes and open minds. He smiled to himself. *They are an intelligent and resourceful people, with simple needs and love for one another in their hearts. I believe that we will still be here long after modern society is a dim memory.*

"Hi, 'Noch, looks like you're ready to go."

"Yes, Monty, I just need to hitch up the dogs and break loose the skids on the *komatik*."

"I wish I could come with you; winter-time isn't much fun when you go away."

"Maybe next year, we can go together; I'm sure Abel would enjoy your company."

"I'd like that! See you in spring!"

"Take care of yourself, Monty. I will miss you."

Monty waved and turned to walk away as Hinoch opened the door to the dog pen.

"Could you give me a hand harnessing the dogs?"

Monty's smile showed his big teeth as he replied, "Sure. Your dogs are easy to handle. My father's dogs act like the wild wolves. You have to be careful around them, or they'll bite you. They're fighting all the time too and they're so torn up, I can't believe they can pull a sled. Look," he pulled up his sleeve to reveal ugly red pockmarks on his arm, "Right through my new sealskin parka! I don't think I want dogs; a snowmobile is better, I think."

Indeed, many of Hinoch's people had not yet grasped the importance of their relationship with their dogs. The animals were poorly fed and sporadically trained. It was not uncommon for dogs to chew through their tethers for a chance to hunt or fight among themselves. When a dog lost a fight, the bulk of the evidence quickly disappeared. For this reason, few Inu ventured far from Nain with dog teams, relying instead on snowmobiles to pull their *komatik*s. The machines had drawbacks too though: an unforgiving reliance on gasoline and a need for regular maintenance, both frequently in short supply. Hinoch knew his people observed his activities with interest. He hoped they learned the value of dogs from his successful journeys. Hinoch knew Monty hung on his every word and observed his every action intently.

He frowned to lend a serious mood to his words and looked at his young protégé. "When a snowmobile is out of gas you go nowhere; when Kringmerk is starving, he will pull your sled hoping to receive nothing more than your praise and respect. He knows that when you are able, you will feed him. One day, you will have your own team Monty. I am sure you will make certain that they are well trained."

Hinoch could see that Monty was processing this snippet of wisdom. He frowned, imitating Hinoch's serious expression, "You bet I will! I can't wait to go out on my own and hunt seals."

"We'll go together a few more times, Monty, so that you learn how to read the ice and how to find the best seals."

"Yeah, I'd like that!"

As they talked, they harnessed the dogs and placed them in the traces attached to the *komatik*. Hinoch's team rarely tangled their traces. As he worked, Hinoch showed Monty the fine points of laying out the harness and began instructing him on important techniques for maintaining control over the dogs. Monty giggled as one of the younger dogs managed to tangle her leg in her partner's trace. She was obviously embarrassed at her clumsiness.

"That's okay, Atin, you should see my dad's dogs. Three seconds after they're in their traces there's paws in the air, dogs on dogs and the worst howling dog-fight you've ever seen. Here, I'll fix that for you."

He quickly freed her leg, whereupon she licked him in the face, starting at his chin, up over his nose and over his forehead in one soggy motion. He sat back on his haunches and squealed with delight, rolled onto his face and washed off with snow. Atin watched this, wanting to join in on the game, but she seemed unwilling to risk another misadventure with the traces. She yipped and whistled through her nose.

"Good girl, Atin," he laughed again, gouts of snow melting and sliding down his face. She wagged her tail furiously, but held her place. Monty realized her conflict was born out of an overwhelming desire to be everything Hinoch expected and the desire to play with her friend. The fact she denied her desire in favour of what she knew Hinoch wanted impressed him. Hinoch's words of only a few moments ago were given credence by Atin's discipline. He internalized his lesson, determined to have a team like this when he was a young man. He removed his mitt and gave her a rub behind the ear, saying nothing, but communing with her.

Hinoch smiled his approval, "Thanks for your help, Monty. Take good care of your brother and I will see you as spring approaches."

"Okay, 'bye." Monty's face became serious. His sole source of refuge was leaving again. He watched as Hinoch moved to the rear of the sled, rocked the skids free and ordered his dogs to pull with a sharp, "Mush!" They waved. He stood, letting the cold seep into his feet, his legs, and his heart. He watched the sled become smaller and smaller, eventually disappearing into the drifting snow. Hinoch moved the team out onto the ice, leaving the random patchwork of dingy buildings behind, moving steadily into the pure, unspoiled wilderness of Labrador. Long after Hinoch had disappeared, Monty stared unblinking at the spot, letting the white overcome his eyes.

The tears, he could tell himself, were the irritation of the onset of snow-blindness.

Hinoch was happy to be on his way again. His team pulled steadily and quietly and the miles slid with a steady hiss under the runners of his *komatik*. Tuk would circle overhead from time to time then fly inland, perhaps to scavenge for food. Hinoch continually scanned the distance for signs of weather, polar bears, or other dog teams. The coastal ice-shelf provided the easiest way to make long journeys in winter.

Inland, it was passable, but the mountainous terrain made travel much more difficult. Hinoch prayed that the winter winds stayed well off shore. If they came, the ice would break up, then re-freeze into a maze of abrupt climbs and drops that would test the strength of his *komatik*, his dogs and himself. Travel would become a bone-jarring series of nearly vertical ups and downs that could cut the miles covered in half. Even at that, the ice shelf remained the preferred route.

The first day, Hinoch reached his third tilt. He fed his dogs from the stores of food in the *komatik* and gave Tuk a few scraps to keep her quiet, then lit the stove in the tilt. Soon, he was cooking the seal meat for his evening meal, relishing the aromas as they filled the tiny cabin. Shortly afterward, he was sound asleep.

In his dream, he saw Abel, his father standing outside his tilt.

"Hinoch, rouse yourself. Danger is near!"

He felt himself float up from his resting place, feeling disconnected from his body. He looked down to see his dogs asleep in the snow near the *komatik*, then he realized he was looking through the roof of his tilt onto his own sleeping form. He was intrigued by this unusual situation, but felt no alarm, or concern. Then his senses told him to look around. Not far off, he saw a polar bear shuffling toward his camp, leaving the characteristic pigeon-toed trail of pugmarks in the snow.

Approach him and command him to return where he came, his father's voice spoke inside his head.

Hinoch descended from his vantage point and alit on the snow in front of the polar bear.

The huge beast stopped, then rose on his hind legs to his full height — nearly twelve feet. Hinoch felt himself rise to the bear's eye level, then he felt a voice, his own voice, boom out with powerful resonance, "You will find no sustenance here, Gaulaqut. Be gone!"

The bear sniffed the air, clearly confused by what he faced. Slowly, he lowered himself to all fours, turned and walked into the distance. The gait was deceivingly awkward, belying the speed and power of Gaulaqut. The stubby tail and massive hindquarters swayed from side to side with each step, the back sloped downward to the front shoulders and the broad head hinged round from time to time on the bear's massive neck. The look in those tiny black eyes tested Hinoch's resolve. In less than five minutes, the white fur had nearly dissolved into the dimly lit nightscape of snow and ice. It appeared to Hinoch that the bear's behaviour had become subdued. He had not appeared alarmed or angered, but subdued, as if obeying a force greater than himself.

Hinoch watched as the bear moved off, then noticed a large, white raven circling over the bear. Hinoch returned to his tilt, feeling himself pass through the logs, becoming part of them as he moved through their fibers. He slipped back into his body where he slept for nearly six hours.

When he emerged from his tilt, the dogs were sitting quietly, waiting for him.

"Good morning, my loyal companions, we have another beautiful day ahead. Let us begin."

He fed them and clipped their harnesses to the central tether. In a matter of minutes, they were underway.

About one thousand yards from the tilt, Hinoch brought the team to an abrupt halt. He stood staring at the pack ice, disbelieving what his eyes clearly saw. In the snow were the pugmarks of a huge polar bear. The animal had walked to this point, then turned and retraced his steps.

An overwhelming sense of peace and power filled his soul. He had learned a great lesson from the spirit growing within.

The second day was equally successful in terms of distance covered, bringing Hinoch to his sixth tilt, where he repeated his preparations for the night. The travel became routine for five more days. The ice was relatively smooth. The storms had stayed offshore, leaving the ice unscarred by the upheavals generated by surging waves beneath and wind above. The skies remained cloudless and dark blue, a hue seen only in the north when the sun is low on the horizon. Each night, the skies were less darkened, the sun skirting just below the horizon, leaving a pink halo that crowned the mountains to the west.

On the sixth night, again, he faced a vision in his sleep. His father's image filled his senses, then he heard him speak. *Hinoch, my son, make haste. We have urgent need of you!*

Hinoch became acutely aware of the agitation in his spirit. He felt it rise through the roof of the tilt. Air began flowing over his outstretched hands. He looked to one side, then the other to see white wings in place of his arms, flight feathers instead of fingers. Hinoch marvelled at the sensations of flight, the feathers coursing through the air, sensing every ripple of its passage over and through them. He flew soundlessly through the arctic twilight.

When he looked down, he was surprised to see the landscape moving past with alarming speed. In what seemed like minutes, he recognized the landmarks of his father's home, the steep valley and the small cabin at its apex. Hinoch passed into the cabin as he had entered his tilt the previous night, to see his father lying on his bed, his mother beside him.

They were gaunt and wrinkled. It was apparent that the summer months had not gone well. He scanned the room and saw that the food supply was desperate. Only a little of the precious rice he had brought last winter remained; the fire was but a few coals glowing feebly on the hearth.

"Father, I am here. Why did you not summon me sooner? I could have brought you food by plane."

Slowly his father's eyes flickered open. Hinoch could see the many souls in them. He could also see that the time was near for him to receive them.

"My son, I have no need of food that I cannot gather myself. It is my time. You are about to succeed me. First I give you the spirits of our family, now hundreds of generations old."

Hinoch saw a warm glow rise from his father's bed, then felt its heat as it enveloped him. He was short of breath from the power of the experience, as his ancestors filled him with new awareness.

"And now, my son, I pass to you the song of the shaman, my spirit, and my powers."

A searing blue-white light enveloped Hinoch, the vision of his eyes became misted in a cloudy-white, yet he sensed immediately that the new vision of his spirit was infinitely clearer. He inhaled sharply and sat upright in his tilt. Had he just been dreaming, or had something profound and surreal just transpired? It took him a few moments to process that something was different. As he looked around his tilt, he realized his eyes recorded only the pitch-blackness, yet in his mind, he could see everything clearly. His rifle leaned where he had left it by the entrance; the stove glowed slightly at the base where the remaining fire lay breathing. Then he felt an uneasiness rise in his throat as he pointed his attention in the direction of his dogs. In his body's eyes he saw blackness, but in his mind's eye, he saw them sleeping soundly in the snow. He could see the logs of the wall, yet he could also see his dogs beyond, simply by refocusing his attention.

Hinoch touched his face as if to confirm his continued existence. Yes, he could touch himself, so he must be here and awake, yet he felt so strangely different, so much an integral part of everything around him. He was at once convinced that he was dreaming and that he was fully awake and alert. No, far more alert than ever before in his life!

As Hinoch emerged from his tilt, the dogs rose and greeted him, then enclosed him in a circle, whining anxiously and licking at his fingers. He moved to the *komatik* and gave them each a ration of seal meat.

He moved the team out of the shelter afforded by the lea side of Cod Island into the minus forty temperatures, driven on a freshening wind that razored at his exposed cheeks. He snugged the hood of his parka and adjusted his welding goggles. He would need to divert his course out of the wind regularly to allow the dogs to shelter their eyes. The wind was northwest, sliding down the backs of the Torngat Mountains onto the ice. No danger of upheavals in the ice existed so long as the wind did not veer to the east. Hebron passed to the east two days later and Hinoch struck out for Saglek Bay, exuberant over the excellent progress, the good weather and his feeling of complete freedom. Despite the severe conditions, the huge dogs made good distance each day, hardening their muscles and thrilling in the physical activity.

Five days after his vision, Hinoch stood at the door of his father's cabin. No smoke rose from the chimney. The tilts had no provisions and his father had not met him on the trail. Hinoch directed his attention beyond the cabin door and sensed the cold air inside the room. There on the bed lay his father and mother. They were gaunt and wrinkled, their features sunken in their heads. As he moved forward, he opened the door, feeling it was more a habit now than a necessity. As in his vision, he saw that the cabin was bereft of food; only a few grains of rice remained in the bag he had brought last winter.

His eyes filled with tears and he kneeled beside the bed, stretching his arms over them. He wept. Gently, his father touched him on the head. He spoke softly, but clearly in Inuktitut. "You are here, my son. Thank you for your haste."

"I have had powerful dreams, Father, dreams of Gaulaqut approaching my camp, then leaving at my command, and of you calling me to your side. I flew to you as a white *Tullugak* and gained vast powers of observation and insight from you. What is happening?"

"You have begun your final voyage into . . . the life . . . of a shaman, my son. I have . . . given you . . . the knowledge over the years. You have gained the sensitivity of a shaman . . . through your study of the lives and spirits around you. All that remains . . . is for you receive my spirits and . . . take my place. I am leaving this life for the spirit world. You will face a huge challenge: to conquer the remaining spirits that I could not. You . . . will meet me again . . . very soon . . . as a large white raven. Sing my song to the raven, the one you learned in your dream, so he will know you. He will unite all our spirits in yours. You will be the sixty-fourth shaman in our family. The most powerful shaman our people have ever known. Our proud history extends over two thousand years into the past. I go now. May our spirits soar forever."

Tuk watched from her perch on the mantle as Abel Shiwack's hand went limp; it slid from Hinoch's head to the skins on the bed. Tuk's intimate and rapidly strengthening link with her guiding spirit told her that Hinoch sensed his parents' spirits. There was nothing to see, nothing to hear, yet Tuk was convinced that a communion was taking place. The room had an aura of warmth, not of the air, but of the atmosphere. Hinoch remained still, his expression changing subtly and his eyes moist as he appeared to watch something beyond Tuk's ken. She concluded the spirits had remained within the small room for some time afterwards, comforting their son.

Tuk ruffled her feathers; she had felt the room cool dramatically. As she surveyed the simple cabin, she realized the spirits were here no longer.

Tuk perched silently waiting for her opportunity. She watched Hinoch kneeling at their bedside with his arms draped over their still bodies. His mother had passed earlier and had seen Hinoch arrive from the spirit World. Her body was cold. Hinoch remained with them until he could feel his father's body becoming rigid as rigor mortis entered his muscles and joints.

Tuk ruffled her flight feathers noisily and her mind spoke to him. *Dawn is near, Hinoch. We should begin to honour your father and mother.* As she watched, Hinoch arose, and gathered up his father's ceremonial walking staff and medicine bag. He took one last look at his father's horribly scarred face; marked for life by the claws of Gaulaqut. He turned then and went outside, where he began to gather wood from the lower branches of the nearby shrubs. He gathered kindling wood for the next two hours, arranging it around the outside of the little cabin.

As the first wisps of smoke rose from the pyre, Tuk sensed a presence beside her. She turned to see a large white raven perched on a low branch, not twenty-five feet away. This was a magnificent bird, larger than any raven she had seen before. His feathers were in prime condition reflecting the arctic winter sun in a play of sunset mauves and reds.

His eyes were the eyes of a being of many souls, a more powerful spirit than she had ever encountered. Her mind spoke, "Hinoch, we are with a *Krauyimatauyok* Torngak."

"Yes, Tuk, I see him also, I will sing the shaman's song as Father instructed." As Tuk watched, transfixed by the events around her, he sang and held out his hand. The raven stepped from his perch, extended his wings and floated soundlessly to him. He landed on Hinoch's outstretched hand.

The glow of the fire was increasing now, but it was transcended by the searing blue-white glow that surrounded Hinoch and the white raven. As she watched, the raven seemed to float up his arm and dissolve into him. The glow increased, then slowly subsided.

After a time, after she saw that Hinoch was again within himself, she spoke, *How are you now?*

I feel my own spirit and its awareness vastly expanded. My father has given me a breadth and acuity of perception that I cannot express, yet I feel at one with all life around me. I can sense its proximity and its vitality. I sense you Tuk and I feel the spirits you have carried with you since we met at the crash site. You are the true descendent of your father and his family, an old and powerful spirit in your own right.

Tuk stood tall on her perch and rattled her flight feathers in an expression of joy, *I have waited a long time for this contact between us. My father told me that you were soon to become a powerful shaman. The spirits I carry are anxious to return to their families. In spring we must all return to the lake to complete the cycle for the lost souls I carry.*

I agree, but now I bear a great sense of loss in my heart. I will never again see my mother and father in their bodies. The fire is taking them forever from me. Yet, conflicting with that heartache is the joy of the new quality of communication I enjoy with them and with all of my Ancestors. I can see them clearly in my mind, even speak with them in my consciousness, as if we are in counsel. The vast difference is in the quality of our communications. Understanding is immediate and feelings conveyed with far greater clarity than I have ever enjoyed before in my lifetime. Words are no longer necessary! Hinoch raised his arms and tossed his head back, laughing with an almost hysterical elation. Tuk took to the air and hovered, anxious to remain the centre of his focus, but his attention had returned to his parents.

He turned slowly, arms still outstretched, marvelling anew at the beauty of this place. *I wish to remain longer, gorge myself on the pure wonder of an existence here. I feel I need to do this so I can better relate the blessing of our traditional lives to my people . . . my people. Their future has been entrusted to me. Now I must lead them.*

His eyes closed and he lowered his arms, then he turned to Tuk and spoke softly. "Tuk, remain my constant companion. Together we will travel back to Nain. Perch on the *komatik* over the smoother stretches and soar with me to find the way to the best ice when the route is not certain." She sensed her time had come, so she flew to his shoulder.

"I now call upon the spirits of Curtis and Paul, resident in this raven."

"We are still here." Tuk jumped, feeling the spirits stir within, alarmed at the disembodied voice. She looked around and saw the filmy image of a young man clothed in leather — one of her spirits.

"Yes, I can see you clearly now. Tell me your story."

His mind formed a thought, then a picture. Hinoch found himself looking through Curtis' eyes, sixty years in the past, at the instrument panel of the old plane and marvelling, as he always did, at the untouched beauty passing below. He could feel the controls of the aircraft in his hands as they tugged and pushed, buffeted by the currents of air flowing over the wings. In a deep, hypnotic state, he became Curtis.

"Goose Bay, Goose Bay, this is Kilo Tango Lima on 126.2. Do you read, over." The speakers in the headset replied in a scratchy voice, "Tango Lima, Goose, read you loud and clear. Runway 27 is in use, winds 280 at ten knots, altimeter 2937, report entering the circuit."

"Wilco."

Curtis slowed the plane to approach speed and began the descent to the airport, now visible in the distance. That evening in the officers' club, Curtis welcomed the camaraderie of the aircrew, waiting for repairs and maintenance, for further orders, for good weather. The forecast was not good, he heard. His frustration surfaced when he woke the next morning to dense fog over the airfield. Paul was still in a good mood from last night, but knew better than to display it.

The departure would be delayed, probably until afternoon, meaning a night flight over the ocean. Curtis was skilled at instrument flying, but always felt uneasy when he had no reference to the ground. This flight would be like flying in a black hole. No lights, nothing to help him verify that his instruments were telling him the truth, for hours on end.

He dressed, collected Paul and accompanied him to the mess for breakfast. Next, they went to the airfield and entered the hangar where the top-secret Mosquito had been taken to keep it from prying eyes. With nothing better to do, they carried out an especially detailed preflight check on the aircraft and reviewed their flight plan in detail. Finally, they went to the weather briefing room to check on the forecast for their route.

Chance of snow squalls near the coast. At these temperatures, icing would be a danger. Paul and Curtis decided to plan a higher altitude for the flight in hopes of finding colder air aloft. In colder air, the precipitation would already be frozen and less likely to coat the aircraft with ice.

Later, in the air, Curtis switched from the Goose Bay navigation beacon to the beacon at Cartwright. With dusk falling, they entered cloud. Shortly afterward, it began to snow and rain. The wind got rough, and the wings began to ice up. The boots on the wings could not get rid of it fast enough. The controls were getting heavy and Curtis couldn't even shake the ice loose. Curtis' fear intensified as the plane began to lose altitude, even at full power. Ice flung from the propellers made repeated staccato noises as it struck the nose of the plane.

Curtis and Paul understood what was coming, but were powerless to change the outcome. Katie-Lee finally refused to fly any further. The trees loomed out of the blizzard, snapping over the plane like twigs . . . rocks ground underneath . . . then pain. Curtis smashed into the control column and, as he felt his own harness break, he saw Paul being ejected through the windscreen.

Curtis passed out. In the morning, he was jolted into awareness by a searing pain in his leg and a heavy, burning sensation in his chest. Slowly, he began to orient himself and assess his situation. The storm was gone and the sun was streaming into the cockpit, warming him. He struggled from his seat; no simple process, because he frequently lost his breath from the explosive blasts of pain his movements generated. He found the emergency medical kit and began fashioning a splint for his leg. This done, he ventured outside to find Paul. He found him in the snow ahead of the plane. His head had been torn open, jagged glass imbedded into his skull, and his back was broken.

Curtis tried to wipe the blood from Paul's face, but the glass cut his hand. He pulled back, alarmed by the strange sensation, a strange surge of energy, like something entering his very soul. Curtis knelt, not knowing what to do. He was still looking down at Paul's body, but he sensed he had the added dimension of Paul's perspective.

Over the next several hours, he buried Paul in a shallow grave and chopped down a sapling to mark it.

With his broken leg and difficulty breathing, he began to gather the supplies they had placed in the aircraft only the day before. Curtis fully realized that without some improvement in the situation, he would not last for more than a few days. He knew he needed to get fresh food if he was to have any chance of survival. Again, Curtis ventured outside, this time to survey the surroundings, which he had totally ignored to this point. He could see a little lake about two hundred yards back from his location. The crash-landing had cleared a path down to its shore.

How to get out onto the water? Curtis thought. Slowly, he looked around, his eyes settling on the teardrop shapes of the engine cowlings. Carefully, he assessed what would be required to convert one of them into a canoe. The left cowling had extra air-scoops for the huge generator on that side. The right side would be easier to seal. He could use the heavy, rubberized canvas ground-sheet intended as a temporary shelter and sleep in the plane. He looked around and saw pine tar hanging from the trees and bark peeling from the birches.

It was a struggle of will against the barrier of pain. Curtis' leg and the burning in his chest threatened to overcome him as he fought to open the fasteners that held the top cowling in place on the starboard engine. For the next day and a half, he forced himself to work for hours carefully sealing up the openings in the cowling. He cut pieces of the ground sheet, then retrieved birch bark and coated the bark heavily with pine tar. Finally, he melted it into place with his lighter, using all the remaining fuel it contained. He felt keen disappointment at the realization that not only would he be forced to quit smoking, but also that it would be much more difficult to light a fire.

Curtis thought, *Damn it, man. If you're going to let that get you down, you haven't got a hope of facing the next few days, weeks, maybe even months. You're alive. Make the best of it! By now, they've probably contacted Dianne to tell her we haven't shown up. She has to be going through hell.*

They've started the search by now, so with any luck you'll be out of here and on your way home in a few days. Let's get the fishing kit into the canoe. Something fresh will sure perk up these dry rations.

He winced and gasped at every rush of pain as he struggled to pull the canoe to the lakeshore. Out on the water, the rush of elation was overwhelming as Curtis landed a nice trout. That meal of raw fish not only restored some strength, it raised his spirits. For the first time in five days, Curtis believed he might just make it. He was determined to maintain his hope, even in these desperate circumstances.

Each day drained more valuable vitality from Curtis. It continued to be painful for him to breathe and the leg had become infected. He regularly forced himself to remain still, listening for an aircraft engine, prepared to light the fuel that remained in the plane's tanks, despite the danger of explosion and severe burns. Other than the hum of insects and the occasional bird, he heard nothing. It was taking too long for them to find him. Curtis knew the fierce winds of that squall had driven them off course. Goose Bay had severely limited rescue resources, so as time passed, he reasoned they would call off the search, meaning it was just a matter of time.

Curtis felt the physical drain of the infection and could not deny the consequent sapping of his will to live. He ran out of dressings and disinfectant. The leg was nowhere near healed; it was getting worse. The bone kept re-opening the wound every time he moved around. He sat disconsolate, looking down on the rotten flesh around the wound and finally allowed himself to sink into despair. He was feeling pain of a kind he had never known, for longer than he could have imagined it lasting, and now as the heat of summer came on, the blackflies were becoming impossible to bear. Despite the hopelessness of the situation, Curtis, refused to give in totally. He fought his way back to the canoe for just one more fresh fish. Out on the water, he let the line pay out over the side and leaned back in the canoe to rest. He closed his eyes, welcoming the sensation as the pain drained away. He did not know whether time had passed when he opened his eyes, but he was surprised to find himself looking down from above.

He was confused for a moment, then filled with wonder as he realized he was looking down upon his own corpse; he was a spirit, floating free.

He looked around and spied Raven hovering nearby, also looking down on the body. He had seen this bird before. He had a nest in a big tree nearby. The bird kept circling and looking down at Curtis' body in the boat. On the second day, Raven landed in the boat and ate some of Curtis' flesh. As soon as this happened, Curtis was drawn down. He realized at the last second, as he entered the bird's body that the raven was taking in his spirit.

Hinoch began to recover from the vision trance. He sensed that from this point, the story would shift to the raven's perspective. In a surreal kind of review, Hinoch relived the life of the old raven. He experienced the bird's elation as he pried lose Curtis' wedding ring and took it to his nest. Hinoch soared with him as he won his mate, wept aloud as Eagle destroyed Raven's joy and cheered Raven on as he exacted his revenge. Then he found himself marvelling in the realization that this was in fact the same bird he had encountered just this spring. Hinoch relived Iniktuk's annual trips to the nesting site, the unending search for the ring and the day he had offered the ring to the bedraggled old bird. He mourned at Raven's death, finding consolation in the knowledge that the spirits would be safe within Tuk as she experienced the transfer of the spirits to herself. The trance ended with her journey to Nain, following Hinoch.

Hinoch wavered on his feet, not knowing how long the vision had taken, feeling he had been motionless for some time, judging by the numbness in his legs. He took a few moments to internalize what he had learned, then spoke softly, "Paul and Curtis . . . are you aware that Dianne married Paul's older brother, Carl, two years later?"

There were two apparitions now: Curtis and Paul. They looked at each other, sharing their surprise, then turned back to Hinoch. *We were like an extended family anyway, we always told Carl to look after everyone while we were away. Guess he did. How do you know all this?*

I met your grandaughter late this fall. She brought me up to date. Hinoch was uncomfortable to be relaying such personal information, but was heartened at Curtis' reaction.

Grandaughter? Wow! What's her name?

Joanna.

My mother's name . . . Joanna, Curtis said, smiling again. *I like that. What's happened to Dianne?*

Joanna told me she is in a senior's home and is quite frail . . . but she is still alive.

Can you take us to her?

Joanna has promised to bring her to Nain this spring. We will all return to the crash site where I will re-unite you.

Wonderful! But is there some way that we can stay there, or do we have to return to Winnipeg?

Hinoch was a little surprised at this question, but responded without asking the reason. *You will be free spirits. You will be able to go when and where you please.*

Will we just float around like after we died?

If you wish, or you may assume the form of ravens. You may become Torngaks.

Ravens?

That is the being of this earth blessed with the capability of becoming spirits in visible form.

Ravens it is then. I just hope Dianne likes flying!

Hinoch smiled in response. *Ravens you shall be.*

The two apparitions began to dissolve as they floated toward Tuk. She opened her wings to accept them into her breast once again. Hinoch turned his attention to his dog team, in need of some familiar contact to ground himself again in the present.

"Come, my faithful friends. It is time for us to return to Nain. Take your places so I may connect your harnesses to the sled."

The dogs moved to their places, almost like soldiers taking their places for a parade. They sat waiting for him to connect them to the main trace.

"Good. Now we go until you begin to tire. The weather is holding calm and clear. We will have a safe and rapid trip home."

Why don't we just fly home? Paul asked. *We can all fly now. I've seen you as a white raven and as a man.*

Hinoch smiled to himself, *Ah, he can speak after all. Perhaps he needed more time to take in his situation.* He replied, *My dogs are my close companions; to leave them alone out here would be certain death. We also need time to strengthen our bonds, you and I. The trip will serve to unite us and make us more responsive, one to the others. Even spirits must sometimes wait until the time is right. As you well know by now, sometimes we must wait many seasons.*

Hinoch paused, sensing something approaching. *Tuk, come down here immediately, danger approaches.*

I am coming, what do you sense that I do not?

Nektoralik, your sworn enemy, approaches from the east. He is descending from a great height and is flying fast.

Then he is attacking. How far is he now?

You must dive to me now. Do not attempt to defend yourself. This eagle is an ancient spirit. He will not be easily thwarted.

As Tuk was about to land, Hinoch opened the flap over the *komatik*, removing his father's walking staff. "Good, now hop in here, Nektoralik is nearly upon us."

Hinoch turned to face the attacking eagle. To his surprise, this was the largest example of the breed he had ever seen. The bird's wings easily spanned twenty feet; dangerous talons extended at least three inches from the powerful claws. Hinoch's acute perception alerted him to the uncharacteristic eyes of this beast; they were golden, almost iridescent.

He held up his father's walking staff and commanded, "Halt your attack, ancient spirit. Nektoralik, I command you to turn back. There is nothing here for you."

The eagle gave his most soul-destroying screech as he extended his deadly talons. He was swooping down upon Hinoch at an amazing speed. The talons struck Hinoch's hooded head, easily parting the sealskin and tearing his scalp from front to rear.

Hinoch staggered; he had not sensed the attack would be on his own person. How had this happened? Warm blood ran down his neck and over his face, yet he felt no pain and no anger. He turned to face the bird's next approach, which he could sense was now from the rear. As he turned, the bird struck him on the back with its full weight. He fell to the ice. A searing pain burned in his neck. His flesh was tearing near his spine. If this continued, Nektoralik would kill him in just a few more seconds. He rose from his body as the white raven.

"Nektoralik, am I what you seek?" he roared.

Instantly, the bird leapt into the air in an attempt to gain height for his renewed attack.

"You are wise to face me Tullugak; I will spare the life of your feeble disguise for the chance to challenge you yet again!"

As they circled, gaining height, Hinoch spoke to his father. *Father, I have been attacked by Nektoralik; is he an old enemy of yours?*

His father's answer came immediately, *Yes, my son. He is an ancient enemy of Raven, possessing great powers of flight. He will not tire, and will continue to rake you with his talons until you fall from the sky unless you deny him the advantage of climbing above you. Climb with all your might and circle him at close range. At every opportunity, pull a flight feather from him until he cannot remain aloft. His favorite defense will be to allow you to approach from above, then he will flip over at the last second and attempt to grab you with his talons. If he succeeds, he will be the victor. Avoid his powerful beak, but at all costs, remain outside the grasp of those talons.*

Thank you, Father.

Soar with our spirits, my son.

Hinoch shouted with his own voice, "Nektoralik, you have engaged Tullugak, the ancient spirit of the raven. You risk the loss of the ancient spirit of the eagle. Why do you press this attack?"

"You are the latest generation of the Tullugak spirit, as yet not fully aware of your powers, therefore you are vulnerable. My ancient arch-enemy is vulnerable."

Tuk emerged from her hiding place as they soared into the sky. She watched in awe as the two huge birds scrambled for altitude, circling tightly around each other. She was witnessing the continuing battle of the two greatest enemies of nature in the skies. As she stared in wonder, Raven suddenly darted at Eagle from above, skimming by Eagle's left wing. Two flight feathers floated slowly to the ground, but Eagle abruptly climbed vertically until all airspeed was gone, then he fell to one side, his wings tucked into the diving position, talons extended. Raven had responded in kind, mere inches from those deadly talons, but he had flapped his wings powerfully as he climbed. From this advantage of height, he plucked yet another flight feather from his opponent. Not without cost. As he pressed his attack a talon raked his breast, deeply gashing this most valuable of flight muscles. White bloodstained feathers fluttered to the ice below.

The dive continued and, as the speed increased, Eagle began to put distance between them. Raven abruptly halted his dive and began again to climb, drops of blood raining from his wound. Eagle could not arrest his descent so easily, due to his greater weight and the loss of three flight feathers from his left wing. As he climbed, he laboured, the left wing producing less lift and reduced control. Raven watched this intently.

With his wound, Raven knew that his endurance would be reduced. He folded his wings to his side and dove on the labouring eagle.

Eagle waited . . . waited, then flipped onto his back at the last second, but Raven had managed to deflect his trajectory slightly. He made no attempt to remove feathers, but remained in his dive, wings extended only enough to influence his direction. As Eagle grasped with his talons, he only captured the tortured air flowing over Raven's right wing. Raven crashed into Eagle's right wing with the full momentum of his dive. With a loud snap, Eagle's wing broke and feathers exploded from over ten inches of his span.

Nektoralik screamed his pain and anger at his defeat as he tumbled. With a resonating thump, he struck the unyielding ice below.

Painfully, Tullugak began to arrest his dive. The impact had stunned him, but he fought for awareness, and the strength to push his battered wings into the slipstream. Slowly, controlled flight returned, just as the ice was looming up toward him. He flared and managed to land, but fell to the ice immediately, exhausted.

He looked at Nektoralik, the nerves of the now lifeless body still attempting to rescue the broken hulk from its inevitable fate. Slowly, the spirit emerged and hovered above the carcass. Tullugak rose and stumbled to Nektoralik. He drove his beak into Eagle's breast and tore the flesh from its host. As he did so, the hovering spirit became part of his own.

"Now Nektoralik, at long last, the battle is over. Our spirits are one and we will be at peace. From this day, Eagle will coexist with Raven and torment him no longer." Tullugak felt his strength return, flooding into his body and his soul. The wound closed and the lost feathers returned to their places. He turned and ambled over to Hinoch, his host, re-entering his body.

Hinoch rose from the ice, covered in dried blood. With his hand, he felt the torn hood and explored the jagged tears running along his scalp. Then he found the deep wound in his neck.

"Tuk, am I badly wounded?"

"You have some serious tears in your flesh and a deep wound near your spine, but as I watch, they are healing."

My son, you have defeated our ancient enemy, Nektoralik, Abel interjected. *You will heal quickly from your wounds, but seek cover for today; you have more spirits to face. They will challenge you as you encounter them, so you must recover before you continue your journey.*

Thank you, Father. I feel stronger already. My next tilt is only a short distance. I will rest there.

He spoke aloud, "Tuk, scan the ice between the tilt and us. Seek out the easiest route."

Tuk rose into the sky and flew to the southeast. Her response came to his thoughts. *The path is clear and the ice is good, we may proceed directly.*

"Then we go. Come, my friends, make all haste for I must rest."

The dogs rose and ran at full speed the three miles to the next tilt. They stopped in the shelter of the trees and sat, tongues hanging, waiting for him to remove them from their traces. Hinoch unclipped their harnesses and gave each dog a large ration of seal meat. He turned then and entered the tilt. His head was aching painfully as he lit the small stove and spread out the sealskins for his bed.

Before falling asleep, he carefully sewed the tears in his hood and removed as much of the dried blood as he could. With his oils, he cleansed himself, paying particular attention to his rapidly closing wounds. He selected herbs from his medicine bag and coated the wounds with them. Soon after, he slept, but it was a sleep filled with dreams. He saw Gaulaqut, the polar bear, Kapvik the wolverine, Arluk the killer whale and a white-skinned man in magnificent, coloured robes.

Father, must I battle each of these spirits as I did Nektoralik?

No, my son, Arluk is your friend. Gaulaqut has faced you once, but realized it was too soon. He will return and he will challenge you now that you are a shaman, but he may also have reservations since you have defeated Nektoralik.

Kapvik will wait until he feels the time is to his advantage. He is your most cunning adversary.

What about the human in the brightly-coloured robes?

I have never encountered that spirit. It is one that has come to you in your own life. You must learn how to deal with it yourself. I was lucky to leave my encounter with Gaulaqut with my life. For the others, I can teach you what I know, but they did not seek me out. I, too, battled Nektoralik, but the outcome was indecisive. I am pleased that what I learned about him has helped you to prevail over him.

Can you teach me more about the other spirits?

Yes, my son. You will sleep now, the sleeping-trance of the shaman. In it, you will learn all you need to help you carry the tradition, then pass it on to your children.

Hinoch dreamed a short while, then awoke feeling strong and refreshed. In one of his dreams, he'd encountered a strange man dressed in long colourful robes.

The tall, robed figure's words had come to him in a commanding tone, *Hinoch, you must return to Montreal and begin to show the world how its blind corruption and ignorance of nature is the very source of its destruction.*

Who are you?

I am the spirit of the lost peoples of the world.

How can I influence the course of the entire world?

Your story must be powerful and compelling. It must clearly show them what they must change to avoid the collapse of nature.

Their most famous scientists have been telling them this for many years. If they have not listened to them, what can an artist from Labrador do that they cannot?

Art has a stronger impact than fact on many people. You must show them through your art how the world should be.

That reality will be totally repugnant to them. They will refuse to put themselves at risk of death merely to obtain food when all they need to do now is drive to the grocer.

Nevertheless, if you do not accomplish this, the world will suffer a violent change in the patterns of nature, causing the virtual extinction of mankind. The image in Hinoch's vision raised his arms above his head

By 'virtual' you imply that the extinction will not be total.

That is correct. Some people, who now live as nature intended, will survive.

Those who now live as nature intended live in numbers that can be supported by nature, in balance with their environment. Modern society forces nature to produce far more than she can sustain to feed their people. For me to instruct them to return to a balance with nature would be to advocate the demise of untold numbers. They will never accept such radical advice.

You must find a way, or millions will perish. The image lowered his arms, striking the ground with his mace. Dust rose from the ground and hovered in the air, refusing to dissipate.

So, I must tell them to reduce their numbers drastically, or many of them will die. How can I convince them to follow a course of action that is a logical oxymoron?

You must show them that the death of the lesser number will save the greater.

Will it? What will they have learned by following my advice? Without a fundamental change in their views of life and their place in the world, they will return to exactly the same behaviour that has placed them in jeopardy. If humankind is to return to numbers that are sustainable by nature, it will take a reduction in population so drastic as to nearly equal the results of a cataclysmic event. I would be far wiser to lead a small group to a place where they could survive the coming events. Then these people could re-populate the world as it recovers with men and women who understand how to live with nature.

You are condemning mankind to death? The image raised a hand to him, palm upward in what seemed a posture of begging.

No, they have done that themselves. I must concentrate on saving the few who understand what nature intends for them.

The image disappeared from Hinoch's dream in apparent agony as it dissolved from view. Moments later, he awoke. As he emerged from his tilt, his dogs, who appeared to be extremely hungry, greeted him anxiously. As he fed them, he noticed the trampled snow all around the camp. They had apparently been actively pacing the area for some time.

Tuk, why are the dogs so anxious?

You have been in your tilt for three suns. They were beginning to fear they had been abandoned. I found some meat from a nearby caribou carcass for them, but I could not bring enough to satisfy their hunger and they would not leave you, even to hunt.

Three suns? How could that be? No matter. Come my loyal friends. For your patience you shall feast!

As he fed the dogs generous portions of seal meat, he asked, *What else has happened while I was asleep?*

Gaulaqut has been waiting out on the ice. He has taken three seals while he waited, so he has been feeding well. He appears to be building himself up for a challenge with you.

His decision to wait will be costly. I am prepared for him now. Father has instructed me well how to defeat him.

Joanna Experiences Changes in Her Life

Joanna finished her flights to and from the outfitter's camp and immediately sought out her grandmother. Dianne was a frail woman of eighty-four years now, but her indomitable spirit would allow no one to condescend to her infirmities. Fortunately, she seemed to be enjoying a spell of relatively good health, probably due to her excitement over Joanna's news.

Joanna entered the small room, made homey and quaint through the addition of many of Dianne's things. Photos adorned the top of her dresser: childhood pictures of Joanna's mother, her late husbands, Curtis and Carl. Several examples of her petit-point, done in younger years, hung in ornately framed pictures on the walls and her favorite comforter lay draped across the back of her armchair. "Good morning Grandma, how are you today?"

Dianne looked up from her knitting; the oversized needles held awkwardly in her arthritic hands and snapped, "Frustrated. This damned old body of mine just won't listen to what I want it to do any more!" She threw the needles and the yarn into her lap.

"You're in fine form this morning. That couldn't have anything to do with you being a bit anxious to hear about my visit with the man who painted Curt and Paul's airplane?"

Her face softened and a tiny smile came to her lips, "Yes dear, I'm sorry I'm so grouchy. Sometimes taking a round out of the staff here is the only entertainment I get! Guess it's getting to be a habit. Come sit by me, here, and tell me all about it. Did you see the . . . the . . .

"The Mosquito?"

Dianne nodded eagerly.

"No, it would have been under several of feet of snow. Nothing much to see now until spring."

"So what *did* you see, damn it!" She slapped her hands into her lap. The needles and the knitting flew up into the air, landing on the floor in a jumble.

"Calm down, Grandma, let me tell the story. I didn't see the actual plane, but he gave you the original of his painting. Look . . . here it is."

She unwrapped the framed picture and showed it to Dianne. She said nothing, but her sallow features blanched.

"That's my Curtis in the mist there. Do you see him?" she raised a wavering hand with her index finger extended. It began to shake slightly.

Joanna took her hand into both of hers after she leaned the picture against the wall on the dresser. "Yes, Grandma. Mom said it looked just like him, too."

"How . . . " her chin trembled slightly, "how did he know what my Curtis looked like?"

"He seems to be some kind of visionary. He says that the photo he took of the plane compelled him to draw the picture. Curtis wasn't visible in the photo, but he sure is in the drawing. Hinoch says he's in the photo, too. He just isn't visible there. He says he must have sensed him and as he worked, he subconsciously drew him into the painting."

Dianne leaned forward, pulling herself upright with Joanna's help. "Tell me everything, dear. I want to know everything."

Joanna made herself comfortable on the footstool, her knees touching her grandmother's. She stared into the grey-blue eyes, remembering the stories she had been told through the years of her grandfather's disappearance. She remembered Grandmother always failing to finish the story, her face buried in a handkerchief, muffling her sobs. She wanted to tell her gently, so she could hear the entire story. She wanted to convince her to come to Labrador. "Hinoch was exploring for a plane wreck that he had heard about from the locals. When he found it, well . . . something strange happened. This raven had led him to the plane, then seemed to disappear. Later, a young raven seemed to adopt him. Now she follows him everywhere.

"So what do some old blackbirds have to do with my Curtis?

Joanna smiled, and spoke softly, gently rubbing the backs of Dianne's hands, "When he was taking some pictures, later that day, he found something in the moss under the raven's perch. Just a minute, I'll show you what he found."

Joanna lifted the thong over her head, then pulled the ring from under her sweater.

Dianne said nothing. She did not move. Her eyes locked onto the motion of the slowly swinging ring like a person being hypnotized. Her eyes filled with tears that ran down her cheeks, then dripped onto her smock, creating small, darkened blotches in the fabric. Slowly, she raised her arthritic hand, clearly wanting to touch the ring, but seeming fearful of somehow shattering the hope in her heart.

"Is . . . is it Curtis'?"

"Yes, Grandma, it is. Look . . . here . . . take it. It's real!"

Dianne slowly closed her hand over the ring. As she did so, her eyes closed and she raised her sallow face toward the ceiling.

"Oh, my dear husband, come back to me. I want to be with you again!" As she said this, her hand tightened around the ring until her fingers became white from the pressure of her grip. She raised and lowered her clenched fist several times as if trying to summon her long lost husband. After several minutes of heart-rending, tear-filled silence, she composed herself.

"I'm sorry, dear, you must think me a silly old fool, but seeing this ring again, I just want to go. I want to go to him." The tears began to flow again, but she fought them back.

Joanna leaned forward and enclosed her grandmother in her arms.

"I understand, Grandma, and I would like to help you to be with him. The Eskimos are a very spiritual people. The man who found your ring is some sort of shaman. He says he knows that Curtis' spirit wants to come home to you and seems confident he can help make it happen. I think it would be kind of, like when we have a 'Celebration of Life' memorial service. You know how you feel. You remember good times and you feel close to your loved one again. I think he might be able to help us."

"Dear, at this point in my life, I don't have much left. I still have faith, though. I sometimes enjoy my age; I don't have to be patient. I don't feel the need to be pleasant to people, or do anything I don't want. At the same time, I don't have anything to lose, and if I can be with Curtis one minute sooner with this man's help . . . well, I'll try anything. Let's go!" Dianne began to pull herself up. Her determination was intact, but her emotions had taken a physical toll, her legs would not hold her. Joanna helped her back into her chair fearing she would fall.

"Hold on, Grandma! We can't go now. I'm sorry, but he's off on some pilgrimage to see his father and mother in the wilderness. He won't be back until spring. We'll just have to wait."

"Wait? I don't have time to wait and I don't want to wait, damn it!" The fire was still in her eyes, but Joanna could see she had endured enough emotion for one day. She tried to console her, but Dianne was beyond being comforted. She was crying again, sobbing now, her emaciated body heaving with the effort of supporting her emotions.

"I'm sorry, Grandma, if we could go today, I'd take you, but he's in uncharted territory. There's just no way I could find him, or the crash site. We've got to wait!"

Dianne stared at her a long while looking defeated and ready to collapse. She began to shake her head wearily as she turned away, then tossed up her hands, "Damn. I don't think I can make it to springtime again." She opened her fist and touched the ring lovingly to her lips. "I guess I'll have to satisfy myself with having his ring. Who knows, maybe I'll find him on my own after I'm gone. I should have lots of time to look then!"

"Grandma, no one can say for sure what springtime will bring. Maybe the hope of going up there will make you stronger?"

"Hope? Dear child, I'm so far beyond hope you'd need a miracle from the Lord himself just to give me a flicker of hope. No, I can feel it, I'll never see spring and I'll never see Curtis' final resting place."

She sighed, seeming to exhale her last breath. So much so that Joanna wondered if she wanted to breathe in again.

"Would you like to discuss what you would like me to do with your remains if you die before spring?"

"You mean you would take me to him after I'm gone?" Dianne paused, clearly deep in thought. "Is Labrador a pretty place?"

"Yes, Grandma, it is some of the most unspoiled country in the whole world. When you walk in the woods, you feel as though you could be the first human being to set eyes on it."

"I like the woods . . . " she smiled with her eyes, remembering some youthful, idyllic experience, "would you do that for me? Would you take me to him?" She reached out and grasped Joanna's hand. Her grip was surprisingly firm, though her hand was cold and clammy.

"You wanted to be cremated, didn't you?" Joanna said. "If you want, I'll spread your ashes, but if, as I suspect, you are as feisty as ever come spring, I'll take you to him. Either way, I promise I'll get you there!"

"Oh, I think that would be wonderful. Promise now. As soon as possible in spring, we go, whether I'm kickin' and grousin' or a genie in a bottle!"

"Grandma, you have the spirit of a lion, I swear. Mark your calendar. We're going in spring!"

Joanna looked at her intently, feeling for the first time that her grandmother was too frail to cling to her life much longer. Her spirit was ready to leave her. In Dianne's clouded eyes, Joanna could see it hovering, awaiting its release. This observation made her pull herself up short. *Where is this coming from?*" she asked herself. *Since that day on the ice with Hinoch, I keep getting these strange insights and dreams.*

Joanna moistened her lips, then leaned forward kissing her grandmother fully on her lips. In her mind, she prayed, *Please, Granny, hang on to your spirit just awhile longer. I'm not sure I could look after it for you. I need Hinoch to help me deal with these things.*

Dianne pulled away and gestured to her bed, "I'm tired now, I want to sleep."

"Good idea, Grandma, this has been a difficult day for you. Here, let me get you comfortable."

"Thank you, dear. It's terribly disappointing that I've got to wait so long to go to my Curtis, but I've waited this long, I'm not giving up now!"

"Dream sweet dreams, Grandma, and keep the ring close by. It will inspire you."

"Yes it will, dear. Thank you so much for bringing it to me."

Joanna helped her into bed and tucked the bedding around her, "You're welcome. Now go to sleep. I'll stay here until you nod off."

She didn't have to wait long, Dianne slipped off quickly and began to dream. A faint smile crept onto her face. Joanna was uncannily sure she knew the subject of the dream.

That night, Joanna slept fitfully. She dreamed of her Grandma and of Hinoch. As the dream progressed, she realized he was instructing her. Next morning, she awoke convinced she must see Dianne again without delay. She showered, dressed and immediately made her way to the home.

"Hi, Grandma. It's me again!"

Dianne looked rested and was in a much more receptive mood. "Hi, dear, what brings you two days in a row?"

"I was dreaming about you last night, about you coming to Labrador with me."

A little moodiness crept back; she complained, "I slept pretty well, but I had so many dreams, I don't feel I had any rest. One thing I do know, though, is that . . . that I'm not going to make it to Labrador alive, dear, but I don't want to go to Curtis as a little pile of ashes and a genie in a bottle. What can I do?"

She could not think of a better way, so she just said it. "Let me take you to him inside me."

"What? How the hell are you going to do that?" she blurted, incredulous.

"Hinoch shared his spirit with me this summer. Maybe if I do what he did and we concentrate real hard, we can share our spirits. Then you can live inside me until you are back with Curtis."

Joanna could see a protest forming, then Dianne's face softened again, "Sounds like a lot of hocus-pocus to me, but I'm not going to argue with you. Let's do it."

"You've got to believe in it and you've got to try and help me, or I'm sure I won't be able to do it."

"Yes, you're right. I've seen a lot in my life that was hard to understand, or believe. Enough to know that I shouldn't discredit anyone else's beliefs without giving them a chance. Now's the time when all I have left is something to believe in; it might as well be this."

Joanna sat on the footstool again; her mind was racing, trying to decide the best way to proceed. "Okay, I had cut myself and he licked his finger with some of my blood on it. I thought he was just trying to clean up the wound, but he had this far away look in his eyes. Later, I started doing things I had never encountered before as if I knew exactly what to do. It helped to save two boys lives. They had fallen through the ice and I handled his dogs as if they were my own."

"You handled dogs!" Dianne patted Joanna's hand, "You don't even like dogs!"

"That's right, Grandma, but not only do I like them now, I seem to get along pretty well with every animal I encounter and I see things in people that I was blind to before." She began to warm to her story and spoke with sincerity. "My life is so much richer since I had that encounter with Hinoch on the ice."

"Sounds to me like you're stuck on this guy," Dianne teased.

"Maybe I am, but I can't see it becoming anything lasting. He has definite plans for his life and I don't think he's thought about me being part of them."

"Don't be too sure." She sat upright and squirmed a little, feigning coyness. "Curtis didn't seem interested at all, then suddenly, he popped the question as we were sitting out on the porch drinking sodas."

"I hope you're right. I've never had such strong feelings for a man before in my life. My heart just tells me we would be good together."

"Yup, you've got it bad, dear. Don't just walk away. Propose to him if you have to. After all, these are modern times. Anything goes!"

She smiled and Joanna could see her spirit dancing in her eyes.

"Oh, Grandma, you always knew exactly what was going on in my mind. I feel like I already have your spirit in my soul!"

"Maybe you do, dear, but let's make sure. Let's try your man's little ceremony. Where's your pocket knife?" She raised her index finger indicating that Joanna should prick it with her knife.

"It's here, but God knows what germs it's got on it. Let me find some rubbing alcohol."

"Get on with it! I'm too ornery to let a few damned germs snuff me out!"

"Okay, close your eyes."

"No, damn it, I want to watch!"

"Okay, okay, here goes." Joanna reached out with the knife tentatively, not wanting to inflict the wound.

"Here, give it to me. I'll do it. You won't even break the skin like that."

She took the knife and calmly ran the edge over her finger, neatly parting the skin. She winced slightly, but made no sound. She offered the knife to Joanna.

"Okay, dear, your turn."

Joanna felt the need to respond in kind, mimicking her grandmother's bravery. She quickly nicked her finger, drawing more blood than she anticipated. Her stomach began to rumble its discontent.

"Hold your finger against mine, like this and close your eyes. Think about my spirit and yours becoming one. Think real hard. I'm going to try and sing a song Hinoch sings all the time . . . if I can remember it."

She took herself back to the cabin in her mind and tried to relive the moments when he was singing. The sounds came to her and she began to sing. The first few notes had hardly broken from her lips when she felt a tremendous rush of consciousness. Visions of people in old style clothing flooded her mind. Curtis and Dianne courting, their wedding, the last kiss as he left to fly to Europe. Joanna sang on, oblivious to time, but flushed with an intricate, complex awareness of her grandmother's life. After a time, exhausted, Joanna fell silent and slowly opened her eyes. The blood on their fingers had dried, requiring a slightly painful pull to break the bond. They looked at each other, seeing their souls in each other's eyes.

"I . . . I've never felt anything like that before in my life," Dianne whispered.

"Me too."

"Do you think it worked?"

"I know it did. I saw things, and felt them."

"Me too. You are head over heels with this guy. You have got to go after him!"

"Just like you felt that day on the porch when Curtis proposed."

"This is eerie."

"You can say that again. That's how I felt when Hinoch cleaned my cut. I've never been the same since."

"I feel wonderful . . . like I'm safe in your care. Anything can happen now and it won't matter. I *am* going to see Curtis again, aren't I?"

"Yes, Grandma, I can promise you that. I'm going to go home now. Take care of yourself."

"Yes, dear, take care of both of us."

Joanna smiled and turned to leave the room. She opened the door and found herself facing a well-dressed young man. He was checking the number on the door

with a scrap of paper held between his index and second
finger. He rolled it into his palm and crumpled it as he
turned on a charming smile. Then she noticed the
notepad.

"Miss Hanson?"

"Yes."

"I'm Ken Wilson from CBC, I'm following up on the
interview we did with Hinoch and I understand from
Lucien that you are the granddaughter of the lost
pilot . . . and this would be his wife?" He gestured to
Dianne, who was leaning forward to see out the door,
suspicion clear in her expression.

"She's too exhausted to talk to anyone right now,"
Joanna snipped, " . . . and I'm not sure I want to talk to
you. So convince me quickly, or I walk."

"Calm down," he raised his palms, "I don't want to
upset anyone and I don't want to exploit the story, I just
want to follow up. We've had thousands of inquiries about
what's happened since. I just want to do a piece that closes
the story for everyone who saw that interview."

"Okay, what d'you want to know?" she softened her
tone slightly as she pulled the door closed behind her.

"Is this woman the wife of one of the lost airmen?"

"Yes, she's my grandmother, Dianne, the pilot's wife."

"What has her reaction been to the discovery of the
location of the wreck?"

"She wants to go there to be with him."

"Like a memorial service or something?" he asked,
raising his pencil.

"Yeah, something like that."

"Well, exactly what does she intend to do out there in
the middle of nowhere. She doesn't look strong enough to

be going into the back woods." He was prying and she began to resent his insinuating attitude.

"Actually, it's a lot more than that." *What the hell, tell him. With his attitude, he'll never believe it anyway, much less write about it.* "Hinoch's a shaman and he believes he can reunite their spirits."

"Oh?" The cheesey grin spread infectiously, "This is interesting. Tell me more."

Her temper was rising, but she was determined not to let this 'city slicker' prod her into an outburst, "It's a long story, but if you remember the interview, he spoke of reuniting the families' spirits. I've seen and experienced the phenomenon myself."

"Interesting. How does it feel?"

Just thinking about the experience calmed her, she went on, "Like you can see the world through someone else's eyes as well as your own . . . and interpret your life with the benefit of their experience as well as your own."

"That must be . . . unusual."

"It is. But I'm getting used to it and there's no way I'd go back. I would feel so . . . so . . . " she shifted her weight to her other foot. This was going on far too long and she didn't appreciate talking about something so personal in the hallway of a care home.

"Diminished?" he offered.

She could see him beginning to drop the attitude; he was being drawn into her story, "Yeah, that about sums it up." She glanced around. No one was paying them any attention, so she relaxed a little. "I feel so much more aware of the world now, that there's no way I'd want to lose it."

"So, are you and Dianne going back to Labrador?"

"Yes. In spring we'll go back and have a ceremony to reunite the family."

"I'd love to bring a crew and shoot this. Would that be possible?"

She was dumbfounded, positive Hinoch would reject the idea outright. "No. No way. Hinoch is very apprehensive about becoming the object of some three-ring circus. The less he has to do with our world, the better he likes it."

"Look, he started this with that interview. Can't we convince him somehow to at least finish what he's started? Look at it this way. Once the story's completed most likely everyone will forget about it . . . and him. He'll be perfectly safe and he can return to his life in peace, but if we don't satisfy the audience with some kind of conclusion, they may well get a bone in their teeth and turn it into a media frenzy. This way we deal with it cleanly and respectfully. Story closed."

The man had some redeeming factors; he seemed to appreciate more of the sensitivity of the situation than she had originally anticipated. She paused, trying to read him for sincerity, "I see your point. Let me think about it. Give me your card and I'll let you know before I leave."

"Thank you. Here's my card. Try to give me a couple of weeks notice so that I can round up a crew and a plane. How hard is it to get into this place?"

"You'll need a float plane or a chopper."

"Thanks. I look forward to hearing from you." Ken smiled, shook her hand, then turned and left, his heels clicking on the tiled floors. She watched him enter the elevator, then began to make her way to the parkade to retrieve her car.

She did not record passing the usual landmarks in her mind as she drove, leaving that function to some automatic mental state. She was concerned about how she would present this development to Hinoch. She pulled into her apartment parking lot no closer to a solution.

That night, winter arrived, covering the city with a sanitizing blanket of pristine snow. Christmas would be coming soon, but Joanna could not get into the seasonal excitement. She ordered flowers for her mother and for Dianne and responded in kind to the few cards she received.

Dianne died in March and Joanna had a quiet memorial for her friends in Winnipeg. She did not announce that her cremated remains would be taken to Labrador. Spring was here. At least the calendar said it was here. The winter had been one of record-breaking warmth and had further distinguished itself by that single, short-lived snowfall. As soon as reports indicated spring break-up had begun in the north, she readied her aircraft and departed for Labrador, landing in Goose Bay on the second day.

Enroute to Nain, she became uneasy. Since her departure from Goose Bay, she had flown entirely in cloud. She was certain of her position, thanks to the new GPS she had installed, and was well clear of the Mealy Mountains below, but she never enjoyed flying on instruments. She always became tense, needing just a glimpse of the land below to reassure her.

Once, she had dreamed of flying over the snow of the arctic. Suddenly the plane had been engulfed by a cloud. Everything had gone quiet and serene. She had drifted along in the mist, feeling disembodied. After an indeterminate amount of time, the mist had begun to clear. Instead of the arctic tundra, she'd seen lush green fields and Camelot-like buildings. Her plane had disappeared. She was floating in the air with no visible means of support. Then she saw a large gateway and a white-haired man in white robes.

She remembered that she had awakened sitting bolt upright in her bed. It had taken her several moments to realize she had been dreaming. She had not been ready to face Saint Peter. She was not ready now. She shook herself from her reverie and scanned the instruments: fuel, exhaust temperature, altitude, heading, GPS position. Everything as it should be. Yet, she could not relax. Her discomfort increased moment by moment as she stared at the white shroud that enveloped her plane.

Nain is only ten nautical miles ahead now, but I'm still in cloud. Damn, I hate this! I guess I'll have to fly out over the sea and descend slowly until I see the surface. I just hope it isn't foggy over the water, or I'll be in it before I can level off. Let's see, the forecast was for scattered stratus cloud at four thousand feet. Well, this is not scattered, it's overcast, so the four thousand is suspect too, but I'll go down to four when I'm clear of the coast and then descend slowly from there. Pray for me Grandma. We're taking a hell of a chance here!

To her surprise, she felt a response. It entered her consciousness like an idea, *You'll be fine, dear, I won't let you get into trouble now, not when we're this close!*

Cheered by this strange affirmation, she descended to four thousand feet.

Well, if the GPS is set properly, I'm about five nautical miles off the coast now. Still flying in cotton batting. Here goes nothing then . . .

She reduced the throttle again, selected the carburetor heat and began a slow descent. She wanted to maintain a healthy airspeed in case she had to pull up abruptly.

I don't want to stall it eight miles out to sea!

Slowly she allowed the altimeter's needle to unwind, indicating her estimated height above the ocean below.

I hope to hell that the local altimeter setting isn't too different from Goose Bay's. I could easily be a few hundred feet out, and that's not healthy. Come on, Grandma. Help me out a little here!

You're okay, dear, just take it slow and keep a sharp lookout. My Curtis always said, "Keep a sharp lookout, even in cloud."

I know that! Where's the damned water!

Easy girl. Just keep looking . . . just keep looking. Watch your rate of descent. It's a bit high, right now.

Joanna glanced at her vertical speed indicator, *Eight hundred feet per minute. Better trim a little more nose up.*

She reached for the crank above her as she shot a glance at her altimeter, *Twelve hundred feet. Damn, I still can't see a thing. Wish I had Hinoch's eyes right now.*

Hinoch's calm baritone voice came to her mind.

Look to your left, about eleven o'clock. There is a small iceberg. You are close now, very close.

I see it! She instinctively levelled her descent. Seconds passed. *There! Shit! Fifty feet! I'm fourteen miles from shore at fifty feet! That's one hell of a long way to skim the wave-tops and it's way too rough to set down out here! Wind's out of the northeast and judging from the chop it's blowing pretty good.*

Gingerly, she began a shallow left turn to begin her low altitude crawl into the shore.

No, dear, remember there's an iceberg over there. Let's go to the right.

Okay, Grandma, that makes sense . . . Thanks.

Joanna felt the puzzlement in her mind, *What is going on here? I'm supposed to be putting every ounce of my concentration into this hairy-assed approach and I'm daydreaming about Grandma and Hinoch. Pull it together, girl, before you ditch us into the drink.*

Hinoch's answer floated into her mind, *You are using more than your own powers of concentration, Joanna. We are with you and will help you. Relax and keep sight of the water. Your present course will bring you between the offshore islands straight into the bay.*

Oh no . . . I'm not flying into the bay. As soon as the water's smooth enough I'm gonna set down and taxi into the harbour.

She flew on, her eyes burning from the effort of staring into the white glare, straining to maintain visual contact with the waves below. Slowly and without her noticing, her track drifted slightly to the south, driven by the strong onshore winds.

Airspeed one-ten. Eight miles from destination. I should see calmer water pretty soon now. I pray I'm lined up with the harbour inlet. Those rocks won't jump out of my way. Whoa!

She banked hard to the right and pulled the yoke to avoid the lone rock looming out of the breaking waves and mist. The right wing-tip struck the top of a wave, shaking the plane like a huge hammer-blow. The nose tucked down and she fought with the rudder to bring the nose up as she leveled the wings. The left float spanked the water hard, killing airspeed. The aircraft yawed abruptly. Joanna kicked the right rudder pedal hard and fought with the yoke to maintain some semblance of controlled flight. The right float struck a wave-top helping to straighten the plane, but a landing was inevitable now. Joanna frantically lowered the flaps and attempted to settle the plane down on the back of a wave crest.

The plane settled onto the wave as she had planned, but as it settled, spray flew back into the engine. It faltered, then roared back into life, but too late. The tail-section swamped under the following wave. The weight of the water sucked the last of the airspeed away. The plane slid into the trough of the waves and the propeller struck the water, bending it grotesquely. MPY pitched sickeningly in the water, the tail held down by the weight of water above it. Air hissed out of every crevice in the old aircraft. It was sinking. Joanna threw off her safety harness, grabbed her precious travel bag and the emergency dingy. She pushed the door open and threw the dingy out, hanging on to the ripcord with a strength borne of desperation.

It struck the water, already taking shape. Joanna held her breath in anticipation of being immersed in the icy waters. She jumped.

Okay, guys, I'm counting on you now . . . Come get me!

Once again, Hinoch's answer filled her consciousness. *I am on my way. You will be fine.*

The water engulfed her. Her abdomen involuntarily contracted, seeming to collide with her spine as she hit the icy water. She was unable to breathe out. She gripped her precious bag and fought to swim for the dingy, the ripcord she clenched her guide to its location. Within one minute, she was inside, convulsed with her body's reaction to the frigid water. The dome over the inflatable craft protected her from the wind, but the soaking she had received meant hypothermia was her immediate problem.

In spite of the cold, she stuck her head out to watch the fate of her beloved plane. As she watched, CF-MPY slipped below the waves leaving only a large dome of air bubbles to mark its departure. She collapsed back into the dingy, fighting to remain conscious.

Come on! You're alive, so fight to stay *alive! You've got to stay awake and keep moving. I know, bale the water out of here. That will keep you busy and when you can dry out a bit you'll warm up.*

She grabbed the baler and began frantically tossing water out the opening. After ten minutes of baling, she flopped down against the gunwale puffing like a marathon runner. It was at this point she realized the dingy was riding more sedately. The waves were subsiding.

Good, at least I'm not drifting back out to sea, she thought. *I'm going to be okay, I feel warmer now, the dingy is reasonably dry and I managed to rescue Grandma from the wreck.* She held up the travel bag and smiled, *You hear that, Grandma? We're okay.*

Gradually, she became aware of a low, intermittent sound.

Waves against a beach. I'm getting close to shore!

She poked her head out again to see the shoreline about three hundred yards away. The waves were running onto the beach, steadily pushing the dingy along with them. Joanna smiled to herself. *My instructor used to say, any landing you walk away from is a good one. Come on, girl. Let's get walking!*

Forty-five minutes later, Joanna was dragging the dingy up onto the beach, where she jammed it between two large rocks.

I need a fire. Hope my matches aren't soaked. She turned to the slope along the shore to see a raven landing on the branch of a tall pine.

"Tuk, is that you?" she called. The bird slipped gracefully back into the air and glided to a rock above her, "Caw-caw-caw!"

"I'm glad to see you again too, Tuk. Where's Hinoch?"

"I am here," he chuckled.

She spun around to see Hinoch walking up from a motor boat he had just pulled up onto the beach. Her toe stuck under a branch and she fell in a lump at his feet.

"This just isn't my day!" she exclaimed almost hysterically.

Hinoch grabbed her arm and pulled her to her feet.

"Are you all right?"

"No, I just ditched my baby into the ocean. I am definitely not all right." She leaned against him and the tears came. She cried aloud, mourning her loss and shuddering from the cold. Hinoch stood quietly, one arm draped behind her waist. After several moments he said, "I've got some dry clothes here for you and something to eat. Go into the dingy and change and I'll get a fire going. In the morning, we can return to Nain."

She looked up into his eyes thankfully, then she jumped back, a look of horror flooded onto her face.

"Your eyes! They're white. What happened to you. Can you see?"

"Not in the traditional way. I see through the eyes of my spirits now. These are the eyes of a shaman. Here, take this and go change."

She took the package he proffered and trudged off to the dingy feeling physically and emotionally numb. As she walked, he called after her, "You will find some oil and towels in there. Rub the oil well into your skin then wipe off with the towels. It will warm you up."

Joanna tossed her arm up into the air to acknowledge him. She was feeling her exhaustion now and she fought to stay awake. Inside the dingy, she stripped and immediately began rubbing the oils onto her body. The small space filled with the aroma of juniper, but with a heady, softer undertone. As the oil covered her body, she immediately began to feel warmer. The rubbing and toweling off enhanced the feeling. She was naked, on her knees in a rubber dingy in the Arctic spring and she felt warm, and wonderful.

She explored the rest of the package: cotton long underwear, soft chamois pants and tunic, and a sealskin parka and boots.

I'm going to be the envy of Nain's high society, she chuckled to herself. She heard the snapping of wood outside and self-consciously pulled on the clothes. In seconds, she felt a second blush of warmth that revived her and awakened her senses to the world around her.

"Well? Do you like it?" she teased, stepping from the dingy. She twirled on the spot, imitating a fashion model.

"You look wonderful. You will be the envy of Nain's high society!" he laughed.

Her jaw dropped open, "Have you been reading my mind?"

"Yes," he replied, "and it is a very nice mind to read."

She said nothing, rooted to the spot, then blushed a full beet red. She could feel her entire body glowing from the flush. She had been more than a little titillated by her experience with the oils. Had he been tuned in then too?

He looked up from the fire and smiled broadly. She blushed crimson.

"Come, sit down here and have some fish. The food will give you energy and warm you."

"I'm about ready to boil over now," she quipped.

Her experiences had been overpowering, but she did not yet know how to interpret them. She only knew that something profound was happening, had been happening since she'd gone out on the ice last fall to hunt seals with this man. She had experienced infatuations, even love, before, but this had a dimension far beyond her previous experiences. She would need time to digest her feelings for this Inuit shaman.

The Lab Air Twin Otter droned off into the distance and Hinoch and Joanna surveyed the pile of equipment at the shoreline of the little lake. The waves from the plane's departure washed ashore, and the lake returned to its usual placid state. They began organizing the random pile dumped at the shoreline.

Moments later, they heard a thumping drone.

"What is that?" Hinoch asked.

"The film crew, I guess," Joanna replied weakly.

Joanna could feel Hinoch probing her mind. She was getting used to this feeling, becoming comfortable with it in fact.

His response was disquieting. "I understand, they have been very persuasive, but I am virtually certain they will record nothing of value to them here."

"I had to give them the chance, Hinoch. They said this'll satisfy the inquiries they're getting. It'll close the story and you can go back to your life here."

"As much as I doubt the practicality of your decision, I agree that, if there is a faint hope that this will conclude the matter, we should allow it. You realize that cameras only record variations in light; they do not see anything else. You and I may see events clearly by virtue of our spiritual link, things that the cameras view myopically, or not at all."

"I know, and how will this ever cure the world's corrupted view of itself . . . " she placed her palm against her forehead, struggling for a way to get him to accept her decision, to forgive her for keeping it from him until now. "Who knows, maybe this might just be what's needed to do it!" She shuffled her feet. Her hands were a flurry of futile attempts at conveying what she knew her words could not. They settled on the toggles of her jacket, twirling them nervously.

Hinoch began setting up their tent, listening to her, but saying nothing in response. She fell silent, feeling increasingly anxious. A few uncomfortable moments later, the tent was ready. He stood and faced her. "I understand that your decision came from your hopefulness. I cannot share that optimism, but I respect it. Perhaps they will glean something that could plant the seed of hope you carry."

Hinoch turned and watched as the helicopter landed twenty yards away. Joanna left his side to approach them as the whine of the turbine died and the rotors ground to a halt.

The reporter and an athletic-looking young man emerged. She greeted them. "Hello, Ken, I'd like you to meet Hinoch."

"Hello. This is Bill, my cameraman."

Bill paused from his efforts to extract his camera from its travel pack. "Hi," he said, clearly more interested in his equipment. "Is the wreck nearby?"

Within moments, the blackflies were attracted to the newcomers. Ken seemed to tolerate them, but Bill juggled the camera as he sprayed himself with a powerful-smelling bug repellent. Joanna was repulsed by the mist that floated toward her and waved her hand to disperse it.

Hinoch smiled, amused at Bill's antics and replied, "Yes, why do you not go to the crash site and take some footage while we get ready. We will wait until you return before we begin."

"Okay, sounds good." Ken said, "By the way, what is this ceremony called?"

Hinoch touched his chin, "The most meaningful translation would be 'Reunion of the spirits', I guess."

"And what will you be doing, exactly?"

Hinoch looked down, reluctant to be pulled into an interview. Joanna stepped in. "I said no interviews and I meant it! I want you to remember that we have promised you nothing as to what you'll record here today. We ask only that you remain at a respectful distance and maintain complete silence. There'll be no interviews, now or later. What you record is what you get . . . Okay?"

Ken seemed disappointed at being pulled up short, but responded, "Agreed, Joanna. My apologies. Which way to the crash site?"

Hinoch pointed and said, "About two hundred yards along this line of new brush. That is the swath it cut through the trees as it crashed. You will find a trail I cut last year."

"Thanks. See you in a little while."

Hinoch and Joanna returned to their tasks, setting up the tent and preparing the rubber dingy for the short trip out onto the lake.

Joanna felt an increasing wonder at her new view of the world. She paused, taking in her surroundings. She looked up at the old snag sensing it had some importance. Tuk was perched there. She could tell that Tuk was hardly able to contain herself. She was a mirror, reflecting the joy residing within her in the spirits she had carried for this long year. Tuk had followed her Great Spirit, Hinoch, for four seasons, waiting for him to find the missing spirit of

Dianne and bring her to this place. Joanna turned and watched as Hinoch laid out the dingy and began inflating it. She went to help him. "Tuk's pretty excited. She knows we're about to free her from her responsibilities," she said to him.

"Mmm, I'm just explaining to her what will happen."

"Oh, sorry. That's why I felt like I was interrupting."

"You are not interrupting. In a while you will be able to join in with no need to vocalize your conversation. I can tell you are beginning to read the thoughts around you. Soon we will converse freely with no need for words."

"Really? The way you keep reading my mind?"

"Yes. We are about to become very close spiritually. The change will be permanent."

A chill ran through her — a feeling that she was being drawn helplessly into a relationship of a kind she had never before considered. She smiled and said, "I'm looking forward to it. I much prefer two-way communication."

"You are concerned," he corrected. "That is understandable. You hardly know me in the terms you have understood up to now, yet you are spiritually linked to me forever — a stark contrast of feelings."

She smiled uneasily, not knowing what to say.

The men were returning from the bush and set up their equipment twenty yards from the lake. Hinoch took Joanna's arm and helped her into the boat. She sat near the middle carefully cradling Dianne's small urn in her hands. Hinoch pushed the boat from the beach and it floated dream-like on the smooth surface of the water. Gently, he paddled to the centre of the lake, directly over the sunken canoe.

Joanna was so excited she could hardly contain herself, and it took several minutes for her to realize the source of her excitement. It came from Dianne's spirit. She could feel her grandmother's happiness in her own heart.

The now familiar sound of Hinoch's song came to her. Her spirits rose within her. Tuk flew to her and landed on her shoulder. Hinoch continued to drone his calming spell. Joanna turned her attention to the water and looked into the depths. Hinoch took the urn, opened it and poured the greyish-white dust it held onto the water. It rode on the surface a few moments, then began to darken and move into the depths below, leaving a trail of descending grey clumps. Next, he extended his hand with the ring hanging from its loop of hide. As the ring swayed over the water, a light mist rose up, then descended into the depths below. In a few moments, it rose again and hovered near the surface, encircling the dingy, then began to rise into the air above.

Joanna looked to her side to see Tuk take to the air. She felt the spirit of Dianne stir within her. She began to feel a chill infuse her being as if she was losing a part of her existence. She wrapped her arms around herself, trying to banish the shivering in her body.

The water rippled slightly, just beyond the ring. She became even more alert, ready to flee, she was so startled. Two faint images of young men rose up from below and stood on the water. The entire area became bathed in a cool, soft blue light.

Hinoch intoned a new and strange song as he became a huge white raven and spread his wings, soaring into the air. A soft amber aura began to radiate from the centre of the mist. Joanna could see the grey clumps of ashes now rising from the depths of the lake and taking form just below the surface. The azure-blue image of a young Dianne rose soundlessly from the waters. Tuk dove to the surface of the water. The image of two young men emerged from her, strengthening their previous images. Dianne walked over to them, where they began to condense into more palpable forms — three young ravens. They took to the air and climbed silently into the sky.

Joanna wanted in her heart to join them, but knew she could not, not yet at least. Hinoch was up there with them now, and as she watched, he climbed until he soared above them with the ring in his claw.

Hinoch voiced a raven's call to them and led them to the old snag, where he settled. Slowly, the old tree came to life and a new nest took form in its uppermost branches. He tenderly placed the talisman in the nest. Immediately, the young female raven landed and entered the nest, burying the talisman in the thick feather-down at the bottom. Moments later, one of the young males joined her and they flew off together. High above the mist, they began their aerial mating dance.

The remaining young male called to Tuk. She watched him soaring above her, doing wonderful aerobatics to impress her with his powers of flight. After a few moments, she climbed into the skies to meet her mate.

A hundred yards away, Bill stopped the camera and said, "How much more fog do you want me to take anyway?"

"Okay. Let's wrap it up," Ken said. "Looks like they're going to be leaving soon. I guess we've got about all we're going to get here. Let's pack up the gear and get it into the chopper. We'll review the tapes tonight."

"Yeah, just what in hell did we get anyway? Some footage of an old plane wreck that we could have pulled from archives? Oh yes, and some nondescript crap where two people row out onto the lake in a rubber boat, a pet crow flies in and lands on the girl's shoulder and then everything gets foggy. Next thing we see are four black crows flying off to who knows where, the boat comes out of the mist and the broad's the only one in it. This is gonna be one hummer of a story, I can tell!"

"Maybe we missed something the tape caught. We'll do a frame-by-frame of the boat scene parts and see what we got."

"Hell, let's just shit-can the whole thing now and save our time. I'd rather watch paint dry! This strikes me as being another washout like opening the safe from the Titanic. Now *that* was anticlimactic footage at its best!"

"Don't remind me. I still say we go back to Nain, take a few days and look it all over carefully. There's something to this story and it could be big. I don't want to walk away from it only to be sandbagged by some other network. We might have to colour it up a bit to make people think something happened. Hell, we've made top-rated footage out of tape with less substance than this. It seemed something was in the urn that caused the fog. We could have a field day with that if we play it right. You know, 'Purported shaman uses dry ice to cause fog over small lake, then releases captive crows concealed in the bottom of the boat.'"

"I don't know Ken, this whole ceremony thing gives me the heebeegeebies. We're in the middle of nowhere and this so-called shaman starts doing magic tricks with fog and has crows flying in and out of the scene. And where the hell is he now? It just doesn't feel right. I've had shivers crawling up and down my spine ever since I met this white-eyed Hinoch creep. He doesn't seem to be a part of this world, somehow."

"Now you've got the juices flowing, Bill. Give me a write-up on your feelings about this guy for tomorrow.

We'll review the tape against your gut feelings and see what we can work up."

"Okay, you've got it, but I still think we're pushing our way into something that will end up flat on its face. How do we put the creepy feeling I've got crawling up and down my skin on video?"

"I don't know yet. Let's work on that and let's try to get a follow-up interview with Hinoch. Maybe he'll say something that'll give us an angle."

"I don't know. I get the feeling that he'd rather deal with a pit full of rattlers than tell us his secrets."

They climbed into the helicopter and closed the door firmly.

"Okay, Paul, get us back to Nain."

The helicopter whined into action, the rotors slowly gaining revolutions. Soon afterward, it lifted off, turned toward the east and thrummed off into the distance.

Joanna felt relief as she watched the helicopter disappear into the thickening fog. She was drained from her experience and edgy about having approved the filming. Ken and Bill had shown their disappointment, adding to her regret.

She picked up a stone and flipped it into the water, watching the rings emanate from the point of its entry, like the consequences of her decision. *I'm sorry I agreed to let them come out here. Somehow, now, I feel that I need to keep today's events to myself.*

She paused looking around at the items they had used during the day. They were scattered about the area, dropped where the need for them had ended. She began rushing around, picking things from the ground and piling them near the dingy.

"We'd better get out of here if we want to get back to Nain today. Let's start packing up the gear," she said.

Hinoch placed his hand on her shoulder. As she brushed past, the strength of his grip stopped her in her tracks. He looked intently into her eyes.

"Do you want to get back tonight? Would you not like to spend a little time here with your family's spirits? I can catch us some nice fresh fish. I'll show you how to find fresh roots and vegetables, then we can relax and enjoy the evening."

She returned his gaze a long moment. She was becoming accustomed to his inscrutable white eyes and took comfort in the quality of this moment of contact. It had a calming effect, erasing her state of near hysteria. She took a deep breath. "You're right. We don't have anything to run back for, do we. Okay, let's set up camp and get supper ready."

Hinoch raised his arm, hand palm down, and stepped slowly through a full turn. The mist rolled in heavy and warm, engulfing the entire area. Perhaps twenty minutes later, they heard the Twin Otter overhead, searching for the landing place, now obscured in fog. After a few minutes, the sound diminished. They were alone again.

That evening, as they sat by the fire, Joanna began to realize the strength of the feelings she had accumulated. She wanted to share them, but could not find the words.

"This has just been too much to absorb, Hinoch. I can't begin to describe how I feel about what I've seen today. I've never felt so powerfully connected to events before in my life. There's no way I could express in words what's happened here. I'd need to find a better way to express my feelings."

Hinoch leaned toward her, "You have related those feelings to me. As a shaman, I have the power to experience your feelings with no need on your behalf to try to verbalize them."

She looked into the fire and tossed her head to one side, "I should feel violated, invasion of privacy and all," she looked back at him, becoming more serious, "but somehow I don't. I've experienced the same thing with my grandmother. Now that she's left me, I feel a bit diminished, a little sad." Her hand went up to her heart.

"You are experiencing things with your sixth sense, your spiritual sense. That is good." He scraped the bones of the fish from the frying pan, the same pan they had shared eating it from, then walked the short distance to the edge of the lake, where he cleaned it in the sand and rinsed it in the water.

"My sixth sense?"

Hinoch returned and placed more wood on the fire. They watched as the shower of sparks fled the flames, seeking oblivion in the blackness of the sky. His gaze returned to her face, "You have heard of it before, I'm sure. The world is full of stories relating to the sixth sense and extra-sensory perception. Your intimate connection to your grandmother heightened your sensitivities today. Your emotions were helping you interpret the events you experienced with your five senses, adding an important spiritual element."

Joanna fidgeted with a strand of her hair. "It's more than that. Ever since we went out on the ice together, I can feel that my perception has an added dimension," she sprawled on the ground sheet, rolling up her jacket to prop herself up. "I'm constantly noticing subtle things around me that help to interpret what's really happening.

For example, I knew the moment I looked into my grandma's eyes that she was ready to die. I could see her soul in her eyes. It was ready to leave her last winter. So we played Indian blood brothers, or something like that and it worked. I ended up carrying her spirit here!"

"In addition to combining your spirits, you convinced her to try to survive the winter. She lived until the end of March on nothing more than the hope you gave."

Hinoch leaned forward and flicked an ember back into the fire with his finger. He smiled warmly, "With no coaching from me, you understood that her time was near and you combined her spirit with your own to bring her here to her husband. You learned much from one lesson."

"All winter long it's been as if something's been growing inside me," she said. "As spring approached, I couldn't even think of opening up the camps until I'd returned to Nain. I got my friend to do the flying for me and came here as soon as I could." Her eyes clouded. "Humph. I guess he'll be doing all of it from now on, since I ditched MPY." She brought herself back to the topic. "I've only spent a few days here, but already this feels more like my home than Winnipeg ever did."

"Your grandfather and grandmother had a spiritual union. When you took her spirit into your own, her goal to be reunited with Curtis became one of your goals." He looked down, tracing an indistinct shape on the ground sheet with a twig, "Take time to reassess your feelings now, Joanna. You have fulfilled your grandmother's final wish. You may find that there is less to keep you here."

"I don't believe that, Hinoch. I feel right now as though my bond is to *this place* more so than it was to a sense of duty for Dianne. This place feels like the home I have never had . . . a home of my own."

Hinoch looked into her eyes a moment; she sensed him penetrate deeply into her thoughts. She dared not allow herself to think what she wanted. She wanted it to come from him of his own volition.

He whispered, "I am aware of your spiritual growth. I am also aware of . . . of your feelings. You will know that they are shared."

Joanna stared into his eyes. She revisited her feelings of the powerful bond that had formed out there on the ice last winter.

She rolled onto her elbows, toward him, and arched her back, looking up at his round, healthy face, "One thing I do know for certain, right now, is that I want to learn as much as I can about you . . . about you being a shaman. I feel like this relationship we have has sprung up of its own accord. My usual way of connecting with people takes time and a slow development of feelings for the other person. Humour me, Hinoch, but my conscious self wants some of that process now. So, tell me about yourself. I sense that your ancestors have been shamans for many generations."

"You are right, Joanna, you know very little about me. I have the advantage of being able to visit your experiences. You have had a wonderful life and you have made the most of it. Your courage and fearlessness comes from your family's background and you are willing to live your life in that tradition." He brushed her hand, perhaps accidentally, but she felt the electricity of their first touch, back in Nain.

"How do you do that — learn about a person's inner workings? I mean . . . can you do it with anyone?" She covered the hand he had touched with the other, rubbing thoughtfully.

"I spoke to you about the sixth sense. Mine is acutely developed. I can communicate directly, with no need for language, with spirits that have been joined with mine. To a lesser degree, I can read the spirits that are around me, but to whom I have had no bonding. Try this. What am I thinking right now?"

She closed her eyes and allowed an image to form. She saw them together through a repeated cycle of light, darkness, then light again. "You . . . you hope that we're able to stay here for several days."

Hinoch smiled and nodded, "You have a keen sixth sense, Joanna. Soon you will read my thoughts with no effort. We will become like a single consciousness, greater than the sum of our souls."

She looked down, avoiding his eyes. She was learning to accept them, but was not yet accustomed to their strange pearlescent glow, "That still kind of scares me. I don't know if I like it yet. Guess it's too late now, though. You're already free to roam the halls of my mind whenever you chose." She looked at him again, "On the other hand, it feels good. Like a connection that's deeper and more meaningful than anything I've ever dreamed. One side of me wants to slap your face and the other wants to revel in the feeling. Does that make any sense?"

"Yes, it does. I did not ask your permission before bonding with you. I knew in my own heart that it was destined, but I did not ask you to permit the ceremony. I apologize to you for that action. I violated your rights as a free individual and will always regret my presumption."

"Like I said, I want to slap your face but I can't because I'm so excited with the idea of being this close to another person . . . to you." She blinked. *Damn, now I've gone and said it.*

She paused, deep in thought again, searching for contact with him. She felt his awareness, then it was as though a door closed before she could enter. For a second, she wondered if he was controlling her access to his thoughts and felt a little left out.

"Well, I can't read your life like a book, at least not yet, so tell me all about yourself."

"I would love to. My family handed down their traditions and history faithfully for over sixty generations, spanning more than two thousand years. Their spirits are as much a part of my daily life as your way of life is to you."

"But hasn't a lot changed since your people lived entirely off of the land? I mean the missionaries coming, converting you to Christianity, and introducing you to our system of trade and barter. That must have been a huge change for your people. Didn't all those changes cause you to lose your sense of spiritualism? One thing I never understood was the fact that you didn't resist the missionaries when they tried to convert you to a Christian way of life."

"No, organized resistance is foreign to us." He grinned, "The best description for our response to the missionaries is universal reluctance."

Joanna laughed, "I like that. But in school we were taught that the Eskimo culture was pagan and pretty amoralistic."

"Many people have referred to us as hedonists and pagans, yet our society is historically one of the most peaceful and accepting societies throughout earth's history. We have never sought to conquer land occupied by other peoples, nor have we denied them access to the lands we inhabit." He pushed the twig into the fire until the end glowed, then pulled it back, holding it up and waving it in front of them. It left a wisp of smoke in its trail. "In contrast, the majority of nations have long histories of conquest and hostile attitudes toward their fellow man."

She took the twig from him and stared at the fading ember. "So you accepted them the same way you accepted everyone and you couldn't understand why they didn't respond in kind. Your customs were very different, but that didn't make them wrong, at least in anyone's eyes except the missionaries'." She flicked the twig into the fire.

"That is a fair assessment. We do not view any other being's actions as right, or wrong. Rather, we regard those actions as expressions of their nature. For example, if someone steals from us, they are wasting their stealth. We would gladly give them what they need. We will even share our women, so long as they are pleased to undertake the experience." Joanna looked up from the fire abruptly. He added, "As a matter of fact, Inuit women are probably among the most liberated and respected human females on earth!"

"I should hope so. I expect nothing less," she smiled coyly. "What's the most important thing to your people?"

He sat up and took a deep breath, "One thing is valued above all by my people: honour. If you call our honour into question and tell others that we are not honourable, then you have earned a deadly enemy. You will be hunted and killed at the first opportunity. Others among us will know why you died, but the person you maligned will ensure that they do not witness the deed."

She sat up and crossed her legs, sensing she had opened a sensitive topic, "So, you *can* be provoked into violence. Killing over a matter of honour seems a bit extreme to me."

"Not many years ago in European society, dueling to the death was common when matters of honour were at stake. human pride is a powerful emotion."

She frowned a little, "You're pretty tough to argue with, Hinoch. You know a lot more about my world than I understand of yours. I can't help feeling that the world would gain a lot if they understood your ways. I already feel more connected to your values than any others I've heard of."

"Yes, my people do live by different rules than many other societies. They have lived and thrived for easily as many years as some of the most ancient peoples in the world. We have thrived by being realists. We do not attempt to make anything into something for which it is not suited. Our needs are very basic — " he raised his cupped hands, "today's food and clothing. Our expectations are equally basic — the freedom to pursue our survival.

"Even our folklore relates to the pursuit of our survival and the perfection of the practice of hunting, fishing and providing for our families. So closely connected to nature are our people that we are prepared to suffer along with nature through the poor years. In contrast though, when things are plentiful, we celebrate and take pleasure in the joys of our simple lives."

She rested her elbows on her knees and nestled her chin in her hands. Joanna was completely absorbed in the idea of such a simple life. She was aware of the tenuous aspect of life in the arctic, but here by the fire it didn't seem to be a great concern. She moved closer, facing him and whispered, engaging his eyes again, "Imagine what the world would be like if we all just took from it what we needed today. You owe the world the chance to learn your philosophy, Hinoch, you've got abilities way beyond understanding. They could be what's needed to save the entire world, make it a better place for everyone."

He frowned and looked away, "I am convinced that would be a wasted effort at a time when it is a luxury that is not affordable." He looked back, "Our beliefs and lifestyle are intimately matched to this environment and this environment alone. They would be largely irrelevant in other places. Even if I were omniscient, I could not demand that the world adopt our lifestyle, or even agree with us." He grasped her shoulders, "It simply would not achieve what is necessary in the time that remains. No, it would be better if the world just left us alone to live our lives as we chose."

She took his hands from her shoulders and held them in hers, trying to ignore the warm sensation of his touch, "It doesn't work that way, Hinoch. You can't just abandon the world by ignoring it."

"Your society has powers that my people cannot begin to understand," he looked down at their hands, then back into her eyes, "nor do they *need* to grasp them. They are irrelevant in our reality. You would find our abilities equally irrelevant in your world. Every societal concept only has validity so long as it is in context. There are very few universal concepts, such as gravity, that operate in the same fashion throughout the universe. Societal concepts are not universal; they are extremely situation-specific. That is why they can generate so much conflict when people are led to believe that *they* are practicing the lifestyle that should be universal."

"Hinoch, I'm afraid you're too negative about the rest of the world. You seem to believe that you can take a few people and retreat into the woods to live the life you choose. That's not realistic. If the world's going to fall apart, you're not going to be able to jump off and avoid it." She pulled away and stood, immediately feeling the chill air on her back. She cradled her arms around her.

He looked up, "I seriously doubt whether anything I could do or say would convince the world's peoples to drastically reduce their numbers and return to a hunter-gatherer type of existence."

She paused, thinking, then asked, "You know, this winter broke records for warmth and there was hardly a single flake of snow. Do you think it's started?"

"I do."

She looked south, into the blackness, "Well, they'll be able to adapt. They always have."

He stood and began moving more wood to the edge of the fire. "In my visions, I have seen great wars fought over dwindling food resources and energy reserves. Many people will die in natural disasters," he stood in front of her, commanding her full attention, " . . . floods storms, disease and drought. All mankind will suffer greatly. Only a few will survive."

"That's a pretty black picture, Hinoch. You have no proof, though. What makes you so confident in your predictions?"

"My visions have never lied to me."

She stamped the ground, "What makes you so damned sure *you'll* make it?" she asked, becoming flustered and more than a bit angry.

"My people focus upon the skills necessary for survival in everything they do. We also emphasize the cumulative effects of passing our spiritual wisdom on to our children, much as modern society passes on scientific and technical skills to their young. In our society, the beneficiaries of the elders' spirits add their own experience and the wisdom it affords. In our view, each life enhances the spirit, then passes it to the succeeding generation."

He paused to gather his thoughts. As he spoke he began to realize that a core issue in his life was about to be explored. He took her hands again, feeling a need for physical contact with this wonderful, open spirit.

"For centuries my family has accumulated vast wisdom and intimate knowledge of nature. This is now a force of nature in its own right. The spirits, of which I am the custodian, are probably among the oldest and most carefully guarded entities on this planet. My life is insignificant compared to the responsibility I bear to make the best possible use of the heritage I embody. I am bound to make every possible effort to live a life that honours my forefathers and takes the greatest possible care for the future of my people."

She said nothing, but stood looking down at their hands, trying to resist the warm, insistent sensation building within.

"My people see their spirit with the same devotion to its future growth. This is our strength. This is how we will thrive even in an environment that no others can endure. This is why we will be here for thousands of years to come. Our beliefs are at home in adverse conditions. In contrast, modern society's concepts and beliefs require a myriad of supporting circumstances and civilized struc-tures that are too fragile and interdependent to survive or adapt to the upcoming events."

She leaned forward, putting weight on his hands, "You're saying that we're heading for extinction, like the animals we've been watching disappear, aren't you?" she said accusingly.

"Yes."

She pulled away and turned her back. "But, you use a lot of technology yourself, GPS and lap-top computers."

"Yes, I feel it is wise to be as prepared as possible. To the extent that technology is of direct assistance to me, I will use it, but I refuse to become dependent upon it. When it fails, I return to my traditional methods. They are often more labourious, or less accurate, but they always work . . . without fail."

She spun around, pointing a finger at him, "So you take what you can use and deny the existence of the parts you don't like. It all sounds pretty non-committal to me. Either you're part of this earth, or you're not. We can't just pick and choose what we'll acknowledge. It's *all* here and I'm going to hound you about it until you realize that fact! You're underestimating them just because you had a bad experience. They'll find a way. I just know it!" She was picking a fight, she realized, but she needed to probe this man's character and she needed to do it quickly.

"Have you ever kept an aquarium?" he asked calmly.

"No, what's that got to do with anything?"

"Do you understand that an aquarium is a miniature ecosystem?"

"I guess so. The fish live in it, so it's an ecosystem."

"Have you ever seen an aquarium that clouds up and starts to kill the fish?"

"Um-hmm, when it's polluted."

"Good, then you also know that if the condition is not caught early, it will seemingly resist your best efforts to reclaim the situation and eventually become an uninhabitable environment. It seems to gain an autonomous, destructive momentum."

"But there's all kinds of stuff to test the water and to make adjustments — with chemicals and filtration."

"Yes, so long as you are attentive to them. Are you equally attentive to the environment in which *you* live?"

She looked at his hand, wanting contact again, but refusing.

"Okay, I get it. You're convinced we're heading into a disaster with our blinders firmly over our eyes and you screaming from the roof-tops about your visions won't make a difference. I hate what you're saying. I hate it," she stamped her foot again, "but I'm damned if I have any answers to prove you wrong."

"My visions tell me we are very close. We would have to do absolutely everything in our power, without reservation, to halt the present trend."

"We being . . . ?"

"Everyone on the planet."

"So, how can you calmly sit there and tell me this? I still say you have to go out there and wake everybody up. For all we know you could be the handsome prince come to wake up the sleeping princess . . . hopefully before she slips into oblivion."

"That is precisely why my outlook is so fatalistic. Human nature has a history of ignoring its oracles. I will be the happiest man on earth if my visions are inaccurate, but that would be the first time in my life that they failed to show me the truth."

"It'd be so helpful if you could show something tangible. Anything, that people would believe!" She picked up a branch and tossed it on the fire, causing an amber cloud of sparks.

"For me to show one of my visions in any form or medium would be meaningless to people other than my own small group of Inuit. What I have told you is based upon a lifetime of growth in spirit and my recent inheritance of the role of shaman. To show anything of my spiritual experiences to an uninitiated public would be useless."

"Still, there's got to be something. Maybe we could find some part of the world that's showing the effects so plainly that it can't be denied."

"The scientists have been showing us these changes in our environment for many years now. No one seems inspired to undertake global changes. Very soon now, the results will be undeniable and irreversible. The best thing I can do is re-create our traditional community, the human beings who live *with* nature, not against it!"

Hinoch scowled, his eyes gaining a pearl-metallic sheen. "My decision is made. I am taking my people back to their original life, where we take only what we need, leaving the rest, trusting in an ample supply being there in the future. I sincerely hope that our location is, and remains sufficiently remote and pristine that we can survive and thrive. Do not for a moment think that I take this decision lightly. I am facing Armageddon and my options are severely limited. I am already mourning the loss of so many people, but I do not see how I can alter the present course of events."

She wanted to drop to her knees and cry, but forced herself to continue, to attempt to test this man, the man she knew could be the love of her life. "That's it? Your mind's made up? You can calmly stand there and

179

condemn the rest of us to death? You are *too* weird!"
Again, she turned her back to him.

There was no change in his voice. He was speaking of
his fundamental convictions and she was pushing, trying
to make him angry. He was passionate about his beliefs,
she could tell, but he remained gentle with her, directing
his passion where it belonged. She bathed in the soothing
tones of his voice, "Nevertheless, these are the facts. I
could cry out and wring my hands, but instead, I choose
to act and save what I can for the future."

Joanna was silent a long time. She turned back and
looked into his eyes. She could see his pain. At least he was
prepared to get on with saving what he could of the world,
as he knew it. In contrast, she knew the rest of the world
was sitting on its collective hands, waiting to be convinced
that action was necessary.

"I pray you're wrong, Hinoch, but assuming you're
right, this is your people's last best hope. How do you plan
to get them to come with you?"

"For several years now, I have been re-teaching our old
ways to the ones who would listen. Their interest in our
traditional ways increased as they further understood how
we lived in the past. There are now perhaps twenty
families that will come with me to return to our old ways
of life."

"You said me. Just yourself? What about me?"

Damn, she thought, *I've done it again. Oh, well,
Grandma said to propose myself if I had to.*

"You would find the spartan life of an Inuit full of
hardships. It is an extremely difficult and dangerous
existence."

She tackled him, wrapping her arms around him,
trapping his arms. "Oh no, you don't! You're not getting

away with telling me that the world's coming to an end, making me fall in love with you and then just walking off into the sunset!"

"Are . . . are you serious about coming into the north with us? With me?"

Tears pooled up in her eyes, then trickled down her cheeks. She swallowed hard and continued, "Damn it, you can read my mind, can't you? Don't you know you hijacked my heart along with my spirit?"

He smiled, that guileless smile she had seen the day he rescued her from ditching MPY, when she realized he had been reading her mind. "Ever since I met you, I knew somehow that my future is here. I don't care about civilized life and all its comforts. Except for flying and my plane, I've never really wanted anything from the world, other than the freedom to enjoy my life in it. Since you made me aware of my surroundings, I know the North is the place for me."

He freed his arms and embraced her. "Then I would be honoured to have you come with us, but my fear remains that the experience will be too harsh for you."

She arched back and sneered, teasing him, "Hey, I'm no sissy, remember, I'm the gal whose survival skills had you so impressed not long ago"

His embrace held. "You said yourself, though, that you needed your survival gear. We will have none of that. Everything we have must come directly from our environment."

She had stepped over the precipice and, realizing her emotions were committed, persisted, "I learned how to survive with gear; I'll learn how without it too."

He smiled, "You are such a hopeful person. I confess I admire that trait in you."

She leaned ahead, relying upon him to support them. "It's in my genes. My grandparents refused to give up and look what it did for them; they have a brand new life together after waiting over sixty years."

Hinoch released his embrace and took her hands. The tingling sensation threatened to take her breath away.

"I confess, Joanna, that I had not allowed myself to entertain the possibility of you — "

"Well you better start." She pinned him on the chest with her forefinger. "And you better wake up and read your *own* mind about me, because I can read you better than you think. Even if I can't read your mind, I know you're thrilled at the prospect of me sharing my life with you and bearing your children."

She feigned pulling away again, but he trapped her in his powerful embrace.

"Yes, I am aware of your feelings, Joanna, and I feel the same toward you, but I fear placing you in such hardship. If you are willing to face the dangers of life with me, we will work together and I will do my best to be a good provider."

She relaxed, allowing herself to mold to his muscular body.

"Well, that's not the kind of proposal I dreamed of, but then nothing else about my schoolgirl dreams of romance has ever come true, either. Maybe that's the way all couples should start out — with just a promise to work on the relationship."

"It is our custom to honour each other, to respect our freedoms as human beings, to revere the spirits of our ancestors and to work for our mutual survival."

She thumped his chest, "Damn it, you always talk like a textbook . . . even when you're proposing! I doubt that many women down south would get that kind of pickup line! I accept. Your place or mine!"

"What do you mean . . . your place or mine?"

"Just an old cliché from my past. It means I accept your proposal. So what do we do now? I guess you're the minister. So . . . are you going to marry us or something?"

Hinoch's face brightened. "Yes, that is an excellent idea! Let us compose our family song and perform the ceremony of commitment."

"Do we light a fire and dance around it with no clothes on, too?"

After an awkward pause, he replied, "If you would like," and he smiled that broad, innocent smile he displayed too infrequently.

She chuckled. "I'll go collect lots of wood. I want a big fire!" She pushed away, more to come up for air than to collect firewood.

As she went about her adopted task of collecting wood, Hinoch crouched down and entered a trance. He leapt into the air as the white raven and flew to the old nesting place. There he met Dianne, and Curtis quietly sitting together enjoying their reunion.

Hello again, Hinoch, said Dianne. *I can't thank you enough for what you've done today. I've dreamed, every day of my long life, about one day being with my Curtis again, but I thought it'd be in heaven. To my amazement, it looks like we've got a whole new life to enjoy together.*

I am happy that you are pleased with today's events, said Hinoch, *and I wish you many years of joy together. I have other news that I hope will please you. I have come to ask you for the hand of your granddaughter, Joanna, in marriage.*

That's wonderful, Hinoch. I'd pretty much guessed we'd be having this event and I was wondering what I could do to celebrate it. You see I know a lot about my granddaughter's workings, when she's happy, when she's sad. This winter she's been like a prize racehorse confined to her stall. She couldn't wait for spring so that she had an excuse to come back out here. I'm so pleased it's working out for you. There's not a lot that I have to give you anymore. My new life doesn't require all the gizmos I used to seem to need. In fact, I have just one thing remaining from my past life and it's pretty much responsible for my joy today.

Dianne paused, her head cocked to one side, eyes blinking as if she were fighting back tears. *Here, I have a wedding gift for you.* She ruffled the down at the base of the nest with her beak and retrieved the gold ring, still attached to the leather thong. *This ring has represented the love in my family for many years now. Recently, it got into your life when you found it in the moss down there. Now it'll be linked to our families' futures. I'm happy to pass it on to you. Make an old lady happy and be good to her.*

You do us a great honour. We will always be grateful for your gift to us.

Good luck, Hinoch. I hope life's full of blessings for you and Joanna.

He looked into Dianne's eyes and thanked her soul for its strength and courage, then he stepped from the tree and spread his huge wings. He floated back to the tent below.

Joanna was waiting, quietly humming his nature song. He landed softly and walked up behind her. The ring dropped from his beak and fell into his open hand as he reassumed his human form. He placed the ring around his neck, under his shirt. Dawn was approaching.

"When did you learn my Nature Song?"

"I don't know for sure. I tried to sing it to Grandma last winter. It seems pretty natural to me now."

"So, it begins, your spirit and mine. We are becoming one great consciousness together."

She rose from her kneeling position at the pile of wood she had assembled, turned and embraced him warmly.

"Let us begin our ceremony," he said.

He returned her embrace. She looked into his eyes, a warm smile emerging on her face. Hinoch began to sing his shaman's song. The vibrations from his chest passed through their summer clothing into Joanna's body. She laid her head on his shoulder and felt herself wilt in his arms, transfused with warmth and happiness.

"Sing with me now," he said. "Simply sing what is in your heart and I will do the same. This will be our family song."

He began and she listened for a few seconds, then joined in with her own words, matching them to the rhythms of his.

"Today I become a bird,
My life is renewed,
I float on the sky
And see life with new eyes . . . "

They swayed together and sang for many minutes then lapsed into silence.

Hinoch reached around his neck and withdrew the ring. "Your grandmother gave me this, with her best wishes for our future."

He placed the thong around her neck and draped the ring onto her shirt. She flipped her hair from beneath the thong and carefully slid the ring under her shirt.

Looking into his eyes, she said, "I've got one of my people's traditions that I want to share with you now, and often in the future." She leaned forward and kissed him fully on the lips. To her surprise, he returned the kiss, warm and full of passion.

"That is one of my people's traditions, as well. Now I know why it is so favoured. Here is another, for more public occasions." He grasped her shirtsleeves between his thumbs and forefingers and rubbed noses with her.

She laughed. "I like that one, too."

"Now, I believe you wanted a large fire, accompanied with some pagan ritual of dancing while naked."

She did not move from their embrace, "Mmmm, sounds good, but I think the fire is strictly optional. I'm plenty warm right now."

Slowly, Hinoch moved to her side, one arm behind her back, the other moving down to the backs of her thighs. She felt herself float effortlessly into his arms. He carried her toward the tent.

"I believe this is another of your customs. The groom carries the bride over the threshold."

"Guess I'll have to get used to sealskin tent and igloo thresholds."

He smiled and kissed her again.

Caw, Caw, Caw. From above came a raucous flurry of calls. Hinoch and Joanna looked up to see Dianne, Curtis, Tuk and Paul putting on a wonderful display of aerobatics, full of spirals, climbs and even Immelman turns. They were obviously celebrating the occasion.

Joanna and Hinoch watched for a few moments, then slipped quietly into the tent.

The thin, veiled fog remained for four days. Joanna and Hinoch spent the time joyfully exploring their relationship and communing with the newly reborn family spirits around them. The morning of the fifth day dawned clear and cool.

"We'll probably be picked up today," Joanna surmised. She snuggled up behind him and slid her hands up under his jacket, "The weather looks generally clear and cold, so Lab Air will probably swing by on their flight to Nain. That should put them here about twelve-thirty."

"Yes, I think you are correct. We should assemble our gear and be ready for him to arrive."

She paddled his stomach with her hands, "I don't know which of us is going to change the most, but if you keep talking like a textbook, I'm going to have to get my hands on a dictionary and a grammar text."

Hinoch laughed. "There are many dialects of the language; we all note the differences as we converse and enjoy each others' turn of phrase. In the final analysis, so long as we understand one another, the primary objective of communication is satisfied."

Joanna shook her head and laughed as she began collecting their equipment. Hinoch began deflating the dingy and preparing the protective cover for its storage.

"So, what're we going to do first when we get back to Nain?"

He handed the cover to her. She opened it and he slid the folded dingy inside. "I will call a council meeting and announce our marriage. We will celebrate awhile, then I will tell our people of my visions and ask them to choose whether they will remain in Nain, or come with us to Ungava Bay."

"How long will they celebrate?"

"Oh, perhaps seven to ten days. We should all be pretty well exhausted by then."

"Wow! Now that's a wedding dance! She paused again, then asked, "How many do you think are ready to follow us into the far north?"

"We may have as few as ten others, or as many as sixty." If we have sixty, I will need to divide us into two or three groups immediately and appoint leaders for each group."

"Why split them up? Wouldn't it be better to keep our numbers as high as possible so we can help each other?"

"That would be nice indeed, but the game would be depleted in no time. We would be forced to travel continuously to find new hunting areas. If we split up into well balanced groups, we can still be of help to each other and we will be able to settle for part of the year in one area without depleting it."

"Will we be able to get together from time to time, just to make sure everybody's okay?" She moved to his side, addicted now to contact with him.

"We will have winter homes dispersed around the tundra, but in summer we will gather at the George, or the Baleine River Bay. Fish are wonderfully plentiful there. We will spend the entire summer catching and drying them. It will be a time of celebration and joy for all of us."

Joanna frowned, and playfully traced his ear, "Sounds like the winters will be pretty slow and boring."

"On the contrary, we will be busy hunting, scraping out hides and tanning them and making tools from their bones and antlers. We will not waste anything for which we have a purpose. Even our waste is given back to nature to feed our future sustenance."

"Seems like our meals will be meat with meat on the side. Kind of hard to keep the menu interesting."

"You will learn there is great variety, all of which can be made very palatable." We will even have the pleasure of a sour salad every time we bag a caribou and plenty of Juniper-berry tea."

"Meat salad too?" she asked, an incredulous look on her face.

"Hinoch smiled, "The stomach sacks will contain chewed mosses and lichens which we hang to ferment for a week or two. The result is a delicious sour salad, not unlike the German dish, sauerkraut."

"Ugh," she grunted, "I can see my digestion will face some real challenges in the near future!"

"Indeed, you will face many challenges, but I will do my utmost to provide well for you and make your life joyful."

"What more could a woman ask?" she said calmly.

She couldn't believe the inner peace she felt, even though she knew nothing about living like a native in the arctic. Give her a plane and she was fully capable of surviving, especially with all the survival gear, but this all sounded mighty primitive. She hoped Hinoch wasn't reading her mind. If he didn't think she was ready to accept this adventure, he'd likely decide to leave her behind. *The hell he will. I'm going, whether I live through it or not!* she assured herself.

At twelve-thirty, she heard the Twin Otter approaching. In a few seconds, it flew overhead, circled and landed smoothly on the lake. As it coasted to the shore, Hinoch prepared to load their equipment.

"This is probably the last time we will use this camping gear. We can give it to the people who stay in Nain. Perhaps they will have need of it from time to time."

"It's pretty light. Why don't we bring it along and just toss it when it's no longer useful?"

"Bread crumbs. We'd be leaving a trail like bread crumbs, leading to our whereabouts, and also, I hate throwing things away that will never become a part of the environment. We will eventually have no metal or artificial goods of any kind. Before our knives wear out, we will need to learn how to sharpen stones and tusks for our cutting needs."

"You don't know how yet?"

"My ancestors know how all these things are done; they will show me as the need arises."

She looked at him in surprise as they climbed into the plane and departed for Nain.

They lifted into the skies and Joanna closed her eyes and relaxed in the back of the plane. Hinoch had gone up to the cockpit with the pilot and was absorbed in his characteristic surveillance of the land below. She smiled. She saw him in her imagination as a caring custodian, overseeing every aspect of the welfare of his charge — the wilderness of Labrador. She was overwhelmed by the speed with which she had been drawn to Hinoch. And the power of her feelings. Nothing in her life had compelled her so fundamentally, with so much satisfaction, into a course of action this replete with risk and adventure. She was an adventurous example of her sex, she knew that, but

WE ARE STILL HERE

even her sense of adventure to this point had been tame by comparison. To this point, she had always surrounded herself with all the training and equipment necessary to deal with the situations she entered. Now she felt as though she had jumped from a cliff with nothing but rocks below. She had no idea how she was to cope with this environment without her safety net.

The strangest feeling she was experiencing was her peace and her calm. She seemed content to trust in the belief that Hinoch would take care of her and teach her all she needed to know. Rather than seeing her leap from the cliff as a fall into the abyss, she saw herself miraculously transformed into a beautiful bird. She saw herself recover from her fall by flying off into the clear skies. Free, totally free and an integral part of her new world.

Her fears were real, yet her resolve to face them was steadfast, made that way by her unwavering faith in Hinoch.

Joanna woke as the plane, now on final approach, spanked a wave, floated a short while back in the air, then settled onto the surface. They taxied to the pier. Joanna was the first onto the pontoon, taking up the mooring line and hopping onto the dock. She slowed the plane, then secured the line to a cleat.

The pilot confided to Joanna as he unloaded their gear, "I heard about your prang. I don't mind saying that you have to be one hell of a prop-jockey to walk away from a forced landing in those conditions. My hat's off to you!"

"Thanks, but it still hurts like hell."

"You were hurt?"

"No, just my pride. I was lucky."

"I hear you. I dusted off my first Otter on approach into Goose . . . damn lucky to be alive, but it took weeks before I quit having nightmares." He smiled broadly, as he untied the painter and stepped onto the pontoon. "Good luck folks, I'll see you again some time!"

They waved, then shouldered their gear. As they walked to Hinoch's cabin, Hinoch asked her, "Will you miss flying?"

"Of course. It's been my life until now, but things are changing fast. I'll get over it. What about your painting?"

"I will no longer paint pictures. Today, I begin painting our future on the tapestry of reality. If I do well, it will be my masterpiece."

"I like that, Hinoch. I think that's the neatest thing I've heard you say."

They stowed the gear in the shed and visited the dogs for a few minutes.

"Monty and Dick have done a good job caring for them. The dogs are putting on weight and show the need for some hard exercise."

"It's going to be awhile before they can pull the sled again. How're you going to exercise them?"

"I will work them with the stone sledge. The General Store needs some more riprap around the footings. We can haul rock and reinforce the shoreline foundations."

"What about our party?"

"That will come first of course. After the meeting, when I know who is coming with us, I will suggest this project as a good means for all of us to become more fit."

"A community works project."

"Exactly. I am going to call the meeting now. Why don't you rest awhile, then come down to the open area near the water. That is where we will meet."

"Okay, I'll freshen up. Anything in particular I should wear?"

"Dress for comfort, we may be occupied for some time."

He turned and quickly walked toward the cluster of small houses arranged against the stone cliffs of the valley.

Joanna turned to go into the cabin and noticed Ken walking toward her. "Hello Ken, how did your tape turn out?"

"Well, not bad, for what we got."

"What d'you mean by that?"

"We got some footage of the old plane and of you and Hinoch in the dingy, then not much else except for the fog and the crows."

"Ravens."

"Pardon?"

"Ravens. They're ravens."

"Oh, sorry, I didn't know there was a difference. Anyway, after the fog settled in, all we saw was a glimpse of four ravens and an obscured shot of what looks like a big white bird. Then you come out of the fog in the dingy."

"That's all you got?"

"Yeah, only thing I don't understand is, where in hell did Hinoch disappear to?"

"He was the white raven."

"Yeah, sure, and elephants can fly too!"

"Listen, with that attitude you'd never understand what happened out there if I drew you a map! You were the one so taken with the story of the lost aviator and how my grandma wanted to see where her husband had spent his last days and rejoin his spirit. Well you've seen it. If you don't get it, that's your problem!"

He took a step backward, "Okay, okay, you don't need to bite my head off. I just don't buy the idea that their spirits are still floating around out there."

"You're right; they're not. Those ravens were the next incarnation of their spirits. They are living happily together again, and Hinoch *was* the white raven. He made it all happen. That's your story." She turned and grasped the latch of Hinoch's cabin door.

"That's not a story, that's a pile of bullshit that can't be supported by anything we got on tape. We'd be laughed out of the studio for even trying to make a story of that!"

She spun around, incensed at his insensitivity, "Well, if you're convinced there's nothing there, I guess nothing's there, so forget it. Forget this too: your whole world, as you know it, is ending . . . a lot sooner than anybody thinks it will. Since you can't get your head around this little story though, I don't know why I'm even telling you about the end of your useless ass."

He grinned, "Oh great, now the sky is falling! What other revelations have you got stuffed into that blonde head of yours?"

"Tell you what. When you're starving in a heat-wave like you've never seen before in your life, just remember this: I told you so! Goodbye!"

Joanna turned and stormed into the cabin, slamming the door behind her.

Damn, why does Hinoch have to be so right all the time. These idiots can't believe anything. They have to see iron-clad proof! A world without faith, without hope, and they don't even know it yet!

Joanna tried to calm herself. She looked out the window to see Ken marching off in a huff down the lane.

Good riddance, I just wish someone more sensitive and observant had had the last chance to save the world. She paused deep in thought. *I can't believe I tore into him like that. I must have really looked like a lunatic, going on about the end of the world. Fact is, I believe we are right. We are the modern Noah's Ark. My children will help to preserve mankind's place on this planet.*

She patted her cheeks, amazed at her own thoughts. *This is unbelievable. Come on, girl, let's get back to earth. I have to get ready for my wedding reception!* She turned her gaze into the cabin and began to look around for the now familiar juniper-infused oils. In the far corner of the cabin, she opened a cupboard filled with stiff, white towels. Beside the towels, she found a sealer filled with an amber liquid. She opened the lid and her nose embraced the sweet smells of juniper and pine.

She removed her clothing, then remembered she had not locked the door. She padded to the door . . . no lock . . . no bolt, just the simple gate latch. She looked around self-consciously for something to prop against it. *There . . . a chair.*

With the chair firmly pushed under the catch, she returned to the far corner and began rubbing the oil vigorously onto her body. Warmth infused her immediately, and the heat of her body vaporized the essential oils. The room filled with a delicious aroma as she rubbed, then she toweled down vigorously. Aglow with the new sensations, she pulled another outfit of clothes from her duffel bag and dressed.

Something came up against the door with a thud, followed by some rather coarse grumbling.

"Just a minute!" she shouted, "I'll be right there!"

She opened the door to face Monty, rubbing his nose and wearing a look of pure astonishment on his face.

"You should fix that door. It's sticking pretty bad!"

"Sorry, Monty. I was changing my clothes, so I locked the door."

"Locked it! Why d'ja do that?"

"Well, you see I'm from the big city, where people are bashful. When they take their clothes off, they like to be sure they'll be able to change in private."

"Sounds kinda silly to me. My family all live in one room. No chance to be *private*."

"I'm trying to adjust, Monty. Just be patient with me, okay?"

"Okay, but don't take too long. Pretty soon, we're heading north and we won't have *any* homes. You wander off for privacy out there and Nanuk or the Amarok will get you. Arrnng!" He made a grotesque chewing motion with his mouth while baring his even, but plaque-covered teeth.

Joanna feigned fear and assured him, "Okay, Monty, I'll stay with everyone else. No wandering!"

"D'you know when we're leaving?"

"No, I don't think they've decided that yet."

"It's gonna have to be pretty quick, we'll need the warm weather to build our shelters at the river mouth and catch our first supply of fish to dry."

"You sound pretty excited about all this."

"You bet. We're going to be real Inuit again. No more tin-pot white men giving us bad counsel. Hinoch'll just give us good counsel."

"Is your family going to join us then?"

"No, just me an' Dick. Hinoch told my dad that he wanted to adopt us and Dad said, "Good. Two less mouths to feed!"

"Your dad wouldn't say that!"

Monty nodded seriously, but showed no signs of sadness at that reality.

"Gotta go now, the meetin's startin' soon!"

"Wait a second, Monty. Can I come with you?"

"Sure, but hurry up!"

"Okay, I'll just grab my coat."

Joanna was alternately attracted to this boy and shocked by him. He was so open and personable, yet so devoid of any manners. He could easily wrap her around his finger she knew, but she felt the need to show him so much that involved discipline. She knew it would not be easy re-shaping this boy's mind, but then again where they were headed, he might do just fine.

They trotted along the pathway to the meeting place. Along the way, Dick and several of their friends joined them. It struck Joanna strangely that these children were going to be included in a meeting where momentous decisions were to be made. As they approached, Monty and Dick slowed to a walk. Monty took her left hand and Dick grasped her right. They led her to Hinoch.

"Here she is 'Noch. We found her!"

"Thank you, boys. Come, stand here with us."

"I understand we've adopted already!" she whispered in his ear.

He smiled. "We will have a large family; some you will bear, many we will adopt. A child is borne to the community as much as it is to one mother and father."

Joanna smiled wryly, "I've been noticing that."

Hinoch turned to the gathering of nearly one hundred and fifty people and introduced Joanna. "This woman has chosen to become a partner in my life; her name is Joanna. Although she does not understand our ways, she is learning quickly. I ask that you include her in everything you do, showing her our ways. She is a strong and courageous woman. You will soon grow to respect her, as do I."

Drums began to play, and a few women began to throat-sing, producing that unique haunting sound only heard in these regions. Slowly the elders approached, one by one, grasped her by her coat-sleeves and gently rubbed noses with her. Smiles were everywhere and she could see that a big celebration was brewing. She quickly learned to snatch a breath before the next elder approached. The diet now consisted largely of seal-meat, which had a distinctly heady, pungent aroma.

The reception line dwindled and Hinoch took her hand and began a shuffling dance, slowly increasing the intensity as the drums strengthened their beat. In moments, a large fire had been lit and the dancers gravitated to it, many others joining.

As the fire's heat increased, the dancing became more intense. Around them, the celebration was taking shape, some people bringing food and others singing. The sounds and activities built to a point at which they were almost cacophonous, but not in an unpleasant or threatening way. Joanna closed her eyes as she danced with Hinoch. She found herself transported into a pleasant place in her mind, to their tent at the lake — warm, safe and filled with anticipatory excitement.

Time lost its grip. Events unfolded as they occurred with no sense of time passing. The night closed in around the village, yet seemed to keep its distance from the fire, not from fear, from respect.

They feasted, danced and communed with each other without reservation. People came and went: they danced, they sang, they watched. People everywhere were smiling, talking and laughing without reserve. Joanna thought of the similarity to some of the better New Year's Eve parties she had attended, with one important omission. There was no sign of alcohol here.

The euphoria came from the endless droning music, and the protracted dancing. The sense of comfort came from the seeming endless supplies of food and communion with her new family. Daylight followed darkness, then once again the cycle passed, largely unnoticed. No one counted the days, they were immaterial to the celebration, so were ignored.

When anyone became too warm, they removed clothing; if they were chilled, they covered themselves with whatever came to hand. Joanna was amazed at the tolerance these people had to cold. She would be bundled up in her coat, dancing to stay warm while others were naked, yet apparently still too warm. She watched and learned that property was not a concept among these people. Women and men had clearly formed close, life-long partnerships, yet remained independent, free-spirited and fully self-determined. She could see a quality of love between men and women, parents and children that was largely unknown in her world.

Her mind began to speak to her, working through the essence of what she was experiencing all around, "*My* wife, *my* husband, *my* child. Nobody here calls anyone *mine.*"

Hinoch spoke to her, but she was not aware of his voice. *You see, now, how sadly that possessive attitude degrades the pure emotion of love. In a very important sense, it takes away the freedom of the partner in the relationship. If you are free to love each other without being possessed, there is no law or obligation between you. You are free, so you have nothing against which you may need to rebel.*

I understand it, but I confess I am very possessive of you, Hinoch. I want you all to myself, she thought.

That is very flattering, Joanna. I confess I like the feeling. I also know that you have a generous heart and will give our children the freedom to be themselves as they mature.

I just realized something. We're sharing our thoughts!

Welcome, love of my life.

Joanna felt giddy with the realization of her growing link with her new husband. It was an almost tangible expression of how she felt drawn to their union.

Joanna surveyed the celebration going on all around them, *I can sure see how casual observers could interpret this as a pagan ritual. They'd have a real problem trying to cope with this much freedom.*

The missionaries were certainly taken aback by our openness and lack of inhibition, Hinoch thought. *They immediately equated what they saw to what they termed debauchery, assuming that we had all the twisted attitudes of Europeans who engaged in uninhibited revelry.*

So they laid down the law, to which you reluctantly paid lip service without ever really accepting?

You have a keen memory and a healthy wit, Joanna. Those characteristics will serve us well on cold winter nights.

I know something else that will be nice on winter nights, she thought as she snuggled up to him. He placed his arm around her waist and hugged her firmly. They kissed to the loud approval of all present.

The celebration seemed to abate of its own accord. People began drifting off to their homes. The singing and drums dwindled and ceased, and the fire began to burn down to a large pile of coals.

"Tomorrow we sleep, then we must begin in earnest to prepare for our journey. I would like to contact Lucien and tell him what I am doing. He has legal access to my accounts, so I will give the money to him and invite him to join us. You must have family you wish to contact."

"Yes, I'll call Mother and tell her what's happening. She told me I would not likely be back in Winnipeg for awhile. Guess she was right, as usual."

"You could invite her to join us if you wish. I would gladly provide for her."

"No, she's very attached to her amenities. I just pray that someone down there knows how to turn everything around and avert this disaster. I won't even be able to talk to her about your visions of the coming disasters; it would just get her all upset. She has a weak heart so too much excitement is hard on her."

"This will be extremely difficult for you If you want more time, I will understand. I could meet you in Hebron at some later date."

She glared at him, "No bloody way! My mind is made up. I'm coming with you . . . *now!*"

Hinoch looked into her bloodshot eyes and saw the fire in her spirit. He was pleased. He reached under her arms and lifted her up into the air like a toy.

"You are indeed a determined woman, and I am honoured that we are going to share our lives together." He lowered her slowly to the ground, then kissed her again, long and hard.

As they broke from their kiss, she mumbled, "If I weren't so damn tired, we'd be making love for the rest of the night, but I don't feel coordinated enough to walk, let alone make love. Take me home, Hinoch!" They ambled off to his cabin, where they remained two full days. When they emerged, preparations began in earnest.

"We will have twelve families travelling with us. We must make haste now, so that we can cover the distance to Ungava Bay in time to catch and dry fish for the winter."

"This might not sit well with you, Hinoch, but when I was in the store, I heard that a freighter's due any day to drop off supplies along the coast. Maybe it won't be the traditional way to travel, but it'll get us over a lot of miles in a short period of time."

"That is a wonderful idea! Thank you, Joanna. Your wisdom will be a great help to us! We must make our bookings!"

Hinoch and Joanna ran down to the General Store, where Hinoch spoke breathlessly to the clerk, "I wish to book passage to Kangiqsualujjuaq on the freighter for forty-four people."

"Forty-four! They'll never take that many; there aren't accommodations for more than five or six, plus the crew."

"I don't care about accommodations, we will look after ourselves, but I must have passage to Kangiqsualujjuaq. Please radio him and tell him to ask his price. I will pay generously."

"He's due in three days, so he ought to be in range. I'll try."

The clerk went to the storeroom where the radio was located. Hinoch and Joanna waited. Joanna surveyed the store, her mind looking at each item in the light of its possible value in their future situation. She selected some painkillers, antiseptics and sterile bandages, knives, ulus, and sewing items.

"Bet I won't get any more of this where I'm going. I vote for a binge now," she muttered to herself. She grabbed six chocolate bars. She carried her basket to the counter, looking into Hinoch's eyes for approval.

"These won't weigh much and they might be useful while we are getting established."

He smiled broadly, "And these?" he asked, pointing to the chocolate bars.

"I'm a chocolate junkie. I'm trying to come down easy," she joked.

"I see. Perhaps you will develop new tastes in our future home."

"Maybe," she answered, somewhat unconvinced.

The clerk emerged from the back.

"Are you going to want meals, or are you bringing your own food?"

"We will bring all our own supplies, but we will need a cooking appliance and some large pots."

"Okay, I'll tell him," the clerk said, disappearing into the storeroom again. A few moments later, he emerged once more, wide-eyed.

"He says, two hundred per adult, one hundred for children under ten. By my tally, that would be about eight thousand dollars!"

"Done," said Hinoch. "Tell him to prepare an open space for us in the hold, with ready access to the deck, sanitary facilities and the cooking area. We will also have need of a large area on deck for cages, for our dogs and our supplies."

The clerk's jaw dropped, "You're going to pay that much?"

"Yes. He has the only ship available for some time, so he can name his price."

Joanna whispered hoarsely to him, "That's a lot of dough, Hinoch. You sure you've got enough?"

"Yes, I am certain. My account in Montreal had nearly three million dollars the last time I checked."

"When was the last time you checked?" Joanna squeaked.

"About four years ago."

"Wow, you really *don't* give a damn about money do you!"

"It has very little purpose in my life. I only need the materials given me by nature to make what I need and to have my people with me. What else does one require?"

"When you look at it that way, not much, I guess, but you've got to be prepared for these stupid questions from me. Remember, I'm not going through simple culture shock here; this is a quantum leap!"

"A quantum leap. What is that?"

"Oh, there was a show on TV a few years ago where this fellow experiments with time travel and gets caught in some kind of loop. Every life he interacts with changes the future and forces him to jump to some other place and time, I'm not sure why. Anyway, he ended up in some pretty weird situations, far removed from his home life. They called it *Quantum Leap*."

"Oh, I see . . . I think," he chuckled as he paid for Joanna's shopping and picked up the box.

"Come, we must get everyone ready. Many of us will need to build cages for the dogs. There is much to do!" Hinoch turned and left the store.

Joanna fell in behind Hinoch. She couldn't believe she'd be packing up in two days for a journey with no return and as far as she knew, no idea of what she needed. *This just gets stranger and stranger!* she thought.

The Trials Begin

The water surged under the ship with a steady burbling sound. The diesel engine thump-thumped in the depths of the hull below. Hinoch reveled in the glassy smoothness of the waters. Whales rolled in the distance and as he looked down into the bow wave, dolphins were darting in and out of view in the dark waters.

So, Father, the journey has begun, he thought. *I have forty-four souls in my charge and my ancestors to lead me to our mutual salvation. I pray that we are enough to prevail. This meager number seems too few should we fall upon bad times, yet they are the most loyal of my people. I could not have chosen better had I selected them myself. Each of our people has chosen by free will to adopt our traditional ways and return to our original home ... the wilderness. Abel, my father, we are returning; show us the land and its riches. Let us become established in our ways before hardship befalls us.*

Do not be concerned, my son. The time of your journey is well chosen. The cold weather will be late this year and the bitter winter storms will be to the south of your new home. Establish your people in the west end of my valley, where the river joins the bay to the north of Kangiqsualujjuak. There will be ample fish, seals and game. They have escaped heavy hunting here for many years now, and are in balanced abundance.

Thank you, Father. I rely upon your counsel.

"What are you doing up here?" Joanna asked as she approached him.

"I am praying for my spirits to guide our journeys."

"Well, couldn't you pick a warmer place to pray? It's freezing up here!"

"I had not noticed. I was so absorbed with the whales breaching and the dolphins playing in our bow-wave. Look, they are still here."

"Wow! It's like it's easy for them to swim at this speed."

"They are swift, to be sure, but they also make use of the pressure wave created by the ship's movement through the water. They are surfing."

"It's beautiful. Everything's so beautiful here." She made a credible pirouette, a smile of pure joy on her features.

"Tomorrow will not be so attractive. See the low clouds on the horizon? They are the clouds borne ahead of a strong wind. The waters will become rough. We must make sure the dogs' cages are well secured to the decks. We may even be forced to bring them below."

Her smile faded a little, "Oh, now there's the recipe for a *real* party! A hundred and sixty dogs in a confined space. I don't think I want to be there."

"I will do my best to control them. I have been connecting with their spirits. Also, my lead dog, Alut, is an excellent Alpha male. He will be a great help."

"He'd better be a real lion. It's going to be bedlam!"

Hinoch turned to her, grasped her arms and chided her, but lovingly, "Be confident. We will do what we must in every situation. If you are hesitant or negative in your attitude, it will detract from our efforts and ultimately from our success."

She looked into his eyes, chastened, "You're right. I'm the woman who shares the life of a shaman. I've got to be a leader too. Okay, I've been told off. Positive thoughts from here on in." She pressed her palm against her forehead and closed her eyes.

"It won't always be that easy, Joanna. We are all human and we will falter. That is why there are many of us: to help each other. We must become one large family."

Joanna looked into his eyes and perceived once again the many souls within them. The changes within her own spirit flooded into her consciousness. Daily she grew closer to him and to his people. Already, she had learned to strip sinews from carcasses for thread and how to tan hides by chewing. It was hard, labourious work, yet she was glad to become part of it.

"We already are, Hinoch . . . at least that's how I feel. We just have to get to know each other better."

She felt her mind flood with warmth. She stepped into his arms. As she closed her eyes, she still saw Hinoch's image in front of her. He was smiling and as she watched in her mind, a large group of people joined him. Not this group, but people she had not before seen. They encircled both of them and began to sing. They sang the shaman's song. His voice entered her mind, *These people are our guides. If we follow their counsel, we will survive.* When she opened her eyes, she was still in his arms, feeling warm and safe.

He pointed to the west. "Look, here is Hebron. Saglek Bay is the next inlet to the north, where my father made his home."

"Do you miss them?"

"In a sense I do. I no longer can see them in the flesh, but I take great comfort in the company of their spirits."

"Why did you not choose to move back here?"

"The people from Hebron hunt this area and it is badly depleted. We would overburden the resources and help to destroy their livelihood. This valley cuts across like a highway to Ungava Bay, we will live at the western end of this valley, and we will visit my father's home from time to time."

"I'd like that. It's important to me to see where you started your life. Let's go below and see how everyone's doing."

"Good idea."

They entered a beehive of activity, everyone occupied with organizing a small area of the hold. The dim light of the caged light bulbs was nearly absorbed in the dark stains of rust and grime that obscured most of the cream-coloured paint on the bulkheads. The only brightly-lit areas were directly below the hatches to the deck above. Men and women worked together, stowing gear not immediately needed; other women tended the children and tried to create small living and sleeping areas. The first night passed quietly.

As dawn approached, the ship began to pitch forward and aft. Simultaneously, it was rolling as it met each oncoming wave. It would seem to lose momentum, then shudder slightly as the bow rose, then it would push ahead to the next wave. Hinoch looked around the hold. Many people were already up, fighting against the ship's movement and trying to get the morning meal ready. He rose and went topside to assess the weather and check on the condition of the dogs. The waves were dark green, with foam tipped tops. As they broke on the bow, a spray would blow back and splash against the tarps strung over the dog kennels, its staccato sound alarming them.

Hinoch slipped under the tarp and spoke to them in his mind, calming them and urging them to rest lying down, rather than attempting to stand and fight the waves. Almost in unison, they lay down and began to return to their sleep. They would be all right for now.

He emerged from the tarp and scanned the horizon. His senses told him that the roughest water lay ahead half a day's sailing. Mount Caubvick was now jutting from the horizon to the southwest. He decided that he would return regularly to reassure the dogs and to assess the weather.

Below decks, things were not going at all well. Many people were already seasick; the odour of their vomit permeated the air, making others queasy.

"Come, those of us who feel well enough, to the decks above. There is a fine northeast wind blowing fresh. In another day, we will have fair, cool weather. Our dogs need our company and attention. Many of them need a walk on the deck and some food. We also need to get some fresh air down here. Opening the hatches will freshen things up quickly."

They emerged to find the crew stringing ropes along the superstructure. A young man with a premature attempt at a beard growing in patches on his face warned, "You'll be needin' to keep a firm hold on the ropes; these decks'll be gettin' slippery as the sea washes over them."

Gingerly, everyone struggled along the rope corridor to the dog cages. In small groups, they removed the dogs and took them on short leads around the deck. As is typical for the Inuit, they soon found an advantage to the weather. The seas quickly washed the decks clear of the dogs' urine and feces.

Hinoch noticed another much more mature member of the crew, known by the name of Tip, closing the hatches above their hold. Tip was a true product of his environment. His seafarer's gait, long, nicotine stained beard and work-soiled clothing made it clear to everyone that he was an old tar. Though his beard was liberally salted with grey, his body was hard and powerfully built, a testimony to his years of labour.

"Could you please leave them open? Many have already been seasick below and the fresh air will help to revive them."

"Sorry, sir. Cap'n's orders," he spoke in a strong Newfoundlander's brogue. "We're to be securin' the ship for weather. He says there be a good blow comin'. Should be lastin' the night."

"Very well then, let me get some more of them topside."

"I wouldn' be recommendin' that, sir. If they're seasick, they won't be too steady on their pins. Next thing you knows, we'll be havin' someone overboard!"

"Thank you for your counsel. We'll probably need to bring the dogs below. We can't risk losing them."

"Your choice, sir, but I hates to see what she's gonna be like down there when things gets rough." He shook his head, looking intently at Hinoch. "You'll be after havin' a real bad night. Animals below decks are often goin' berserk in storms. That many half-wild dogs'll be raisin' a lot of hell!" He raised his hands to his ears, wincing at the thought of all the noise.

"We'll be able to control them. Will you give us a hand to move them?"

"Oh no sir, not me. I'm partial to *keeping* my nether parts, I am! Just be takin' 'em one by the time and make certain you hangs onto the ropes with your free hand. You'll do fine, bye."

They had been forced to shout to be heard above the wind. Hinoch knew there was no more time to waste. He went to his dogs and clipped a rope to his lead dog. He stumbled and fought to regain his feet. The water washed him hard against another dog's cage. The dog snarled and lunged at him. He glared with eagle's eyes into the cage and the dog instantly retreated, lying down at the rear of his space. Hinoch scrambled to his feet and led his dog to the hatch. Gripping him by the harness, he lifted him over the lip and handed him down to Monty, who was waiting below. Everyone on deck followed suit, bringing individual dogs to the hatch and lowering them to the hold. In about thirty minutes, they were all safely below decks.

Soaked, battered and sore from their falls and slips, the people filed below after the last dog was lowered. They entered bedlam.

Alut was surrounded by other male huskies — the challenge was clearly afoot. Hinoch rushed to approach the dogs as one lunged at Alut headlong. Alut crouched to the deck then lunged, roaring at his attacker. They struck with a thump of muscular flesh against bone. The husky's fur shook with the impact. Alut grabbed him by the throat as he rebounded and with one powerful wrench of his head, tore the entire front of the huskie's neck away. The husky expelled a spray of blood as he tried to scream in pain. Another dog sprung at him from the rear, mounting him and biting down on his back. His hold was tenuous on such a huge animal. Alut shook him loose in an instant, as he broke the neck of a second attacker. He turned and shattered the third dog's foreleg with one bite.

Then, before he had time to react, Alut took his neck from the side and choked the air from him, pinning him to the deck as he slowly succumbed.

The remaining males retreated, slipping and scrambling on the blood-soaked metal of the deck. He now stood, his white fur bloodied, head lowered and teeth bared, facing the remaining males. They fussed among themselves for space at the back of the pack, showing no taste for another challenge to Alut's authority.

Hinoch's powerful baritone voice began his shaman's chant. The ship's hold resonated with the deeper notes as he sang and within seconds, the dogs were noticeably more peaceful. People began taking them to separate areas against the hull, placing themselves between the dogs to help keep them segregated.

Hinoch addressed his people. "Feed the dogs well tonight. We want them lazy with their stomachs busy digesting seal meat. That goes for us as well. Eat as much as you can, then settle down for the night. The weather will become rougher until just before dawn, when it will abate."

Hinoch helped Monty and Dick as they dragged the dead dogs up the companionway to the rear superstructure and the deck, dumping them overboard.

Hinoch returned below to find Joanna and Noel working to clean up the blood and torn bits of fur and flesh. He decided to consult Captain Hunt. He left his people and returned to the aft ladder leading up into the superstructure and the wheelhouse. He entered the wheelhouse and scanned the faces of the crew. They were intent on their duties, but showed no real concern about the coming storm. Captain Hunt stood leaning against the bulkhead carefully watching his helmsman's activity. His sailor's cap sat jauntily askew atop his white hair.

He bore the scars of a life at sea, two broken fingers and a deep gash that extended from his ear to his chin. He had earned that from a parting steel cable during a storm many years ago. Now in his early sixties, he was putting on weight and his skin resembled the tough, wrinkled hide of a walrus.

"Good evening, Captain, do you have any more suggestions or requirements of my people for the night?"

"No, bye. Just stay where you're to and keep the hatches on, no matter how bad it gets. These here waves could swamp her in minutes if a hatch is left off."

Hinoch looked out onto the foredeck as a wave swept onto the ship, green water easily ten feet above the bow railing. It broke onto the deck with a rumble, tearing some of the dog cages from the deck and pushing them aft.

"She'll be no fun, I'll be tellin' you, bye. You'd best be figurin' out how you'll be passin' the rest of the trip with the dogs down below. By mornin', the cages not gone overboard'll be kindlin'."

"Yes, we will need to work out some method of easily controlling them and segregating them. Would you mind if we tie their harnesses to the pipes and bulkheads under the decks?"

"String 'em up if you likes, bye, but if you damages the ship, you'll be payin' for repairs. So don't be pullin' things down for temporary cages or nothin'."

"Thank you. We will not damage the ship. After all, we need it to take us to Kangiqsualujjuaq. One more thing. Could I ask you to turn the heat off in the hold? We are accustomed to cooler temperatures."

"Aye, I'll be after tellin' the engineer to shut 'er down straight away."

Hinoch returned to the hold and began to formulate the best method of tethering the dogs. He called upon the other men in the group and showed them what he had in mind. Within the hour, the dogs were in their pulling harnesses and on short tethers around the hold, spaced far enough to avoid any more physical contact should an argument break out. Conditions were far from comfortable, but with some effort, it would be possible to keep things clean and livable.

Alut was the only dog allowed to roam the ship. Hinoch continued to ask of him what he had been destined to do from birth: assume the role of Alpha male. He roamed at random, rumbling huge bass notes at any dog that was not resting quietly.

The ship tossed and pitched, struggling to surmount each arriving wave. The sides and deck repeatedly rumbled from the impact of huge waves. At times, the entire massive structure seemed to lurch to a halt, then slowly regain headway as the bow dipped down to meet the next onslaught.

Some slept, others spent their energies voiding their stomachs, continuing to heave even after nothing remained to expel. Joanna moved from one to the other, helping them to clean up and get as comfortable as possible. She seemed to experience no ill effects whatever from the tossing, pitching steel cavern they found themselves trapped inside. Hinoch moved to her side.

"Joanna, you seem unaffected by the storm, or the stench down here. How do you do it?"

"I don't know. It used to bother me, but I'm okay now, I guess. You seem to be doing all right."

"I have felt much better, I confess. I think that I'm too busy to allow myself time to be ill."

"Whatever works for you, but shouldn't you try to get some sleep?"

"Perhaps later when the storm settles a little, but right now there is too much happening for me to rest."

"When will it ease?"

Hinoch looked forward. He was looking beyond the ship that confined them. "We are not making much headway, so I think we will be in these conditions until after sunrise. Calmer weather is still five hours away." He looked back to Joanna, searching her face for any sign of concern.

She returned his gaze calmly, "Well, I'll try to get everyone settled, then I'll get some sleep. You can stand the first watch and I'll relieve you in a few hours."

"Fine, sleep well, you will need your rest in the days to come."

"You too, Hinoch, watch you don't burn both ends of the candle for too long; we can't afford having you sick."

"I will be fine. Later I will sleep."

The morning waters bore no sign of the anger they had possessed the previous day. A low swell remained, which hardly caused the ship to rock. The water's surface had resumed its glassy sheen, with dark, unfathomable depths.

Slowly, people emerged from below, taking in the fresh air and exercising the dogs. Others remained below, cleaning and preparing the morning meal. Hinoch had slept about two hours when the fresh air from above wafted through the hull, rousing him. He surveyed the activities, again headed by Joanna, with satisfaction. She was busy moving among the people, helping wherever she could.

As he tried to arise, he realized he had Alut as his blanket.

"Come, Alut," he said, "let us take in the fresh air above."

The dog raised his head and looked at Hinoch, alert and eager, but he seemed unwilling to get up. Hinoch attuned himself to the dog's spirit. He noticed a mat of blood-soaked fur on his back; his hindquarters were becoming numb and unresponsive, making it difficult to walk.

"Rest, Alut, close your eyes and let me find the source of the injury." His hand passed slowly above the dog's spine, without touching it until he confirmed that the increased energy of the blood-soaked area was also the source of the nerve injury.

"Here it is," he said as he examined the wound, "a broken fang is penetrating to your spine. Rest still. I will remove it."

He took out his small caping knife and quickly shaved the area, then opened the wound enough to expose the tooth. Alut turned his head to watch, but made no sound, enduring his pain in complete silence. Hinoch bent down and clamped the fang in his teeth. He turned it slightly, feeling it dislodge and pulled it free. Quickly, he crumbled some herbed moss from his medicine pouch and packed the wound carefully.

Rest here, my friend, his mind spoke to the dog, *the feeling will return soon, but you must avoid movement for awhile. I will assume your role in the minds of the other dogs until you are healed.*

Hinoch examined the fang, nearly one and one-half inches long. It had broken off at the root. This had been the last wound inflicted by that dog.

Joanna approached, clearly concerned. "What's wrong with Alut?"

"He has a small wound on his back that needs to heal for two days. I have told him to remain quiet."

"I have some First Aid training. Can I help?" she bent forward and gingerly touched the blood-soaked pad of moss on Alut's back.

"Thank you, he will be fine. I have packed the wound with medicines that will prevent infection and help him heal. He will enjoy your company, though. Feed him generously and spend a little extra time with him." Hinoch rose and began to move away.

"Okay. What're you going to do now?" she glanced at him briefly, then resumed her examination of the wound. She was intrigued that such readily available items could be used instead of bandages and dressings.

"I am going to calm the other dogs and fool them into thinking Alut is still on the job."

He completed his rounds and returned to Alut, who was still bright and alert. Again, he held his hand above the area of the wound and closed his eyes, seemingly in deep meditation. When he moved his hand away and stood up, Alut also stood and joined him at his side. Slowly, they walked to Joanna.

"He will be fine. It appears that the spinal cord was not punctured, just bruised."

"What was wrong with him?"

"One of the dogs he fought bit him on the back and broke a fang off between his vertebrae. I found it this morning and removed it, then packed the wound with herbs and moss."

Joanna touched her fingers to her temples, "I've been so busy. I just realized I haven't been connecting with you much since the storm started."

"You have been fully occupied and you have done wonders helping our people. I am certain we will have ample time to communicate in future."

She nodded, smiling, then bent down to examine Alut's wound once more. Hinoch knelt down beside them. "That's wonderful! He seems to be recovering very well. I noticed you held your hand over the wound. What were you doing?"

"It is an old healing technique we call *Inunrautik*, which roughly translates as 'ancient first ancestors'. The Orientals practice a similar technique, which they call Reiki."

"A friend of mine studied Reiki. I never really paid much attention to it, though."

"It is a very powerful healing technique, if you believe."

The ship's whistle blew a deafening blast. Even below decks, it brought everyone to their feet in alarm. Hinoch and a few others went topside to see what was happening.

The morning was cool and calm with a light coastal fog. As they watched, they began to see the shoreline, darker blue details rising from the shadows ahead. As their eyes became accustomed to the glare of the fog, small details of the cliffs began to emerge. Birds flew in clouds to and from their nests in the near vertical crags of rock, washed white by their dung. The ship's whistle blew again, the echoes reverberating from the nearby cliffs two seconds later. They were less than one-half mile from shore.

They sailed that entire day near the coastal mountains, whose shadowed white peaks poked up into the cloudless skies above the mat of fog.

"Tonight we will turn south-southwest," Hinoch advised. "If this weather holds, we should arrive mid-day tomorrow."

"The calmer weather is sure a blessing. Things are going much better below," Joanna said.

"Good, we don't have enough material left to rebuild the cages on deck. The dogs must remain below with us."

The next day, they approached the George River inlet. Ahead, they could see the fog bank floating above the waters at the mouth of the harbour. Again, the ship's horn blew, but the echo was much more subdued. The coastline was much lower here, with only small hills to return the echoes.

"I'm always arriving in a fog, lately," Joanna joked.

"Things will become much clearer as we approach our new home. The things you have been feeling and seeing in your dreams will begin to make complete sense here."

"It doesn't matter what I say, you always take me seriously, don't you?"

"Yes, I do, unless you are laughing. That is my nature."

"I'll remember that." Joanna surveyed the tiny wooden pier they were approaching and as they gently nudged up to it and docked, she gained respect for the ship handling skills of the captain. "He pulled up like he was parking a car. I stood off farther than that with my plane and sometimes ended up paddling like a mad fool to get close enough to tie up."

"He has had a lot of experience at this kind of thing," Hinoch said. "I remember him bringing this same ship to dock when I first came to Nain as a boy. He had less white hair then but he was skillful even at a young age, I have heard. It is time for us to start unloading. We will take the dogs ashore and leave them tethered to the dock while we unload."

In two hours, they had unloaded their belongings and had begun to pack everything into bundles that were more portable. The village was much smaller than Nain, with only a trading post and a few small shacks. The weathered boards and disrepair of the buildings reflected the isolation of the place. As the fur trade had diminished, it had become unprofitable for the traders to maintain an outpost here, so they had abandoned it and the people who had moved here. Little remained. The village people, mostly elders, came to the dock to see the arrival of the freighter, and were overjoyed to see so many disembark. Everyone fell to the task of unloading passengers and freight.

The supplies and equipment would need to be carried to the edge of the village where they could camp while they prepared for the journey inland. The dogs were all laden with bundles lashed to their harnesses and every man and woman carried what they could. Three trips later, the pier was cleared of their belongings and the work of setting up camp began.

In only a few hours, sealskin tents dotted the shoreline of the harbour and a centrally-located campfire sprang up as the men took fishing lines and hooks, baiting them with seal meat. They returned to the pier and began jigging for flounder. The sandy bottom yielded well and, by sunset, there were enough fish to feed everyone.

The women had gathered berries, greens and roots from the low shrubs that dotted the landscape, inhabiting sheltered gaps between outcroppings of rock. The food they had gathered was steaming in a variety of pots when the men returned with the fish that were quickly added to the brew. Within the hour, everyone had gathered around the fire.

"Mmmm, this is good!" Joanna remarked. "What do you call this dish?"

"I do not know. Perhaps the women have a name for it, but to the men, it is another day that we are not hungry."

"So I shouldn't get too involved with menu planning, then. Dinner is whatever gets dragged into camp at night." She grinned mischievously as she play-acted dragging a large object over her shoulder.

"You might say that," he responded, feigning having missed the point of her charade.

As darkness settled, the people remained by the fire and talked about their experiences on the ship. The villagers had joined in the evening's activities, eager to hear any news from the outside world. Many of Hinoch's people had never been aboard such a large vessel before, so the stories were indeed animated. Later, as conversation waned, songs rose with the sparks from the fire, warming everyone's heart as they celebrated their new friends and their future together.

Joanna pulled her feet back from the fire and warmed her hands against the soles of her boots. "I'm starting to understand a little more of the language now, but I guess my accent is pretty poor. I have to repeat myself several times before I get my message across."

"You are doing well. Several people have remarked to me about how quickly you are learning." He looked into her eyes. "Do not be anxious, you have all the time in the world now to learn our ways and we have equally plentiful opportunities to teach you."

"Yeah, guess I won't be running around shopping and paying bills anymore, will I?" she said, looking at the weathered old trading post.

"Exactly. We are all together. Every day will be filled with the immediate and pressing business of providing for our needs. Tomorrow, we will make travois for the dogs to pull. Each dog will be able to pull nearly two hundred pounds this way. The men will pull the rest in the same fashion."

"Isn't the travois an Indian invention?"

"Yes, but it is useful for our present needs, so we will plagiarize the design. I assume they will not object and I am certain they will not litigate."

Joanna hooked his arm and looked at him coyly, "Let's go to our tent and sing our song, maybe rub noses awhile."

Hinoch smiled, "An excellent suggestion. Shall we?" They rose quietly and slowly wandered to their tent, but they did not go unnoticed. Smiles beamed in the firelight as the people nodded to each other, taking great pleasure in their leader's newfound happiness. The fire began to fade soon after, and the people began clearing the food away and moving off to their tents and their loved ones.

Next day, the camp was a hive of activity. One group went beachcombing for logs to use as poles. Another group went hunting and the remainder foraged in the vicinity for firewood and edible plants. By early afternoon, the poles had arrived and the construction of the travois was well underway. The pot was on the fire again, with deer, roots, and berries steaming in another broth.

Joanna busied herself with scraping the hide and stretching it out on the rib bones of a long-ago beached whale for drying. Her progress with the task was carefully monitored by Noel, the female elder of the group, with approval and occasional assistance. Hinoch had bagged the deer, a young buck, with one arrow. According to the story in camp, it had been an amazingly long and difficult shot. The story of his prowess as a hunter was being passed along with considerable pride. She understood only snippets of the chatter, but gathered that Angatkro, the shaman, was an excellent provider.

When Hinoch returned, she displayed her efforts with considerable pride.

"Well, do you think this will make good summer shirts and pants?" she asked.

"You have prepared this hide very well. You have not cut through or torn it anywhere. Yes, why not make yourself a new outfit? Your traditional clothes will wear quickly in the interior."

"Don't you want something from it?"

"Noel will show you the best parts of the hide for clothing; the rest will be used for wrapping and storing utensils and tools. Did you pull the tendons from the meat for tying cord?"

"Yes, they're drying right now. Monty and Dick tell me they nearly got a deer too."

"They managed to stalk a buck to within thirty yards. They are becoming more skillful each day. I am proud of our adopted sons." He surveyed the activity around them, "We are making an excellent start. The travois will be ready tomorrow morning. If all goes well, we will be travelling the next day. Your suggestion to take the freighter has put us at least twelve days ahead in our trip,

223

plus we have been able to bring more supplies than our own boats would have carried.

"Believe me, some of these ideas I'm having kind of amaze me, too. I seem to be learning things far more quickly than I ever used to. It feels more like I'm being *reminded* how to do these things when they show me. I somehow feel like I've seen a lot of this before. The ship idea must've come from some basic logistics training in my flying days. You know, use the best suited, most cost-effective mode of transport."

"Well, it is wonderful to see you adapting so quickly. But remember, we have plenty of time. There is no need for you to push too hard. You must always remember to conserve something for the next day. Sometimes the demands of tomorrow will be more important than what you spent your energy upon today."

"I am conserving some energy for us. I hope you are, too."

Hinoch smiled broadly and grasped her arms, then he gave her a long, warm kiss.

"We must always conserve something for ourselves. You give good counsel, Joanna."

Joanna grasped his hand as they walked to the fire for their evening meal.

Early next morning, Hinoch examined Alut to ensure that the wound had healed sufficiently for him to pull a full load. He was healing nicely. The skin was still red over the wound but it had begun to knit, and the scab, filled with herbs, was already beginning to pull loose at the edges. He made a pad of soft deerskin to fasten under the harness. This would soften the pressure on his back as he pulled.

Joanna peeked over Hinoch's shoulder, "Mmmm, that is healing nicely and I can't believe how quickly. He seems pretty much his old self again."

"Yes, the herbs have worked well and fortunately there seems to be no permanent damage. We can attach the travois to the dogs and load them. About one hundred and twenty-five pounds per dog will be a good amount for the start of the trip."

Hinoch and Joanna worked with the loading of the travois ensuring the dogs were hitched comfortably to the lead poles. This done, they went to the others to help prepare their dogs for the journey. Each of the people also had a small travois to pull, but the dogs were doing the majority of the work.

"This will condition them," Hinoch assured everyone, "By winter, they will be able to pull our new *komatiks* like the wind!"

Shortly after sunrise, they moved northeastward into the bush. Initially, travel was difficult and slow because the bush often snagged the dogs' harnesses and the travois poles as well. Much time was spent freeing anxious dogs who suddenly found themselves unable to move ahead. The people struggled on, overheating from their exertions. The blackflies were having a field day with their captives in the calm air of the bush. The scented oil everyone had applied had washed off quickly with their perspiration, leaving them exposed to the tiny insects' olfactory radar.

In the afternoon, they embarked upon a steep climb up the coastal hills. Many of the dogs could not pull their loads up these sharp inclines, so the process began of depositing supplies to be recovered on subsequent forays.

Slowly they made their way upward, carrying what they could.

Once they reached the plateau, they came to a shallow, fast moving river. The water bounced over the rocks in ripples scarcely a foot deep in most places, yet the stream was fully one hundred yards wide. The horizon spread out almost perfectly flat as far as the eye could see to the east. In the distance, some sixty miles beyond, the Torngat Mountains loomed. The terrain was rough, rocky and peppered with low bush and many sharp little valleys. From here, progress would be less strenuous.

"We will make camp here, near the river. Everyone has had a difficult day and we will all suffer from sore muscles tomorrow. A few more days of this level of activity though and we will all be fit and feeling our best."

"I sure hope so," Joanna puffed. "The first time up that hill wasn't too bad, but the two trips that followed were killers. I'm bushed!"

"Did you not save any energy for tonight?" Hinoch teased.

"'Fraid not. I spent it all today."

"I confess it will feel good to rest tonight. Perhaps tomorrow?"

"Yeah, tomorrow," she waved weakly as she flopped onto her travois.

Hinoch went around to everyone, then spent an hour with Monty and Dick, helping them set up camp for the evening. He quickly assessed the situation and concluded that this had indeed been a demanding day.

He decided, "I must make the next few days as easy as possible, even if what we accomplish is not up to expectations."

The evening meal was quick and simple. They sat around the fire, their muscles knotting and cramping from their exertions. The only distraction was the sunset. The horizon glowed crimson, with spectacular highlights in the virga hanging from the clouds. As the sun lowered, the strands of cloud glowed brightly in a plethora of shades of red and mauve. In the subdued, coloured light, everyone moved to their tents where the coming night's rest was the universal priority.

Joanna dreamed . . . The summer's heat at home in Winnipeg was at record levels, plants that normally flourished fought to sprout and survive. The people of the city were suffering from the intense heat and violent weather. Terrible dry thunderstorms seemed to develop each night, robbing everyone of sleep. As she dreamed, she suddenly found herself in her home, her mother lying on the floor in obvious pain. She crawled to the phone and dialed 911. She heard her mother's voice cry out, "Come quick . . . heart . . . it's my heart . . . " The phone dropped to the floor beside her mother's lifeless form.

Joanna sat up in bed, her eyes mirrors of her sorrow.

Hinoch's thoughts brought her back to her present situation. *Your mother has just died. You want to be there to give her a decent burial. It is not too late. I can take you back to Hebron and you can fly back. I'll meet you there again in say, a month?*

No, Hinoch, I've made my choice. Mother understood that I wasn't able to return to Winnipeg. She's at peace now. My place is here. She leaned against her man and he hugged her. The tears rolled slowly down her cheeks, tears of pure sorrow for the loss of her last remaining blood relative. After awhile, she tentatively explored Hinoch's feelings.

"You're sad, too, but not just for my mother. What is it?"

"I have been feeling the weight of my responsibilities. I was awake when you sat up."

"It's more than that, Hinoch. Remember, I can sense a good deal of your feelings and I can tell you're upset. What is it?"

"I have had a recurring vision. We will not have good weather for many seasons. Hunting will be poor and we will lose many of our numbers to poor health and starvation. I know in my heart this is the time to bring my people here, but the reality of losing any of them rests heavy on my conscience."

"But you had other visions telling you that things will be even worse further south. If I understand what they told you, it won't be easy anywhere but, here at least, we've got a chance of making it." She shivered at the thought of facing hardship and snuggled into him to drive away her negative thoughts.

"I want to see us succeed; I do not want my people to suffer and die. That is definitely not what I want."

"I don't think we have much choice, Hinoch. What we want isn't important. If we go back to Nain, your dreams tell you *none* of us will survive. If we stay up here *some* of us will survive. I think a slim chance is better than no chance."

"You are correct, but I must make my people clearly understand the dangers they face. If they do not agree with my vision, I will return them to Nain."

"That sounds fair to me. Do you think many will go back?"

"I hope not. We need everyone we can bring with us to help establish our community."

"I hope they all stay, too. I really like these people."

She leaned over and pulled him down to their bed, then kissed him tenderly. They remained in each other's arms for several moments, quietly.

Joanna said, "Tomorrow is a new day. We'll face whatever it brings. I'm certain we won't lose anybody to turning back. They were committed to coming and I think they understood it wouldn't be a cakewalk out here. Hell, look at me, I'm catching on and the bonus for me is that I've never felt so free before in my life. There's no way *I'm* turning back!"

"Excellent," he mumbled, "I have at least one vote of confidence."

"And tomorrow, you'll get the rest."

Hinoch was up early the next morning. He gathered everyone before the first meal of the day and addressed them. "Good morning, my people. Today we will travel only a few hours to work out the pains from yesterday's exertions. I must also tell you that I had a vision in the night that showed me the hardships we are about to face. The world is undergoing dramatic changes and the weather will not be our friend for many years to come. Many of the beasts of our world will not be plentiful and some may disappear entirely. Some of us will not survive, but my vision tells me that many of us will persevere and prosper in future generations. I give you a second chance to consider your future. If any of you wish to return to Nain, I will arrange your fare on the freighter's next trip."

The group was silent. Then, one of the elders, Melauk, returned to his preparations for the day's travels. The others followed suit. Within the hour, the dogs were stringing their way across the tundra, accompanied by the entire group of people. Not one person had opted to return to Nain.

Hinoch set his course to the northeast to intercept the large valley that he knew led back into the mountains. Food was plentiful and hunting was good. Only a few hours of hunting and gathering provided for everyone.

"We've been travelling seven hours now. Everyone seems to be doing well and we're all getting over our aches and pains," Joanna said.

"Yes, Joanna, we will see the shores of the next inlet very soon now. Maybe two more hours travel."

"Good. I'm feeling fine, but I'm looking forward to some more of that fresh fish and a change from all this walking."

Hinoch surveyed the horizon, excitement about their impending arrival clear on his face.

"There will be plenty of fish to eat here, but the work will be long and hard. We must build racks to dry the fish and kayaks and *umiak*s to hunt for seal and whales. Later, as winter approaches, we will need new *komatiks*."

"Say, when do we have holidays? I'll be about ready for some rest and relaxation once we get all that work done!"

"Yes, when we are ready for the winter, we will celebrate."

"Slave driver!" she batted his sleeve. Hinoch turned to her in surprise. She continued, "That's an awful long time to wait for a break. Couldn't we do something sooner?"

Hinoch grinned, clearly amused at her accusation. "Perhaps we will have a short celebration when we arrive at the river basin."

"Good idea. I think everyone's about ready for a short rest."

"I believe you are correct, but I am anxious to begin our preparations for winter. I don't want us to be caught unprepared when the cold weather arrives."

"That's true, but my mother always used to say that getting enough rest is part of being able to do your best." Her eyes clouded with tears, the pain of her mother's death brought back by this mention of her.

"Your mother was wise," he said softly. "We will follow her counsel when we arrive."

Next morning, Joanna woke abruptly, her stomach in her throat. She lurched outside and jettisoned the entire contents of her belly. In her haste, she had not even grabbed her shirt. She stood naked in the fresh morning air. To her surprise, the bracing effect on her skin quickly helped her to feel better. She stood and surveyed the surrounding land with wonder.

"This is my home. I'm becoming a part of it. She stretched her arms upward and felt the delicious sensation of her muscles tightening as she stood on her tiptoes. "Jeez! I'm naked as a jaybird out here! Part of the land or not, I better get out of sight before somebody gets an eyeful!"

She glanced around, instinctively covering up with her hands. Hinoch draped her shirt over her shoulders and she yipped in surprise.

"Damn, you can sure sneak up on a person. Try to give me some warning, okay?"

"Sorry, you left in a hurry and I was concerned. You know, you are with child."

"What? No, I just couldn't process something in last night's supper. I'll be fine." She paused, looking into his eyes, "Really? Am I?"

Hinoch nodded and smiled. She jumped into his arms and kissed him — a long, passionate kiss. After a few moments, they retired to their tent.

A short time later, the day began. People roused from their tents and began preparation for the day's travels. It had been noticed that Hinoch and Joanna were not out and about so, when they emerged, they were greeted with hoots of laughter and a generous amount of teasing. Even Monty and Dick, who had emerged from their own tent some time ago, joined the ribbing.

Hinoch smiled and accepted the teasing a little sheepishly. Joanna blushed and was obviously unnerved. Hinoch spoke, "Thank you for your concern, my people. We have one short day of travel remaining, then we will celebrate our new home. Let us begin!"

They struck camp in record time and the miles passed with relative ease. They were becoming fit and invigorated from their new levels of activity. The mood was universally a happy one.

"Look!" Monty yelled, "I can see the water!" We're getting real close."

"You are right, it is the water. You have keen eyes, Monty. You will be a good hunter."

Monty grinned and ran back to the others to inform them of their impending arrival.

Later, as they approached the inlet, Hinoch turned to Joanna, "We will build our summer home here, at the edge of this valley. It will be sheltered from the storms and hopefully it will be high enough to survive the rising waters I have seen."

"Won't it be a long way to haul water?"

"No, we will go to the water when we need it. We will not need water in our home."

"What about washing?"

"There is no need. We will clean ourselves with oils. As you have already learned, it is actually superior to soap and water in this environment. We will wash our clothing and utensils at the water's edge and carry them back to our home."

"What about diapers?" This kid's going to produce a mountain of them!" She patted her still flat abdomen.

"The women will show you — you will not use diapers. Moss is much more absorbent. No diapers, no diaper rash, no powders or lotions required."

Joanna's face showed her frustration, "I've still got a lot to learn. It's just so damned easy to fall back into the thinking I grew up with."

"That is understandable. You must not discard it entirely. If you think creatively, you will find elements of your previous life that will apply very well to our present situation." He meshed his fingers, indicating a blending of ideas. "Come, we will go down to the water and make camp, then we will celebrate our safe arrival."

"Look over there, out near the coast. What's that white spot moving along the shoreline?" Joanna asked.

Hinoch scanned the distance, his eyes becoming serious. "Your eyes are also becoming much keener. That is Gaulaqut, the polar bear."

"We'll have to watch out for him, won't we? That's the one beast out here that fears nothing."

"Our dogs will warn us if he approaches. And he does fear one thing — he fears me. One day soon, he will challenge me for supremacy."

"You're not going to fight a polar bear; we don't even have a gun! Be reasonable! You'll get shredded!"

C.J. BEUHLER

This is not an ordinary polar bear; this is Gaulaqut, the Great Spirit of the polar bear. I must assimilate his spirit to help insure our future. This is my legacy to add to the spirits I pass on to the next generation. Each spirit I assimilate adds to the wisdom and skills future generations will enjoy."

"So, what are you going to do? Have a meeting with him?"

"My spirits will combat his spirit. Hopefully my person will receive no more wounds than I suffered in my encounter with Nektoralik, the eagle."

"What will I see?"

"You will likely see me approach the polar bear and enter into combat with him. Just remember, it will be my spirits, not me. I have surpassed his abilities. He will not seriously harm me."

So, I'm going to watch you wrestling with a bear, but it won't be you, it'll be your spirit? I'm afraid that's not much comfort. I don't want you anywhere near that monster and I definitely don't want you getting messed up. I like you the way you look right now!" she poked her finger into his arm affectionately.

"I am the leader of my people. I cannot and will not jeopardize their survival. I must face this spirit for their benefit. To be part of Nanuk's clan brings yet another species into partnership with my people. We will never have to fear him again! We will be able to work together for our mutual survival."

"I hope you're right, Hinoch. It just seems too risky. Remember, I probably wouldn't last ten minutes without you, so I'm uptight about the thought of losing you."

"Your concern is appreciated. I will be careful."

She completely lost her temper, "Shit! Don't you get it? You're *really* all I've got out here. If you get killed, I might as well lay down and die too! I don't want to do that! I want to raise lots of kids with you and grow old with you. If you keep taking these chances, I don't see a lot of future for us!"

Hinoch glared at her. "That is one of the realities of our life. We must take chances every day to survive. I have a great advantage. I know from my ancestors' wisdom when, where and how to take those chances. My odds of survival are vastly greater than these people," he gestured to the people, who were becoming alarmed. "You are taking far less risk with me than any of the other people here. Take heart in that and have courage."

She looked around sheepishly, then down at her feet. She kicked at a stone, "I blew it again, didn't I? Sorry," she poked him in the chest with her extended fingers, "but I still don't like it. You make damned sure you can win before you take him on!"

"There is no need to be sorry. You are my partner and your concern is valid. It is important, however, for us to disagree in private in future if at all possible. I do not want to have the others see discord between us. It may breed discord and disobedience among them at a time when action is imperative. I must concentrate upon disciplined leadership, so there will be no question when immediate action is necessary for our safety."

"You're right, of course. I'll do my best to keep a lid on it until we're alone. But then, watch out. I'm half of this partnership and you're damned well going to know it!" She slammed her fist into her palm.

"I am fully aware of that fact. It is what I had hoped would be the basis of our life together." He pulled her to him and rubbed noses. The concerned looks of the people melted into looks of happiness as the couple embraced and resumed walking together toward the valley below.

As the sparks rose into the sky from the fire that evening, songs rose with them, offering thanks to their ancestors for their safe arrival. Joanna watched the children play on the beach, dreaming of the not too distant day when one of them would be hers. The people enjoyed what would prove to be a rare opportunity for some leisure and relaxation. Tomorrow would bring a pressing workload of preparations for the coming winter.

The Great Battle of the Spirits

That night, Hinoch did not sleep. His sixth sense was active, aware of the presence of a rival spirit. Gaulaqut was near and intent on challenging Hinoch's powers. Hinoch silently looked over at Joanna to ensure she was soundly asleep, then rose from the tent as the white raven, consciously blocking her from his thoughts. He flew into the half-light of the arctic night. As he flew, he spotted Gaulaqut quickly. He was still near the mouth of the river, but moving toward their camp.

"Gaulaqut, you are approaching my camp, what is it you seek?"

The huge animal stood on his hind legs, stretching fully twelve feet into the air. His sleek white fur gleamed in the night — such a beautiful beast, this Gaulaqut, yet so dangerous, capable of surprising speed and deceptive power. "I seek you, young shaman. You have tried to escape me without success. Now I will have my victory over you. Come down here and face me."

Hinoch hovered on the wing, no more than ten feet above, "My powers are in my ability to soar above your domain and choose when it is beneficial for me to come to earth. You are a supremely powerful beast and you are threatening my safety; why in all prudence, would I come to earth now?"

"Because you seek the powers I possess. I will not give them up unless you can defeat me in battle. Your cunning and trickery are well known, Tullegak; they will not work against me."

"I possess other spirits. Which do you seek?"

"I seek all of them, as you seek all the spirits I possess. You must face me as yourself, shaman, or I will enter your camp tonight and take whatever pleases me."

Hinoch circled lazily, considering his options, attempting to further anger Gaulaqut. He was risking his life for the Great Spirit of this species, the creature that had very nearly killed his father. His people were completely reliant upon him; if he were killed here tonight, they, too, would likely perish. He thought of his departure from Joanna with regret and wanted to go to her and apprise her of the situation. He attempted a delay in the battle. "I will meet you here. Wait for me one hour."

"No, I will continue toward your camp. If you do not meet me before I arrive, I will destroy everything I encounter."

"Do not fear, Gaulaqut. You will not have that opportunity."

Gaulaqut swatted the air, his claws whistling in the wind, "You feeble human, you will not stand a chance against me. I fear nothing."

Hinoch placed himself directly above the bear, forcing it to crane its neck to see him. "You will learn to fear me before I take your spirit."

"Ho! Threats. Are they all you can muster Tullegak? I wonder whether your puny spirit is worth my trouble."

Tiring of the strain of looking up, the bear lowered his head for an instant. Hinoch did not reply, but abruptly dove and raked Gaulaqut's eye with a claw. The huge bear swiped at the air so fiercely that Hinoch again heard the claws whistling close by.

"You are too slow, Gaulaqut; brute force does not always triumph!"

The bear roared in pain and anger, "Now you must make haste, Tullegak. I will make my best pace to your pitiful little camp of weaklings. Many of you will die tonight!"

"Then join me now in battle, Hinoch roared back as he landed behind the bear and reassumed his human form. Instantly, he bent down and picked up a rock. Gaulaqut was preoccupied for the moment with the loss of his eye, rubbing his head against the soft fur of his foreleg, smearing it with blood. He sensed Hinoch's location behind him and felt rage burst inside. As Gaulaqut turned to charge, Hinoch threw the rock, blinding the bear's other eye. Gaulaqut roared, but continued his charge. Hinoch easily stepped aside, drawing his machete and striking a vicious blow as the bear passed. The blade sank between the bear's ribs and punctured a lung. Blood sprayed Hinoch as the bear's breath hissed from the wound. Gaulaqut spun around instantly with a flailing blow from his massive front paw. It clipped Hinoch's forearm, breaking it and pushing the jagged end of the bone through his skin. Hinoch's machete flew through the air, beyond his reach.

Gaulaqut swatted again, like a boxer attempting to land a series of blows, but he made no contact. Hinoch had anticipated the next blow and had stepped aside. "So, human," Gaulaqut whispered fiercely, "you are cunning and quick, but you break like a blade of grass under my feet. Now you die!"

Hinoch's head was swimming from the pain. He held his walking staff firmly in his good hand, and pressed his broken arm against his back to reduce the pain. Pinned to his back in this fashion the broken limb was less prone to flop around and the jagged bones were less likely to worsen the wound. Slowly, he raised the sharply pointed tusk at the end of the walking stick, holding the rounded burl at the top in his good hand.

"Answer me, you field mouse. Where are you?"

Hinoch crouched slightly and remained perfectly still, saying nothing. The huge bear stood to his full height, sniffing the air, but all he could detect was his own blood and the scents of pine and juniper. Foaming blood spewed from his side with each panting breath, yet he did not feel weakened. His rage was sustaining him. Suddenly, under his ribs to the front he felt a sharp pain that travelled deep inside his chest to his heart. He swung a mighty blow and made sound contact, hearing the human land many feet away to his right. He began to feel faint as he turned and charged in the direction of the sound, but he smelled human blood. He fell upon the scent and opened his jaws wide.

∾∾∾

Joanna wake up. Wake up!

She rolled over to find the bed beside her vacant. *Hinoch, where are you?* she thought.

I am out here, near the river mouth. Gather some people, and the dogs. I need your help!

Joanna threw on her clothes and bolted out of the tent screaming at the top of her lungs.

"Help! Help! Somebody. I need help!"

In seconds, heads poked out from the tents and people began to emerge.

"Quickly, bring the dogs. Hinoch needs our help!"

She ran to Alut, released him from his tether and harnessed him.

"Come, Alut, come!" she shouted as she ran to the west and the river mouth.

What am I doing? Am I dreaming and Hinoch has just gone out for a pee, or did I really hear him call? No, something's wrong, I can feel it!

She ran along the sandy shoreline, stumbling over rocks and branches with Alut loping easily beside her.

Where are you, Hinoch? Tell me how to find you.

Look for Gaulaqut, he has fallen on top of me. I cannot breathe!

My God, that bear. He went after that damned bear . . . She screamed her anger into the wind, "Hinoch, I'll *kill* you!"

Tears streamed from her eyes. Her breath began to rasp in her throat, the cold air burning deep into her chest. Her stomach began to threaten its morning ritual.

"Not now, damn it, she puffed, "I don't want to die choking on my own puke. I've got more important things to do!"

Her senses told her she was close. She scanned around the embankment, looking into the gloom of the early morning light for any sign. She spotted the huge white bear, then the river of foamed red on its side and saw its jaw slowly opening and closing on Hinoch's lower leg. He was entirely under the huge beast and it was chewing on him!

She screamed, "Stop it! Stop it!"

Alut charged past her and fell upon the bear's throat, choking off the airway and pulling the huge head to the side at a strange angle. A soft blue haze seemed to engulf the scene briefly. A huge blue-white polar bear rose from the bloodied corpse. Slowly, it sank back down and seemed to slip under the bear.

As Joanna floundered through the loose sand up to the scene, she first noticed the glazing in the bear's torn and bloodied eye, then the jaw stopped moving. She stumbled to Alut's side, grabbed the bloody gash in the bear's ribs for a handhold and pulled with all her might. Her grip threatened to slip from the hot, blood-covered meat inside the cavity, but she clawed her hands, digging her nails into the flesh and pulled with all her strength. Slowly, the bear began to roll down the slope of the embankment until she and Alut had to release their grips and jump clear to avoid being pinned. Immediately, Alut went to Hinoch and began licking his face, whimpering with concern for his master.

Joanna was kneeling beside them in an instant, checking for signs of life and silently crying. Hinoch stirred, then took a short, painful breath. He was bleeding from the mouth.

"Broken ribs," she said, assessing the situation, "and a compound fracture and God knows what else." She fell back onto her heels, raising her trembling hands intending to hold her head and calm herself. She stared at the blood, horrified, then tried again, *Come on, girl. Hold it together. You have to think. What do I do first?*

Hinoch's words floated into her mind. *I will be all right. Bind my ribs with the skins of my pant legs and put a splint on my arm. The rest will heal in its own good time.*

She began to follow his guidance as the rest of the group arrived. The men immediately began to deal with the bear in preparation for taking it back to camp. Noel came to Joanna's side and helped as she worked to bind Hinoch's ribs, slicing his pant legs deftly with her *ulu*. Next, she concentrated upon controlling the bleeding from his arm.

"I have gained the spirit of Gaulaqut, the greatest hunter of the north. We are now assured of success!" Hinoch rasped, becoming delirious from shock.

If you don't die, or end up crippled for the rest of your sorry life! she grumbled in her thoughts. *Damned men. You can never tell them anything. They insist on doing things in their own bull-headed way. Why the hell do women love them so?*

"Ouch!" He protested as she set the bones in his arm with a firm pull and Noel tied a rough splint onto his arm.

"Don't complain," she barked. "You're lucky I didn't decide to hell with you and leave you to smother under that overgrown rug!" Noel cringed at her anger and her fearlessness in showing it, but she kept to her task, saying nothing.

Hinoch managed a smile and, with his good hand, he caressed her cheek. "Yes, but think how warm our bed will be now with that bearskin on it!"

"Oh no, you don't. I'm gonna burn that damned thing. I don't ever want it anywhere near me, ever again!"

Joanna finished tying the splint, then allowed herself to succumb to her feelings. She threw up.

She squatted on her heels as though paralyzed as the people tied the now gutted and cleaned bear to the leads of the dogs' harnesses. The dogs were eager for some work. They strained and jumped in their traces, barely able to move the massive load. The women had lit a fire and were preparing some hot water and tea less than five yards away. Alut sat with Hinoch, where he had fallen, still licking the blood from his face, and hands.

She watched, feeling strangely detached from events, as Noel returned with warm water, began washing Hinoch and tending to the wounds on his chewed ankle. This done, she returned to the fire and retrieved a cup of tea, which she offered to Hinoch.

"No!" Joanna shouted, "He has broken ribs! No liquids!" Noel turned abruptly, spilling some of the tea. Joanna's tone had alarmed her.

Joanna saw Noel's fear and regretted her forcefulness. "I'm sorry I shouted," she spoke more softly, "but it's very important that he have nothing to drink for two days." She smiled and wiped the hot liquid from the woman's arm, then took her hands, smiling to reassure her. She received a tentative smile in return. Then Joanna looked down at their hands. She had smeared blood over her from her own bloodied hands. She asked for some water and rinsed herself, then tried to clean up the mess she had made.

Noel accepted her gesture, then simply said: "*Kujannamik*, thank you." She rose and returned to the fire.

Our bond grows strong. I was able to wake you from a sound sleep. The words came to Joanna's mind. She turned to Hinoch, speaking her words aloud in protest.

"Yes, you did, I just wish it had been for something pleasurable, not . . . not this!"

He answered her aloud, "I would have died under Gaulaqut's carcass had your sixth sense not heard me. I see that as a wonderful thing that people rarely are able to share. Hopefully, in future, we will share many pleasant thoughts as well."

She tried to smile, but her anxiety pulled it into a sneer, "That would definitely be my preference. My nerves won't take much more of this crap!"

"You are strong. This land will test you many more times, but you will find that you can withstand every challenge that comes. The courage you displayed this morning assures me of that."

"Okay, just not too often. This wasn't morning sickness," she said pointing to the vomit nearby, "I just about tossed my toenails just now! That was my nerves protesting at me being yanked out of bed and run hard and covered in blood and polar bears and . . . seeing you half dead. Not a great start to the day for a civilized girl!"

"Nevertheless, it will be a great day in our history. The day our clan conquered Gaulaqut."

She shook her head and growled, "Men!"

At that moment, another of the men, Tunet, by name, arrived with a pair of dogs and a travois. Work began to transfer Hinoch to the travois and make him as comfortable as possible. Tunet, Noel, and Joanna removed their jackets and stuffed them gingerly between his chest and the poles, pausing for him to regain his composure each time he winced or groaned. Once he was firmly in place, they harnessed the dogs and began walking alongside, restraining the dogs with strong leashes. Joanna was surprised to find her jacket soaked with sweat, despite the chill of the dawn. The trip back to camp was a slow and painful one for Hinoch.

The following morning, Hinoch attempted to rise from his bed. Joanna jumped up from the cooking fire and yelled, "Oh no, you don't! You're going to stay out of trouble for the next five days if I have to lash you to the ground like the Lilliputians did!" She entered the tent, bent over him and threatened to push him down.

Joanna spoke with such determination that Hinoch settled back into his bed, saying nothing. The pain in his chest was also a very convincing factor in his obedience. He concentrated on his meditations, exploring the vast experience of the spirits of Gaulaqut. He entered a shaman's trance and travelled with Gaulaqut as he hunted, seeing first-hand how the great bear used his colouration to best advantage when the snow was sifting across the landscape on the wind. How he hunted only into the wind, relying mostly upon scent to locate his prey and how he relied upon surprise to cover the last few feet with one leap.

He learned that his father had foolishly engaged in his quest for Gaulaqut on a snow-swept landscape, moving about, following footprints rather than waiting under cover for the bear to find him. He watched, gripped with fear as Tullegak rose from his father's unconscious form and valiantly sought to distract Gaulaqut. As Tullegak swooped and dived, risking death, his injured father recovered sufficiently to escape, paddling out to sea in his kayak. Hinoch's relief was so complete that he drifted from his trance into sleep.

Two days after the incident, he awoke, his mouth parched.

"Here." Joanna said, "You can have some liquids now. Drink this broth. You're going to need your strength if you're going to insist on these mad adventures."

She knew she had to examine the wound on his arm, but was reluctant to remove the splint for fear of moving the bones. She instructed him to remain perfectly still as she carefully removed the splint from his arm. It was infected. The exit point of the bones was red and puffy. The claw marks on the other side still had sand from the beach in them. She went to retrieve her supply of bandages and disinfectant.

"I will heal better with my herbs; my body is accustomed to them. Please bring me my medicine bag."

Joanna looked at him a moment, then turned and handed him his medicine bag. She had thought of protesting, but remembered Alut's almost miraculous recovery and relented.

"Here, take this moss and tie it in place over the wound with this piece of boiled caribou hide. With this, you make tea. If you will keep it warm by the fire, I can drink from it hourly."

Joanna said nothing, but complied without hesitation.

"I need you to speak with me." Hinoch said, grabbing her wrist, "I know you do not understand why I undertook such a dangerous course of action, but please believe me, it was necessary for our future survival. I do not take unnecessary chances. I value your future and the future of these people far too much to be foolhardy."

Her mind responded, *I just can't get my head around why you went out alone and why I sense that you purposely blocked me out until I was your only hope. These men would have helped you.*

Unfortunately, the speed and power of Gaulaqut would have been at its greatest advantage had there been many of us. By myself, once he was blinded, I had a much better chance of avoiding him, while remaining close enough to strike deadly blows.

You only partially succeeded.

Yes, when you stand close to the fire, you sometimes get burned. Please, come lie down beside me. I need you here to comfort me now.

As she lay down, he held his hand above her abdomen. "Our child is strong and healthy. He will be our next leader."

"He?" she asked, "How do you know it's not a girl?" Then she quickly added, "And why couldn't a girl be our next leader?"

"It is a boy. You are right, though. There is no real reason a woman could not be our leader, but it has traditionally been men who lead."

"Maybe one day, one of my girls will change that tradition," she said, a coy, but determined expression on her face.

She made herself comfortable beside him and soon they were both asleep.

The following day, the torn skin of his arm was pink and healthy looking. The wound was healing far more rapidly than Joanna could imagine, or believe.

"You seem to be breathing more easily today. Has the pain gone?" she asked, gently pressing her hands up and down his chest.

"Not entirely," he winced a little, "but it is much less than yesterday. Soon I will be able to resume our work."

"Not so fast. I want you to rest until all the pain is gone and your arm is healed. That's a major bone, it's going to take time to knit. It may never have its original strength." She helped him to stand, pulling on his good arm.

Hinoch turned his attention outside their tent and asked, "How are our people doing? Why have they not been coming in to seek my counsel?"

Joanna cleaned out the contents of the caribou skin sleeping mat, then folded it and spread out a fresh bag. "I told them to do their best and let you rest. They're doing fine, we're getting lots of fish and the racks are nearly finished to dry them. The men have two *umiaks* finished. Talk about fish stories. They say they're going to get a whale!"

"I sincerely hope so. One small whale will give us our year's supply of oil and *muktuk*."

"You're kidding, right?" she asked as she began stuffing caribou moss into the sack.

"No, whale oil and skin and bones — the entire animal — is very important to our survival."

"I can't believe it! How did you people ever survive this long, killing bears and whales and God knows what else?"

"Until now, we avoided polar bears as much as possible. Now I possess the spirit of Gaulaqut. We will no longer fear them."

Joanna remained unconvinced. "I don't know if that's wise. I'm going to maintain a healthy respect for them anyway." She quickly sewed the new mat, spread it out and bade Hinoch lie down again.

In a matter of days, Hinoch was back on his feet, supervising and guiding his people through their preparations. By the end of seven days, he was at their sides working as though nothing had happened.

During a break in the work, Joanna took him aside and quietly asked, "Are you sure you're all healed up? I can't believe that broken bones can knit in so little time."

"Yes, I am fine." He smiled confidently. "Tomorrow, we should go together to pick the location of our future home."

"Okay, should I call a realtor?"

They laughed. It was the first laughter they had shared in seven days.

Hinoch pointed to a nearby cut in the valley wall, "Let's look up this valley. It doesn't seem too steep and it's less rocky."

"Yes, I believe this will be a good place. There at the top, see that cleft in the rocks? We can dig back into the wall there and share the heat from the soil in the cold weather." They stood at the entrance to a small coulee. The entrance gradually inclined as the cleft in the valley wall narrowed. There was a small promontory mid-way in the opening. From this point inward, there were high, steep walls along both sides.

"We're going to dig a cave?"

"Partially. Our ancient ancestors, the Yup'ik, dug into the ground whenever possible to help insulate their homes. It meant that they did not have to burn scarce supplies of wood and oil."

Joanna frowned, not entirely sure she liked the idea of living with minimal heating. "Makes sense, I guess. I just hope we can dig up here."

As the couple approached, they could see they were not the first people to select this site. Joanna pointed out the remnants of log buildings nestled against the sides of the small meadow, dug into the walls of the small coulee. A tiny village had once been here, a lodge there, at the apex of the coulee, a storage shed there on a small ledge in the wall, a small fire pit in the centre, for celebrations. They wandered slowly around the open space, imagination drawing images in Joanna's mind of the people who had been here, inner vision showing Hinoch their history.

Hinoch smiled with both realization and pleasure, "This will be a good home again. The spirits of the ancients who lived here are welcoming us. They say good hunting has returned and whales abound off-shore in winter."

"Who are they?"

Hinoch swept an arm grandly, "They are my ancestors. They lived here many years ago. They have led me back here."

Joanna turned and gasped. "Look at the view! No wonder they chose this place."

Hinoch turned and was also filled with wonder. The sun to the west sent a dimpled silver ribbon upon a blue ocean dotted with white caps. To the east, the same sun reflected from the distant mountains at the upper end of the valley. Green landscapes shaded into hues of blue further inland, topped in turn by the snows on the mountains and the sky above.

Hinoch shared the moment with her. "Yes, they chose this site wisely."

The two of them stood entranced by the pristine beauty this promontory offered. "My visions are clearer than ever now," Hinoch whispered, "We are recreating a centuries-old village of my people."

Something in the gravel at the base of a smooth rock caught Hinoch's eye. "Look! Here. Harpoon tips, arrowheads and old oil lamps that have been here for many hundreds of years." He continued to rummage through the gravel, extracting bits of stone and bone that would have no significance to a casual observer. Joanna joined him and began sifting through the rubble. From time to time, she held up a piece for Hinoch's evaluation.

Hinoch paused, overjoyed with his finds, "These are the designs we will follow for our own tools." He sorted the best examples from the fragments and placed them carefully in his medicine bag. "Come, we must tell our people," he said as he took her hand and started back down to the valley. What was to become their home site was less than one-quarter mile from their present camp. The coincidence was not lost upon Joanna. She looked at her husband, now playfully tossing a rounded stone into the air as they walked and realized all her concerns would be answered in time.

Work began in earnest. The people gathered materials and hauled them to the village site. The dogs became stronger with each passing day, able to pull massive loads up the long, gradual slope to the small meadow above. Once the debris of the old buildings had been cleared, the village began to take shape with surprising speed.

Hinoch divided the people: the good hunters were assigned to supplying the needs for food, both for the present and for the coming winter; the young and strongest were put to work gathering materials for construction of new buildings.

Everything they needed was in abundance, so work progressed with haste, sparked by the urgency of preparing for the onslaught of winter. Hinoch now possessed the brute power of Gaulaqut. He was able to move and lift tremendous loads continuously without tiring. The little village took shape once again.

As they worked side-by-side one day, plugging the gaps in the walls of the lodge, Joanna expressed her insights. "Just like you said, your ancestors are showing us what we need to know as that need arises. I had a dream about this place last night. The people were celebrating and a big fire was burning right over there." She turned her suntanned face to the north of the meadow and pointed to the fire-pit with mud-encrusted fingers. "They were dancing and singing, but it wasn't our people. It was them, the ones who lived here before. Then as I watched, they came and gathered around me smiling. Next thing I knew, I was flying up into the air and falling into a huge skin they held stretched out below me. Everyone was laughing and I went higher and higher, then I woke up." She looked at him, seeking an interpretation.

"You are having a vision. Pay close attention to it. More will come and you will learn a great deal."

"What does it mean?"

"You are being welcomed by my ancestors, but there will be more and you will know the true meaning of it when it is finished."

"I used to hate stories that couldn't be told in one sitting. They bored me. I hope this story is more interesting."

"This vision is important to you. It is unlikely you would be aware of it if it were a simple, trivial dream."

That night, the ancient people came to her again. She woke and roused Hinoch.

"You were right. It is important. As I bounced up and down, I found myself holding a baby boy. Then I was holding a baby girl too, but when I let her go, she flew away, a little bird. After awhile, the boy wanted down. When I let him go, he was at least ten years old. He got down and helped them to toss me even higher. Then I had another little girl with me and she was happy to stay in my arms until the bouncing stopped.

"Continue to pay heed to your dreams. Your spirits are becoming strong and will tell you much more about your life."

That day, Joanna was acutely aware of the importance of children in the camp. She watched them at play in the meadow and was fascinated by their joy and their unadulterated innocence. She imagined her own children at play and asleep, all the while becoming more aware of the import of her visions. This tiny village depended on the cycle of life entirely for its future; each loss of a life represented a significant loss to the potential of this community. She promised herself that the little girl of her vision — her little girl — would not fly away before she was ready to survive on her own.

Summer stretched on into fall, cool, wet and foggy. Joanna became very round and began to find her work increasingly difficult. Without being asked, Noel happily took up the physically demanding parts of her workload, taking an abiding interest in her progress. Other women were also expecting, but Joanna was easily the farthest into her pregnancy. The buildings were finished, including the common house, wedged securely into the cleft at the rear of the meadow.

A low-roofed, mud-chinked shed on the west side of the meadow was already nearly full to capacity with dried meats, hung from the rafters. One corner had sturdy shelves reserved for whale blubber and seal meat. These would be stored frozen during winter and processed into oil before the spring thaw. The remaining space was reserved for hides and sinews to be used for repairs to the kayaks, *umiaks* and *komatiks*. The other side of the meadow boasted a small sweat lodge and a lean-to, storage space for the harnesses and sleds in summer and the boats in winter.

The lodge was large enough to hold everyone and had only one common area inside. The logs were heavily chinked with coarse moss, mud and twigs, then the outside was covered with interwoven branches and moss as an insulator. The only light inside came from the smoke vents in the roof. A central fire pit provided heat for the few cooking utensils. In mid-November, the people began living communally for the first time since Joanna had joined them.

In the second week, Joanna confided to Hinoch as they walked back to the village from the river, "I'm having a real problem with all of us being together in one room like this. When do we get any privacy to . . . well, you know?"

"Have you noticed any of the others needing privacy?"

"No. Definitely not!" She blushed.

"We are one large family now. We live, eat and do everything else together. We do not need what you are calling privacy."

Undeterred, she spoke her wish, "Couldn't we just build a little cabin off by itself somewhere? Someplace where we could be alone?"

"My parents chose to isolate themselves from their people. They would accept nothing from anyone who lived other than by the old methods. They died for their choices, love of my life. That reality tortures me every day. We need our people every bit as much as they need us. You must learn to live without your privacy."

She stopped and grabbed his arm, "What did you say?"

"You must learn — "

No, before that, something about love?"

"Love of my life?"

"That's it. You don't know how I crave hearing you say that!"

He lifted the heavy caribou skins that covered the entrance to the lodge as he continued, "You will hear it often. It is the truth."

Suddenly, it didn't matter to her who was watching.

It was a late November night. The sky was clear and the frost heavy on the ground, but there had been no snow yet. Winter was definitely late. The fire glowed in the small meadow and the people sang and danced. An inaugural celebration of the hunt was underway. Hinoch and Joanna presided quietly near the fire. Joanna was now very near her full term and any energetic activity was out of the question. The celebration was well into the third day when she tugged at Hinoch's sleeve.

"Look, do you see them?" she whispered, pointing beyond the fire.

"Yes, they have been here for some time now. They are happy to see our celebration."

She looked around, following their movements, "They're floating all around us and smiling. It seems so welcoming. I thought ghosts were spooky, but they're nothing like that."

As she watched, the vision of an old woman came to her and, bending down in front of her, placed her hands on Joanna's rounded belly. The vision spoke to her.

"In twenty suns you will have your boy — a fine, strong boy with golden hair."

Joanna looked at Hinoch, unable to form words. He spoke.

"Thank you, ancient one. We will name him Abel."

The old woman smiled, showing her broken and worn teeth, "Your father will be honoured." Then she was gone.

"I can't believe it. Are they going to tell us everything?"

"We will know much of what our lives promise. It is the blessing of the shaman," he said, placing his fist against his chest.

Joanna grasped his fist, holding it against his heart and leaned toward him, "You haven't told me something. It's about my vision isn't it, the little bird? We're going to lose one child aren't we?"

He looked down, "So it would appear, but if we are on guard, we may be able to prevent the loss. Your visions may yet show you how the loss occurs. If we can prevent it, we will."

"I can't bear to think of having a child, then losing it. So much can happen out here. We will need to be on guard for them all the time."

He returned his gaze to her eyes, "Vigilance will help, but they will require freedom to explore and learn about their world as well. Life is a wonderful exploration. Unfortunately, there are also risks, some of them great. We focus on the joy of life and accept its dangers. To forego the best things of life in fear of the possible consequences is not in our nature. With good fortune, we grow older and we encounter only minor scrapes, learning from them how to recognize the greater dangers and deal with them."

She couldn't resist the opportunity to needle him, "Like you dealt with Gaulaqut? You should have been killed, you know." She gave a little push, trying to signal him not to take her too seriously.

He smiled, just a little, "I knew I could prevail over him, but I did not foresee being pinned under his dying carcass. Fortunately, you are sufficiently connected to me to hear my thoughts and brave enough to save me when I go too far."

She looked at him, accepting what had been intended as a genuine compliment. "I hope that goes both ways. I'm pretty green at this lifestyle, so I feel I could easily walk into trouble without seeing it."

"You are wise to be cautious. Stay near our people at all times and learn from them the dangers around us. They will keep you away from harm."

As he spoke, there was a commotion behind them. The people were rushing to the edge of the meadow, looking out to sea. Together, they rose and joined the others.

In the first light of morning, they gathered on the promontory, as yet uncertain of what had been spotted. A small, elongated dot was visible to the west, approaching the entrance to the valley. Low in the water, behind the approaching boat was another body, awash in the small waves, yet increasingly visible as they neared. Hinoch threw his arms up. "A whale! The hunters have a whale in tow!" We have our supplies of oil and *muktuk* for this winter." He spun around, grabbed Joanna and pulled her into a bear-hug. "We are truly ready for the season now. When the ice comes, we will need only a few seals and fish for fresh food." Hinoch's reaction was shared by the people. Hugs were shared all round and laughter filled the morning air.

Hinoch was clearly overjoyed, but Joanna understood that he would have been happier to participate. The task of managing the establishment of their home had precluded him partaking in the hunt, since his visions directed the construction.

"Next year, I will be able to join them," he smiled happily, watching the boat intently.

"Yes, that will be good for you. You love to hunt, don't you?"

"It is my nature to hunt, to provide well for my family and my people." He patted her belly playfully. She grinned and feigned pushing his hand away, then her face went pale. She grunted.

"Hinoch, how many days has it been since our celebration?"

"It would be sixteen. Why, are you having contractions?"

"Mm-hmm. At least I think so."

"Come inside, let me examine you."

He lifted her into his arms and carried her into the common house, placing her on their sleeping mat. He placed his hands over her distended abdomen and closed his eyes. When he opened them, he was smiling.

"Our boy is strong and healthy. I believe you have just been punched. There is no sign of him turning to enter the birth canal."

Joanna's colour was returning. She felt clammy and not a little queasy. "Well tell him to knock it off. Mom can't take that kind of punishment. Not at this stage, anyway!"

Hinoch stretched out beside her and pulled her to him, smiling contentedly. "He is a strong spirit. Our son will prove to be a handful. It would appear he has already started to challenge us."

"Oh no, can't we have an obedient child to practice on? Why do we have to start out with the challenging one?"

"He will be obedient and a source of lifelong pride to us, but he is strong and will be adventurous enough for both of us. His nature will lead him at least as strongly as will we."

"So I'm outnumbered from the start. Two bull-headed men to cope with." She thought for a moment. Then she spoke to her belly and to Hinoch, "Well just you wait. It's all girls for us from here. You're going to get yours, guys!"

During the nineteenth night, Joanna awoke to the strangest sensation she had yet experienced in her pregnancy. She felt as though an enthusiastic gym class had been unleashed in her stomach. Her water broke and the first contraction came. She instantly learned that the punch of three days ago had been mild in comparison. She doubled over and moaned.

Hinoch was instantly awake and examining her.

"The time is here, Joanna. Our boy is coming into the world today!"

She tried to smile, but managed only to grit and bare her teeth.

She gasped, "I've decided I don't like this after all. Let's take him back!"

She screamed in pain. In an instant the entire room was up, people in various states of attire crowding around to offer their assistance. Noel quietly pushed them back, then kneeled at her side. She pressed a gnarled finger into her lower back near the spine. Joanna looked at her amazed.

"Thank you. That helps!"

Hinoch replied, "It is only temporary and will not work for an extended period, but we will hope it is a short labour. Abel is anxious to join us!"

"I'll vote for that!" Joanna whimpered.

The old woman pushed Hinoch away, but Joanna would have none of that. "He caused this, he can watch the results," she declared, still gritting her teeth.

Hinoch reached into his medicine bag and ground a pinch of herbs between his fingers, then rubbed them under her lip. His Nature Song filled the room, calming her. The people sat around in a circle to see the birth of the shaman's son. Joanna felt the pain of the next contraction, searing through her body, but it did not seem to matter. She screamed again, but she felt joy. She was entering the world of motherhood.

Two long hours later, Abel entered the world, declaring his arrival in a loud, clear voice. Hinoch scooped him up as soon as Noel tied the cord and held him high for all to see. He had wisps of hair, but it was clear that it was not the dark hair of his father, but the fair hair of his mother. The people were pleased.

"My people, here is Abel, our son and our future leader. May his spirit soar forever!"

In unison, everyone rose and cheered. Abel did not cry, but looked about wide-eyed at the strange world he had entered. He smiled. Hinoch returned him to his mother and covered them warmly with fresh skins, then he went to the corner of the cabin and retrieved a bundle. He opened it to reveal the magnificent white robe of the polar bear.

"Son. This is my first gift to you. It will warm you and keep you safe from the elements for many years. One day, too, you will possess the spirit of this magnificent beast to give you wisdom and strength. The people murmured their approval of the gift and began discussing the need for another day of celebration. Noel indicated that they should make their plans outdoors to give the new mother and her baby a chance to rest.

Later that day, it began to snow. It fell, soft in a windless evening. The new day dawned transformed into a wonderland of white sprinkled with diamonds reflecting the light of the blazing sun. The children were playing in the meadow and below at the beach the men were flensing the whale. Hinoch surveyed the scene, his heart overfilled with joy. His smile rivaled the brightness of his surroundings.

That night, many of the people were busy making snow goggles from the rib bones of the whale. The narrow slits across the width of the goggle reduced the amount of light sufficiently to prevent eye irritation. With fresh snow on the ground, many were feeling the gritty sting of irritated eyes, after a day in the arctic sun. The fresh bones were less brittle and more workable than others they could have scavenged from the beach. Stories of the hunt and successful killing of the whale dominated the conversation.

Joanna was interested in everything that was in process, asking many questions. "What will become of all this blubber?" "Won't all this meat go bad?"

Hinoch patiently answered each question in turn, taking advantage of the time to hold his precious boy cradled inside his shirt. "Most of it will be kept frozen until it is needed for lamps or cleaning oil."

"Are they really eating that stuff raw?"

"Yes, it is a delicacy to us. We call it *muktuk*. It has a rich, almost sweet taste. Here, try some."

"What do you call it again?"

"*Muktuk*"

She hesitated, then decided from the looks of pleasure on everyone's faces that it couldn't be too bad. She bit a small piece from the chunk Hinoch had proffered. Her tentative look faded as she savored the morsel. She was finding the taste very rich indeed, slightly salty and with a background sweetness that lingered on the tip of her tongue.

"Not bad, not bad at all!" she said, a hint of surprise still in her voice.

He watched her take another bite, "Have you found a substitute for chocolate?"

"Not yet and don't remind me. I only have two bars left!" she mumbled, her mouth full. She propped up on her elbow and looked across the room where the women were splitting the baleen apart. "What are they doing?"

"That is the *baleen*. It has a natural brush-like characteristic that is excellent for grooming hair, finishing hides, or when left in a block, even for straining the oil to make it clear and free of debris. When the smaller pieces are trimmed properly, they can also be used as dental picks."

"Talk about all-purpose. I'm beginning to understand how important a whale is."

"Yes, it is one of the most important animals to us when it comes to supplying a large number of our needs."

"What other animals are important?"

"They are all useful to us, but the antlers of deer and caribou make excellent tools and tips for our weapons." Hinoch produced a piece of antler he had been carving, "Here is the head of a harpoon. You can see here that the shaft of the harpoon rests in this indent," he demonstrated, placing his index finger in the indent. "The cord is attached here and runs up the shaft. It is held in place by the tension of the cord, wrapped up here on the handle. When the harpoon is thrown, the hunter pulls on his end of the cord releasing the wrapping on the handle. This, in turn, releases the point from the shaft. The shaft pulls free of the animal and floats to the surface to be recovered later. Meanwhile, the hunter holds the cord until the quarry tires, and then pulls it up to the surface." He released his finger-hold on the top of the point, letting it fall from his index finger to the sleeping mat.

"Wow, who said the primitives were primitive!" she said, picking it up for closer examination. "This looks like a finely designed piece of technology to me. It had to be somebody pretty smart to come up with this."

"Yes. Or the accumulated wisdom of many people over time, slowly improving and perfecting the first basic idea."

"Mmmm, that makes sense, too. Just one more example of why you're so closely linked to your ancestors." She returned the harpoon point to him.

"Yes, we are the sum of our predecessors in many ways."

The winter season progressed, but without its customary severity. Many days saw people outdoors without their heavy winter clothing. Joanna recovered quickly and was consumed with the demands of the boisterous package she had delivered. He was a robust and energetic boy with an unflagging appetite. It seemed to her that he was constantly demanding either nourishment, or cleaning. When he slept, she often slept as well, exhausted from his energetic routine.

Abel was nearly two weeks old when the first blizzard of the winter arrived. The afternoon was dominated by a lead-grey sky and a long, rolling surf onto the seashore. The wind had not yet arrived, but Hinoch knew it would not be long.

"We must prepare to be inside for many days. A great storm is coming that will prevent any but the most necessary of outside activities."

The dogs were fed well and encouraged to bed down in the snow. The people moved the remaining whale-meat and the usable parts of the carcass into the storage building. Immediate food supplies went into the house. As the last of the chores were being completed, the visibility began to drop rapidly, the snow being borne in the teeth of a freshening gale. In a matter of moments, the visual details of the area washed away in a stinging blanket of white. Everyone moved inside.

Hinoch looked around, counting noses to be certain everyone had found a way to the log house. He did not see Adilat. He looked outside with his shaman's vision. She was some two hundred yards to the north, stumbling away from the lodge. He ran outside and fought desperately against the wind and deepening snowdrifts. He called upon the strength of Gaulaqut to help him reach her before she came to harm. He became the bear, loping through the deep snow with ease, closing the gap with amazingly quick bounds. Moments before he reached her, she tripped and fell. He moved beside her, shielding her from the shrieking wind and nuzzled her to get her to look at him. She did not move. He sniffed at her and smelled blood. As he rolled her over, he saw her face twisted in pain. Protruding from the snow, he saw the stump of a sapling coated in the blood he had smelled.

She had tripped over a rock buried in the snow and had fallen full force onto the ragged, splintered spear jutting nearly ten inches up from the ground. He reassumed his human form and scooped her up into his arms. Lacking the huge pads of the bear's feet, he struggled to return to the lodge. It took him a full twenty minutes to retrace the ground he had covered so quickly as Gaulaqut. He arrived to the anxious faces of his people.

She had died in his arms, along with her unborn child. The time of the storm passed with everyone mourning their first losses. It was a bittersweet time because of their recent good fortune. Hinoch conducted a ceremony to celebrate the passage of the woman's spirit to the family.

The storm tested the new structures for two full days. The branches laid around the walls quickly filled in with blown snow, adding to the insulation and the warmth within. Everything held up well against the storm. Hinoch was pleased.

"When are we going to light a fire? I'm frozen!" Joanna whimpered.

"We don't often use fire for heat; it consumes too much fuel. That is the main reason for communal living. It provides the heat of many bodies in a small space."

"That's all fine, but I'm used to central heating with a thermostat I can crank up whenever I feel chilly. A room where our breath freezes to the walls and frozen *muktuk* to eat are not doing anything for my core body temperature!" She slapped her arms around herself, trying to generate some warmth.

"Then you need to bathe and wrap up in fresh skins. Here. I'll help you."

"No thanks, I'll tough it out until tonight, when everybody's asleep."

"You are still suffering from your lack of privacy."

"No, I'm getting used to it. I just prefer to bathe when no one is looking. I feel that I just look different enough that I'm a curiosity. I get much more attention when I'm undressed than any of the others." She looked around the room.

"That may be so, but you must also consider that perhaps your self-consciousness makes you feel as though you are being watched." He leaned toward her, winked and confided, "I know I certainly enjoy the occasional glance."

"You, I don't mind. I kind of like it, in fact, but, in my head, that's a private pleasure, just for us."

"I understand, but we would not do well living as a couple separate from the others. There is not enough fuel to heat even a small cabin for an entire winter. Even our celebration fires must be much smaller here than in Nain. Remember what happened to my parents."

"Then humour me and let me bathe in the dark."

The winter proved to be one of contradictions. Although the weather was forgiving with light winds and little snow, the game seemed to remain nearby. Food was plentiful and there was no need for the group to disperse. The men went out onto the ice several times, returning with good catches of seals and fish. As spring approached, food remained plentiful and good stocks of dried meat had been set aside for the coming summer. Three more children were born —two boys and a girl.

Hinoch realized their good fortune, but was certain that, ultimately, their survival would depend upon wise use of

267

the available resources. He planned this to be a summer of exploration. The hunters needed to learn when specific game entered the area and where they passed on their migrations. Everything was in abundance and some other things, such as blackflies, were too populous for the comfort of many.

Scented oil worked for a time, but in the warm weather, perspiration soon washed it away, leaving people vulnerable. The heavy workload compounded the problem. The entire summer languished in warm humid weather and frequent heavy rains. Unused to these conditions, many people were in declining health as autumn approached.

Joanna had taken her remaining cloth garments apart and had sewn a tent for Abel to play inside when they were outdoors. This was only partially successful, since he was so precocious that it was nearly impossible to keep him under its protection. He was bitten quite badly several times and received a sunburn on one of the few sunny days of the summer. These things did not seem to affect him adversely. By autumn, he was trying to stand and walk in emulation of the elders he saw around him. The younger children were at his mercy when he played, since he had the advantage of his age and size. In spite of this, they all adapted and thrived in the summer heat, unlike their elders.

Many days climbed into the mid-seventies and the people had to learn to consume adequate amounts of water daily to avoid dehydration. As the time for winter approached, everyone waited for the ice and snows to relieve them from the heat. Their eagerness was not rewarded. The heat persisted well beyond the time for it to retreat under the oncoming armies of arctic wind, ice and snow. Abel's first birthday came and passed with no one wearing more than light chamois shirts and jackets.

Hinoch decided that fishing and drying the fish should continue until the ice arrived. His visions had warned him to adapt the pattern of his hunting and fishing quickly to the changes he perceived, yet to be cautious in what they took, so as not to deplete the species. He roamed the land relentlessly, taking careful stock of each species, its numbers, behaviour and general condition.

It was February before they took a whale. There was a great celebration when it was brought to shore and prepared for the winter.

Hinoch asked his father: *Abel, we have had a strange summer of great heat and to this time we have not seen snow. What is happening?*

My son, the time of hardship is beginning. The world has suffered great droughts. Famine and disease are spreading from nation to nation. You have done well this season, but you must begin to increase the quantities of dried food you gather each year. Store it up high in the lodge and ensure it is kept dry. Save more seal oil, since the whales will not fare well as the oceans warm.

Thank you for your counsel, Father. May your spirit soar forever.

Indeed, Hinoch watched with rising sorrow as year after year, the weather made the traditional times for hunting uncertain. As he had feared, first the whales began a final decline into virtual extinction as the oceans warmed and their salinity became diluted by the melting ice caps. Many of the species of fish failed to spawn because the water was too warm, altered chemically by the vast quantities of melt-water as the ice cap on the Torngat Mountains steadily waned. Hinoch made the best of every changing element of their environment, but food and materials for tools and weapons became increasingly difficult to obtain. By the tenth year of their time in Ungava Bay, he was seriously considering moving the camp but had not found a location with any more plentiful game.

Although they struggled, they managed to establish themselves, gradually, as each season passed. Timid winters became the norm, with few snowstorms, little offshore ice and declining seal and whale populations. The bounty of *muktuk* and seal steadily declined until they became a rare delicacy. Summers far too temperate for this latitude followed one on the other, decimating the fishing. They adapted, gathering plant growth, and hunting inland, creating the danger of exterminating the deer and caribou. Each year forced new adaptations and each year there was less.

In the winter of Abel's tenth year, Joanna had a baby girl, Noel. That was an especially difficult year. Food became increasingly scarce and the weather was a constant, unpredictable threat.

Joanna remembered her visions and feared the worst. Hinoch was rarely at home. He was incessantly combing the area for one more meal. One early morning, Noel woke her, fussing weakly. She did not know what to do, so she whispered, "Hinoch, wake up, I need you."

He roused and instantly was aware of his daughter's distress. He cradled her in his hands and began quietly singing his Nature Song. She began sucking her thumb and soon drifted off to sleep. He cradled her in his arm and lay back.

Joanna snuggled them, tears in her eyes, her fear evident in her expression, "She's so frail and I hardly have any milk to give her. She can't grow into a strong woman this way."

"I will go hunting again, out to sea. Perhaps there will be something for us in the deep water." Hinoch surveyed his small group. All were thin and many of them lacked the energy to hunt or fish. He was not much stronger, but called upon his last reserves to try. At least he would try.

The people were beginning to rouse, so he called his adopted sons, "Monty, Dick, come and help me prepare a dog team."

He went outside.

Alut, now an old dog, greeted him, clearly suffering from age and deprivation, as were the majority of his dogs. They also had not fared well and pups to replenish the teams were scarce.

"Here my companions. This is the last of the seal meat. You will need energy for this hunt. We must seek the life I sense far out on the ice."

"Monty, you and Dick wait here until I have been on the ice most of the day, then hitch up the rest of the dogs and come to help me bring the catch to the lodge."

Hinoch's team moved slowly down to the river valley. The snow was still thin in spots, so Hinoch had to pick his way, avoiding exposed rocks that would damage the runners. He purposely kept their pace measured to conserve as much as he could of their remaining strength. There was some ice, but it would be thin and treacherous; he would need all his skill to avoid falling through. It was for this reason he had selected Monty and Dick to follow him. They had learned to read the ice almost as well as he.

"Alut, we will stop here. I sense life below in the deep waters. This open area in the ice could be a breathing-hole for a large seal, even a small whale. Here, I will wait here. Where is my harpoon? I feel so tired."

Time passed. Hinoch tried to keep warm, poised unmoving at the edge of the ice, but his body resented giving up energy for his comfort when his very survival was so insecure. He remained at the hole, unmoving for what seemed an eternity, the sun sliding in a red glow along the horizon.

Slowly, a form loomed in the waters below, a young Beluga whale.

"Unh," he grunted at the force he put into throwing the harpoon. The point struck home as the whale wheeled to escape. Hinoch pulled the heavy line free, releasing the shaft and looped it over the runner of the *komatik* to help him apply friction.

I cannot stop the line from paying out. This whale will soon take it all! No, I cannot lose the line. I must stop him. Gaulaqut, help me, give me your strength!

The line finally slowed. Hinoch's mitts were nearly cut through and he could feel the heat searing into his fingers.

"This is the last of it," he gasped as he wrapped the last strands of it tightly around his wrist. He was abruptly jerked face first to the ice and the *komatik* began to slide toward the open water.

Now, Gaulaqut, help me pull! "Alut, help me pull!"

The gaunt old dogs rose, then heads down, bellies almost lowered to the ice, legs vibrating from the strain, the team began to pull. Hinoch gained a purchase with his free arm and pulled too, freeing his cheek from the ice. Then slowly, he began to recover to his knees. Crab-like, they moved across the ice, the taught line cutting a deep groove in the ice at the water's edge. For one second, Hinoch felt the strain relent. He jumped to his feet, wrapped a second loop over the tip of the runner on the *komatik*, then painfully unwrapped the line from his mitt. Heat scorched his fingers as the blood began to re-enter and bring its warmth to them. He began pushing the sled. He could tell that after nearly two hours, the battle was swinging their way. He called the dogs to stop and stumbled back to the hole in the ice with his ice knife in his hand.

He peered into the hole seeking to catch sight of Kenalogak, the Beluga whale below. The harpoon's tip had done its work, opening a large gash in the whale's side, from which blood flowed freely. The whale was now subdued from loss of blood and lack of oxygen.

I must work quickly now. Pull her up onto the ice. "Alut, pull once more. We are nearly there. We will have food for the rest of the winter!"

Hinoch pulled with all his might to raise the dying whale to the surface. He knew that once she began to emerge from the water, the loss of buoyancy would multiply the effort needed to bring her up onto the ice.

"I must save some energy for the final effort," he mumbled. He began to realize that as the head of the whale rose onto the ice, he was seeing her through a strange black tunnel that became smaller and smaller. He crumpled to the ice.

～～～

"Hey, 'Noch, you did good!" Monty grinned down at him.

Hinoch stared up at him and could only whisper, "The whale, must get the whale."

"Dick and I got her up onto the ice. Nice throw, she didn't stand a chance! We fed the dogs and we're letting them rest; then we'll pull it in to the valley. The people are waiting."

"How long have I . . . been sleeping?"

"We got here just as you were laying down for your nap."

"Thank you for your candour, Monty. You are a good son."

"We knew when you went out you'd find something, so we gathered up all the dogs that could stand on their own and came out after you. We just followed your trail. Here, have some *muktuk*."

Hinoch took the piece of meat and ate thoughtfully. "We must thank her spirit. She is one of the last of her kind and we have jeopardized their future by taking her." Hinoch drifted back into a coma-like sleep. In his dreams, Alut came to him, strong, white furred and happy.

Goodbye, my good companion, goodbye, he said in his dream.

"Come on," Monty commanded. "Let's get back to camp. We've got lots of work to do!"

He lifted the carcass of Hinoch's prized dog from the ice and placed him beside Hinoch's sleeping form in the *komatik*. Slowly Monty and Dick struggled to return to the village.

Hinoch awoke in the lodge house, looking into Joanna's tear-filled, sunken eyes. "My love, we have food. We will survive now until spring."

Slowly, as he regained his senses, his sixth sense told him Joanna was grieving. Grieving the loss of their little daughter. The food had arrived too late for her.

"She is gone?" he asked aloud.

Joanna nodded, bowed her head and cried, the wailing, sobbing lament of a new mother with no child to nurture.

Hinoch tried to lift himself from his bed, but the effort was beyond him. He extended his bruised, blood-blistered hand to her, beckoning her to lie down beside him. She demurred; instead, she rose and retrieved some *muktuk* from the women nearby. They ate amid her sobs.

The slender, nearly vertical bow of the sloop cut through the waves at a steady six knots, impelled by the east-northeasterly breeze flowing over the large Kevlar airfoils. In the pilothouse, Lucien watched the horizon with trepidation. The ocean became more unsettled and the heat was oppressive, the humidity high. The waves, trapped between opposing flows of wind and tide, acted as though they didn't know which way to go, and rose in sharp peaks at least two feet high, slapping against the hull of the boat. Lucien stared at the storm clouds, his fear rising with the freshening northeast wind. Before the news media fell silent weeks ago, he had heard of these monstrous storms out on the oceans.

The world as he knew it was gone. Businesses had long ago boarded up their doors and services he had taken for granted had simply ceased to exist. There was no law, other than the universal need to survive. The wind bore dust instead of the smell of plants and flowers; vehicles and personal valuables littered the streets. The truth was upon them.

He had never been a serious sailor and had never ventured this far out into the ocean. His yacht, built for pleasure, was a statement of blatant opulence. It was sixty feet of luxury that, like everything else, had been reduced to its primary function: transportation. Even its high-tech navigation systems, dependent on the satellites floating uselessly in space above them, had been replaced by the age-old systems of charts and dead reckoning.

Frantically, he poured over the charts of the area, attempting to identify a safe haven within running distance. There was nothing. Using a set of dividers, he stepped off his estimated daily sailing distance, based on their previous average speed of six knots. To this point, he had been within sight of land as he'd travelled down the St. Lawrence, with frequent opportunities to triangulate his position. Now overnight, the tides and winds had taken him beyond sight of land.

Using dead reckoning from his last known position, he estimated them to be one hundred nautical miles offshore, southeast of Battle Harbor. The depth sounder was not registering. Either it was not working, or the depth exceeded its maximum range. Lucien was well aware that the depths indicated on charts less than six months old were suspect, due to the steady increase in ocean water levels over the past number of years. He kept the depth sounder operating primarily for its ability to warn of shallow waters.

He turned to his emaciated, sickly-looking crew. Tom and Sue were a common-law couple he had known for many years. Tom was his business manager and friend. He relied on Tom to keep his creative ideas grounded in reality. Sue, it seemed, relied upon Tom for similar support. She was a highly-strung woman who retained a good deal of her beauty, despite the fact she was malnourished. They were huddled together on the divan, their light summer clothing badly worn and soiled. It was all they had left.

Ruti sat patiently on the lounge chair, her head propped in her hands. Lucien, the confirmed bachelor, had only recently begun to admit his feelings for her. He had met a number of beautiful, cultured women who would have been happy to receive his attentions, but none had spoken to his heart as clearly as Ruti. It had first begun when he'd observed her spiritual connection with Hinoch. Some day, he hoped, he would enjoy the same kind of contact with her, but for now, he had to focus on their survival.

"We need to lower all the sails before the storm hits, and set a storm jib. It will help steady the boat. The sails are roller-furled, so I just need you to help me control the lines. We have lots of diesel, so we'll motor until the storm blows over. Remember to snap your safety harnesses to the rail and work quickly, but carefully. The wind's getting up. We have to go now."

Sue whimpered, "I haven't got the strength to fight with those things! I'm afraid to go up there. Let's just leave the sails and close everything up tight. This is a big boat, it should be okay." She pulled self-consciously at her matted red hair. It had begun to fall out. Her skin was dry and transparent.

Lucien knew he had to maintain control. His crew was not accustomed to following orders unquestioningly. "No, *mot-dit!*" He mustered his most confident tone. "Too much wind will capsize us, or break the mast. We don't have enough diesel to motor all the way to Hinoch's village, so we must protect the sails."

Tom spoke in a weak voice bereft of tone or timbre. "Why the hell are we going to the Arctic, anyway? Surely to God it's got to be in worse shape than just about anywhere else." He had a prematurely bald head and several skin sores. He had contracted AIDS, one of the many diseases that had begun to roam the earth unchecked.

Lucien was in the best condition, simply due to his ability to pay the astronomic prices for food. At the outset of the droughts and food shortages, he had used his wealth to help provide for his friends and employees, but it rapidly became evident that this wouldn't change the facts. The world as he knew it was crumbling around him. He had to save what he could. He hoped it wasn't too late, that he could find Hinoch. He surveyed his crew, wiping the sweat from his forehead, "We don't have time for this. You all agreed this was our last chance. Well, we are taking it. You all know there's no going back and I trust Hinoch's abilities. If there's a way to survive, he'll find it."

"He only told you once where he would go. We don't know if he really went, or if he made it. This sounds like a total gamble to me. I vote we turn south and hope we can outrun it."

Lucien knew he had to take command and show leadership. "This boat is going to Ungava Bay, or to the bottom trying. At least *I* will be trying!" With that, he stormed onto the pitching deck, clipped his harness and moved forward to furl the jib.

Tom spoke softly, trying to soothe Sue's frayed nerves, "He's right, you know. We're out of options and if we just huddle down here like scared rats, we'll die for sure. I vote to at least try." He climbed the companionway onto the rear deck and moved forward.

Sue and Ruti looked at each other, desperation in their expressions. Ruti spoke first, "I don't want to sit and do nothing either. I always feel better when I'm busy. Let's go."

They both donned their safety gear and went topside. Ruti had retained a good deal of her vitality. Her growing relationship with Lucien had provided her a healthy environment until the final days when the raiders had attacked Montreal for its stored resources.

The police, military and even organized crime groups had banded together, staging raids on the cities. With their weapons and tactical skills, it was easy for them to obtain the food and supplies they needed. When Lucien saw this, he realized that perhaps he had waited too long. He considered himself fortunate to have made their escape without attracting attention.

Later, the sails safely furled, they contemplated their rations for the day. Lucien carefully opened a can, hoping to conserve the juices for supplementary fluids. "We each get a share of this can of peas and four crackers. The desalinator is starting to work a little better, so we can each have a cup of fresh water."

Sue lamented, "Remember when we used to go out for anything we wanted, at any time, in the best restaurants in Montreal?"

"That was then," Tom said flatly. "This is now. Enjoy your peas. At least we have *something* to eat, thanks to Lucien."

"At least someone appreciates me," Lucien tried to sound humorous, but it rang of too much truth. He had spent his last cash reserves buying three cases of canned vegetables. He changed the subject, "I've set the autopilot to follow a northeast heading, that's where the wind is shifting. I've been told the best thing to do is to keep it heading into the waves."

Ruti interjected wistfully, "I just can't help thinking I'd much rather roast on a beach in the Bahamas and starve, than freeze to death in the Arctic *before* I starve. I've lived up there. I know what it's like!"

"I agree it sounds nicer," Lucien said, "but everyone we talked to who could get out said they were heading to the tropics. They're probably stacked on top of each other in Nassau. The place is going to be a hotbed of contagious disease and larceny."

Sue sat on the divan, her long legs crossed beneath her. "I know, Lucien," she said, forming fists and grinding them against her knees, "but I've never felt like this before. I've never had to deal with having no options. This has to be the *definition* of desperation, we've been forced into trying to get someplace that has about one chance in a million of being survivable."

"Yeah, that fits all of us. We've always had unlimited choices until now," Tom put in, "But there are no options left except this boat." He slammed his hand against the table to reinforce his point. "It belongs to Lucien, so *he* says where it goes. He says his friend knows how to survive. If we find him, maybe we'll survive too."

Sue whimpered, "For the last while, I haven't been sure I want to survive. The life I love is gone, maybe forever." She looked down, rubbing her soiled feet.

"Sue," Ruti soothed, placing her arm across Sue's shoulders, "we all feel that way sometimes, but we can't give up." She lifted Sue's chin and turned her head, to look into her downcast eyes. "Who knows, tomorrow we might catch a nice big, juicy fish and gorge ourselves on sushi."

"Ugh. Who can eat that stuff?" Sue mumbled as she pulled away from Ruti and stood, holding her hand to her mouth.

Tom blurted, "*We* can. We're hungry enough to eat our sneakers."

Sue toppled against the bulkhead as the boat lurched into a wave. Her head struck a corner, opening a gash in her pale forehead. She moaned in pain.

Tom inspected the cut quickly, then said, "Just a minute, I'll get you a bandage."

Sue held the palm of her hand over the cut, clearly more upset by her circumstances than the wound. She closed her eyes, squeezing out the tears.

"Things are getting nasty out there. Lucien, you sure that autopilot thingy can keep us on course?" Ruti asked.

"If it can't, I can't do any better," he replied, raising his hands in a helpless gesture.

Tom wiped Sue's cut with a damp cloth and quickly applied the bandage, then he gave her a reassuring pat on the cheek, "There, you'll be as good as new in a few days."

She smiled at Tom fleetingly, then looking for a diversion from her personal misery, Sue added, "The way machines have been failing all over the place, I've kind of lost faith in them. Maybe we should keep an eye on the direction indicator — "

"That's the compass Sue," Tom interjected. Then, realizing Sue didn't appreciate the correction, he added, "and that's a good idea. We should take turns keeping an eye on things."

"I don't think that'll be a problem. I doubt if anyone's going to be able to sleep tonight," Lucien predicted, revealing some of his own doubts about their situation. The seas were becoming heavy now, striking the hull, causing the boat to lurch unpredictably. They all had begun to hang on to permanent fixtures to avoid being thrown off balance.

"Well, we should try," Ruti advised. "If we don't sleep, we'll go downhill even faster. I'm going to prop myself into a corner and try, at least." She began stuffing cushions into her corner of the divan, wedging herself into the already tiny space.

The boat was struggling in the wind and waves by now, the bow knifing into green water, slowly rising as its narrow leading edge penetrated the other side. As the wipers cleared the windscreen, Lucien looked ahead in growing terror. This was heavier weather than he had ever seen before and it was clear the bulk of the storm still lay ahead. Bile rose into his palate. He choked back the fear being generated by what he saw bearing down on them. Massive blue-grey clouds tinged with wisps of white rolled and boiled like the dust from an explosive building demolition. The yacht was quickly being dwarfed by the burgeoning waves, staggering to the crest, then surfing down only to plow into the next. The wind was blowing hard now, howling in the rigging and sending streamers of water flying from the wave tops.

Dusk settled, hastened by the looming darkness of the storm. It was useless to look out now, so Lucien turned his attention to the compass, autopilot and the engine gauges. The RPM was steady at two-thousand, but he could not decide whether he should adjust it. He placed his hand on the control stalk, then gingerly removed his grip. The autopilot was working steadily now, swinging the rudder back and forth almost frantically. He prayed to himself that it could maintain their course.

The boat lurched, coming to a virtual standstill as a massive, unseen wave engulfed the bow. The boom of the water as it hit the deck was deafening. The safety glass windscreen in the pilothouse became laced with tiny lines. It bulged, then tore open under the pressure of tons of water. Lucien gasped as the cold water rushed over him.

Seconds later the women's screams of alarm pierced the roar of the wind. Sue and Ruti turned and tried to run ahead of the small wave that surged into the lower cabin. In an instant, the lounge was calf-deep in water.

Tom scrambled up the companionway and yelled above the wind, now threatening to best all other sounds in the pilothouse. "Pumps! We need to start pumping water out of here! Lucien shielded his eyes and squinted at the water-soaked console, its lights flickering on and off as water seeped into the circuits.

"Here, here it is!" He flipped the switch. The red light came on momentarily, then flickered madly. "I don't know if it's working or not. Go below and lift the floor panel in the centre of the lounge. You should be able to see if it's taking the water out."

As he shouted, the next wave blew into the pilothouse with such force that he lost his balance and crashed to the deck. He lay there stunned, his view of the console obscured by the water rushing down from the huge opening above. He thought he saw the compass slowly spinning, the autopilot not responding. He scrambled back to the captain's chair and fought with the wheel, but the autopilot was still engaged, frozen at twenty-five degrees to port. He could barely move it and the power switch did not disengage the system.

The boat turned ninety degrees to the oncoming rogue wave. Lucien felt the deck pitch under him, "She's going over! Everybody hang on!" he screamed. He fell to the side of the pilothouse, then flopped onto the ceiling. The boat seemed suspended momentarily, then began to fall into the cavernous airspace under the curl of the wave. The mast pierced the waters below like a dart, then the deck slammed into the water.

The howling wind stopped abruptly, replaced by green water rushing into the cabin in a solid wall. The diesel stopped and the lights flickered on battery power, then went out. Below, Tom heard the grating sounds of wood, fiberglass and metal as the heavy equipment in the engine room tore loose from its mountings. As the boat struggled to right itself, Lucien was borne on the torrent of water into the main lounge, his lungs convulsing for air.

Finally upright again, the boat porpoised madly in the raging seas. The water continued to surge into the boat, now streaming from both the hull below and above. Every time he tried to breathe, there was only water. He stubbornly held his breath, bumping into cabin fixtures in the icy blackness. Someone grabbed his ankle; he kicked free, clawing the water trying to reach a pocket of air. Finally, lungs bursting, he exhaled, then drew in nothing but seawater. The salt burned in his sinuses and constricted his throat. He choked. Then, as he blacked out, he screamed his protest soundlessly into the water.

〰〰〰

Hinoch paused over his evening meal, his face suddenly pale. He got up from his place at the head of the group and quickly walked outside.

Lucien, my brother, where are you. What is wrong?

He stood in silence watching the Northern Lights dance in the skies. His vision began to come clearly to him. Lucien was dead, drowned at sea. Sadly, he turned to go back inside. Joanna met him at the entrance.

"You had a strange look on your face. Are you okay?"

"I am fine, but I have just lost my brother."

"I didn't know you had a brother."

"Lucien has been a Song-Brother since I went to university in Montreal."

"What happened?" She placed her hands on his cheeks; he drew her to him in a firm hug, seeking her comfort.

"I saw him in his yacht; there was a storm, then darkness. After a moment, there was black water rushing all around me. I couldn't breathe. That is when I came out here. I don't feel his spirit any more. He will be lost forever."

Joanna wrapped her arms around him as he looked into her eyes, tears streaming down his face. "I'm sorry for your loss, Hinoch, I know. It still hurts when I think of mother having a heart attack alone like that, but we can't second guess our decisions. We chose your course of action based on what we knew at the time and you *did* ask him to come with us when you called to tell him of your plans. It was his decision to wait."

"I should have tried to warn them all. Even if they wouldn't listen, at least I could say I had done my best. This way, I must live with my doubts and my guilt. I have never felt this way before. It is painful to know that I have condemned untold numbers to death with my choice."

"You knew, then, that it was impossible to save everyone. You chose to save us and that's what you've done!" Joanna's eyes filled with tears, remembering her anger and frustration as she agonized over leaving with Hinoch for the far north. "I couldn't come up with a better solution. I couldn't think of a way to make them listen. I didn't like the reality you saw, but I had to accept it. I justified my choice by recalling the Bible story of Noah's arc . . . how he anguished over having to choose who would survive the flood. It wasn't easy for him, but he followed his visions and saved what he could for the future. You, my love, have done exactly the same thing." I've learned to accept our decision, now you must learn to accept it too."

They walked slowly out to the promontory, arm in arm and surveyed the darkness.

SLOWLY, THINGS IMPROVE

The heat of summer subsided slowly into autumn, another year in which temperatures were far above what nature could endure. Hinoch went about his daily activities, saying nothing of the internalized guilt he carried over the loss of Lucien. Joanna was the only one who knew of his loss and only she understood from her own bitter experiences how he was grieving.

The elders requested a council meeting to discuss their concerns. Monty was the first to address him. "Hinoch, the Council of Elders is concerned. Tides are rising higher each year. Now high water nearly fills the valley to the hills. If it rises any higher, we will need to pull the boats up into our meadow to keep them safe."

"If whale and seal hunting do not improve, we may no longer need boats. It has been three years since we have taken a whale and the seal catch is less than one-quarter of the original numbers we took when we arrived. Fortunately, deer and caribou are not in serious decline. The plants upon which they graze have become more lush from the longer warm seasons and they seem able to endure the heat quite easily. I am convinced that for the present, we need to concentrate our hunting efforts inland. We must cut fresh saplings for bows and arrows and make lighter spears with throw-sticks."

"Then we can pull the boats up and store them?"

"Yes. I am going to lead a hunting expedition inland above the falls for deer and caribou. We will travel in three groups of men, women and children. If we have good hunting, we will set up a camp to dry the meat for this winter. If you encounter a large herd, light a smudge to alert the rest of us, then attempt to push them down into the valley. We will converge on them there. I hope that we will have success. We will meet each night to plan the hunt for the next day."

As the elders left the lodge, Abel ran to his father and grasped his sleeve, bouncing with anticipation, "Father, will I hunt with you this year?"

"Yes, Abel, it is your twelfth year. You must learn the skills of the hunter. You are already proficient with the fish-spear. This year we will teach you how to hunt deer."

"With the spear? Can we start now?"

Hinoch smiled, soaking up his boy's enthusiasm. "Yes, we will start now. This spear will have a different tip. You will find it is better balanced for throwing. The throw-stick will increase your range."

"How does it work?" Abel's eyes were full of curiosity, eager to learn.

Hinoch retrieved a spear and throw-stick he had made. As he moved to the old hide stuffed with moss they used as a practice target, he showed Abel how the spear fit into the groove cut in the throw-stick. "See here, the end of the spear rests against the notch at the back of the stick. You hold the spear in place with your forefinger until the moment of release, at the top of your throw." He parodied the movement, showing Abel how to retain his grip on the throw-stick while releasing the shaft of the spear.

Abel paid rapt attention to his lesson and quickly learned the timing of the release. His throws were initially erratic but, by the end of the session, the aim was improving. As they returned to the lodge, Abel proudly took his father's hand, "I have dreamed of hunting with you many times, Father."

"Then let us begin by making you some spears of your own, matched to your throwing arm."

Joanna looked on with concern as Hinoch and Abel worked at making these primitive weapons and as Abel learned how to throw them accurately. It seemed more benign somehow, for him to stand knee-deep in the river spearing fish than to be hunting a warm-blooded mammal. She knew she should not express such concerns though. To do that would be to deny him his birthright as a free, primitive man.

In three days, they were ready and embarked on their hunting foray into the interior. Hinoch directed one group to move up the north slope of the valley, another the south, while his group held back along the south shore of the valley. He frowned as he saw the falls at the head of the delta. They were only a few feet high in contrast to the past, when they fell nearly fifty feet to the exposed sands of the old tide line. He noted on the positive side, the river above the falls had dwindled to a width of only one hundred feet and nowhere could you fail to see the rocks in the stream. This confirmed to him that the ice cap on the Torngats had almost completely melted. The low water flow would make it easy to wade across the river at almost any point.

The morning passed with little activity and Hinoch's group stopped for lunch. As they sat chewing their dried fish, they relaxed in the bright sun, thoroughly enjoying the day. The weather thus far had been rainy and cool, but today promised to be clear, calm and warm.

Abel clutched his new spears tightly in both hands. They had quickly become his prized possessions. "Father, how will we get close enough to use our spears and arrows?"

Hinoch pointed to the high land alongside the valley, then as he spoke, he drew the valley sides in the sand at their feet. "The groups above will flush the game out, hopefully directing them toward us down here. The group from the opposite side will attempt to prevent them from turning east," he indicated a blocking action in the sand, "forcing them to find cover in one of these coulees. Our job will be to predict which one they will enter." He drew a coulee and pointed to spots along the side walls. "We will place ourselves along the edge as they enter from below. With luck, they will begin to feel safer and slow their pace as they climb. We will attack them from the sides and above, giving us the best possible shots."

Abel looked up from the map, "What is the greatest range I should attempt?"

"Only as far as we have been practicing. Your spear will drop rapidly beyond the distance we have found for you to be most accurate. A wounded animal is an animal in agony and one that is lost to us for food. We want to be as certain as we can of a killing shot."

Hinoch reached out and took his son by the shoulders, looking squarely into his eyes, "One other thing. Under no circumstances are you to attempt to recover your spears until I have given you permission. Others may release a shot just as you step into their path, with disastrous results."

Abel nodded, then his focus shifted to the hills, "Father, look to the north. Is that smoke?"

"Yes, son. Come everyone, we will move up into this small valley, nearly to the top. Those rocks at the sides will provide us with cover. Remember, wait until you are almost certain of a killing shot. Come now, hurry! Joanna, take the women and children and hide to the west of this opening. If the deer appear to be inclined to move toward you, show yourselves and move slowly to the north."

The animals began to emerge into the valley. Eight does and two large bucks. The bucks would be primary targets for their heavier muscle and the precious antlers. The deer were not spooked by the people behind them. They were merely staying out of their way, keeping their distance. Slowly, they moved down the north slope, stopping occasionally for a nibble of grass, then looking behind and checking for the progress of the people following them. The people travelling the south slope moved quickly to distance themselves to the east before descending into the valley. As they began their descent, the deer noticed them and increased their pace slightly, heading to the small coulee leading to the south.

Hinoch's group had made a strenuous climb up the sides of the valley. The wind was almost calm, a breath of air from the north — a perfect day for the hunt. The wind would not give the deer any clues as to their location. Hinoch placed everyone for concealment and the best clear shooting range. Abel stayed with his father. Everyone settled down, trying to calm their heavy breathing and seeking the best position in their hideout for using their weapons.

They had not settled many minutes when the lead doe became visible below. She appeared ready to enter the coulee. Their best escape was to the west, but the women and children hidden at the base of the hill showed themselves. As the deer approached the entrance, the women began moving slowly out into the valley to cut off that escape route. Now becoming concerned, the deer moved quickly, hopping stiff-legged into the coulee, climbing toward the hunters.

Hinoch could sense the building tension among his group, so quickly signaled for everyone to wait until the bucks were in range of the lower archers, Monty and Dick. They were to release first, hopefully claiming the bucks, then the does further up the coulee became fair targets. The best archers were below, so chances were good that both bucks would fall. The lead doe emerged onto the steppe at the top of the coulee as the bucks came into range.

Monty and Dick did well, taking the animals quickly and quietly. Nevertheless, one buck managed a danger snort as the arrow hit home. The does sprang into full gallop. Hinoch signaled the attack and all stood up to take aim. Hinoch pointed to a large doe and told Abel, "That one is your target; she will come close, so wait for your best shot."

The boy stood, braced himself, and set his spear for the throw. Hinoch waited also, his bow at the ready. His intention was to finish the animal should Abel's shot miss the mark.

Hold steady, my son, he thought to himself. *Wait . . . wait. Now!*

Abel could not have timed his throw better and the aim was good. The lance penetrated the doe's chest just above the heart, angling down, piercing one lung and the heart. Hinoch relaxed his bow, his shot unnecessary. The doe fell a short distance away and died within seconds.

"That was a perfect throw, my son!" Hinoch roared as he lifted him up in the air, tossing him a full four feet up, then catching him as he fell. He hugged him with the love borne of a father's pride in a child's achievement. Abel beamed, his eyes glazed with the excitement in his soul.

"Let's clean her and take her down to the women." Abel unabashedly hugged his father, "Mother is going to be pleased. We have not made too many holes in the hide."

Hinoch bent down to set Abel on his feet, "Yes, your first deer is well-taken; she did not suffer and she will be large enough for plenty of meat and summer clothing."

Hinoch stood back as his boy set to the task of cleaning the deer, giving him instruction on how best to open the belly and remove the entrails. They had pulled the deer higher on the slope, so that gravity would assist in extracting the vital organs and bowels from the cavity made by Abel's razor-edged caping knife. The heart, liver and kidneys were set aside as a treat for the dogs. As Abel worked, he became covered in blood, but he showed nothing but enthusiasm. He had cleaned many fish by now, but this was his first contact with a warm-blooded animal; the heady smells of the deer and the contents of its bowels did not deter him in the least.

Hinoch surveyed the scene. Both bucks had been felled and three does — half of the animals. He climbed the steep incline to the steppe and observed with his raptor's vision that one doe was wounded, but was not far behind the others. She would survive. The wound was minor. He turned back to continue supervising his son. There, not twenty yards away, the boy had stopped cleaning the doe. He crouched like a cat, set to spring.

Hinoch could see the source of his son's intent. A fawn lay quietly, hoping to be overlooked. As he watched, the boy pounced and captured the tiny animal. Together, they rolled down the small remaining slope, coming to rest at the bottom. The fawn struggled vainly, but the boy was already strong and fully capable of restraining it. To Hinoch's surprise, Abel pulled a cord from his pocket and tied it around the animal's neck. He had expected him to take its life with his knife. The boy looked up and saw his father.

"Look, Father, I caught a little one. Can I keep it?"

"No, son. We cannot provide for it. It is too young and requires its mother's milk. We have nothing that will sustain it."

"One of our dogs has milk. She will feed it."

"She is more likely to eat it. Her priority is to feed her pups. I suggest you release it. With any luck, the remaining does will return and adopt it before the wolves find it. If we take it back to camp, they will never dare return for it and one of the dogs will certainly kill it."

The boy stood for a moment, the tiny animal confined in his strong, blood-covered arms. He was clearly thinking over his father's words. Hinoch rarely denied him anything he wished.

"You are right, Father. It has had a cruel day today, but to confine it and watch it die anyway would be even more cruel." He quickly set the fawn down and slipped the cord from its neck. The petrified little animal stumbled only a few feet away, then tried to hide again. Abel looked at it for a few moments longer, then returned to his kill.

Hinoch returned to his side and helped him to sever the knee joints in the legs. "These will be our handles. We leave them completely attached to the hide and remove only the upper limbs."

They worked systematically severing the major bone joints and separating the hide from the flesh in one piece. Once it was free from the carcass, Hinoch began placing the sectioned meat back into the hide, "Here, this is how we use the hide to carry the meat. I will help you pull it down to the women if you wish."

"Thank you, Father, it's a long way down; I would probably be pretty tired."

As they worked their way down, the others joined them, pulling the caped out hides along where the ground permitted, carrying them where it did not.

They paused to catch their breath, sitting on two rocks facing each other, the deer on the ground between them. Hinoch leaned forward and placed his hand on Abel's shoulder, giving him a little shake, "You have made me very proud today, Abel. You have shown that you have the heart of a hunter, the compassion of a loving man, and the wisdom of an elder. Today, you have learned how to hunt, shown that you care for others and demonstrated that you can make decisions that fit with nature. This has been a great day for us!"

The boy smiled up at his father. His heart filled with joy and pride.

∾∾∾

Forty-seven years later, Hinoch stood remembering that cherished day with his son as he contemplated his present reality. He was an old man. Joanna was ill. He knew his children were concerned, as was he.

"Abel, do you know where to find your sister? She is not responding to my thoughts and your mother has need of her."

"Yes, Father, she is near the water, probably concentrating on fishing. I will not be long."

Hinoch looked at Joanna leaning in the doorway of the common house, clearly diminished by the years of hardship she had endured. "Come. Let me take you to the lookout point. You have always marvelled at the view. Let us enjoy it again together."

She raised her hand, inviting him to assist her, "I'd like that, but these old eyes don't take in the scenery as well as they used to." As they made their way to the promontory, she asked, "Are you going out hunting again today?"

"Yes, the game has started to rebound as conditions improve. We are back to our original numbers. I believe the hard times may have come to an end. We should have plenty to eat this season. See, the waters have subsided almost to the levels they occupied when we first came here."

"That's good. We stand to lose more people if things don't improve soon. Some of us are too thin to survive another hard winter."

"You are especially thin. You must eat well to restore your weight."

Joanna frowned, revealing her fear of the new reality she was facing, "I know, but lately I just seem to rent my food. It passes through and I don't seem to get much out of it."

Hinoch caught her expression and looked down, unwilling to accept what he knew could not be avoided, "Your ancestors did not have such a high protein diet. When you were young, your internal organs were strong enough to cope, but now, they require more plant-based food — food that we simply do not have."

"I never imagined that I would live long enough for my constitution to give up on me. With all the crazy damned adventures I've seen out here, it's a miracle that I made it this far!" She chuckled, shaking her head, "I consider myself lucky to have seen eighty years."

"You are wise and you know that your time is near. Your daughter will make your remaining time pleasant and peaceful."

Joanna stopped, dropped his arm and turned, fire in her old eyes, "The hell, she will. She has better things to do with her time. I've had sixty years of adventure. I've developed a taste for it and I'm damned if I'm going to turn into a vegetable now! Dianne will help me, but she's not going to coddle me. I won't have it! She had her finger pressed into his chest when a memory of a similar scene came back to her. She smiled and patted his chest softly, "And speaking of taking it easy, when are *you* going to relax and spend a few idle days?"

"I cannot. We must constantly assess the state of our environment and adjust our strategies."

"Your son is nearing sixty years. When will he be allowed to do these things?" She looked at him knowingly, "I know, I keep thinking the young women have a lot to learn yet, and I'm their elder. I don't want them putting me out to pasture, either. My joys are the same as yours: seeing our people thriving in our home and seeing our children becoming their leaders. The time's here for us to let them spread their wings and go it alone."

I agree, Dianne's thoughts broke in, *We're doing fine and you have not devoted nearly enough time to each other since the hunting started to improve. We all know what to do, at least for now. Why don't you take a few days and just enjoy some time together. Remember, you always taught us to save some energy for the end of the day when we are all together. It's time to do what you tell us to do!*

Abel chimed in: *I can look after things for at least a few days. Take an* umiak *and go on a fishing trip together.*

Hinoch and Joanna beamed at each other, *All right, but no wild celebrations because we're away. There's too much work to be done!*

Abel prepared an *umiak* and stocked it with food and a small sealskin tent. Dianne helped her mother negotiate her way down the coulee as Hinoch assembled his hunting and fishing equipment.

"Remember, son, I will be available to your mind's eye for counsel at any time, if you have a question."

"Thank you, Father. Enjoy your time together."

As Hinoch paddled the *umiak*, Joanna made herself comfortable, then looked into his eyes. She reviewed her many years of joy and sorrow with this miraculous man. Her heart was content.

"We're old, Hinoch, and I'm not very strong anymore. I think I'm about ready to go to the spirit world. How about you?"

"I still have much to teach our children. You are right though; my strength of body sometimes fails me sooner than I expect. We are indeed old, but we have lived well and we have created a wonderful, strong community of our people. We number nearly one hundred now and we hunt the entire area of Ungava Bay."

"Your masterpiece is nearly finished isn't it? Remember, when we were starting out? You said you were finished with painting, your next work would be to re-establish your people as they were meant to live. If you did well, it'd be your masterpiece." She raised her arm, pointing back to the village, "You've done well, Hinoch. You have your masterpiece."

He turned, admiring the beauty of their home setting. The air was cooling slightly and a mist was rising from the warm waters, lending a dream-like element to the vista of the valley. "Yes, the pride soars within my heart every time I look at what we have achieved together, love of my life. Our reason for being here comes to an end. Soon it will be time to pass on our spirits to our children and let them enrich those spirits with their lives."

Joanna's gaze moved upward, "Look, up there. Ravens . . . hundreds of them! My family's here to see me off."

Hinoch looked up, but saw no birds.

Joanna continued, still gazing into the skies, "I remember you telling me about Lucien dying in that storm at sea. He'd fled Montreal and tried to sail to Labrador, to seek us out and join our group. I remember your sorrow. You even doubted your decision to save your own people at the cost of losing so many. It's so sad to see the ones you love go like that. All the others that died too. The hardest reality I had to face in my life was the realization that you were right, there was no turning back for them . . . "

Joanna became silent. Hinoch could see her spirit was restless. "I'm tired, Hinoch. Let's make camp so I can rest."

Hinoch did not react. His gaze was fixed upon her face, his memories of their years together playing through his mind. He saw her flying her plane, sprawled on the ice, shooting seals, cutting her eye; he saw her eyes light up when he told her she was with child. He cried out soundlessly as she wept for their dead daughter. Their life had been filled with the heights of unbounded joy and was tinged with the worst of sorrows, but they had survived and thrived, living as the people should.

After a few moments, he seemed to return to the present. He looked into her soul.

I see your spirit is ready to leave you. Do you want to return to our home to be with our children?

"What's wrong, can't you speak the reality your eyes are showing you? I am going to die today. I am scared, too, but that won't change anything. I am taking comfort in what we have accomplished. You should be happy, too. Today is the beginning of my latest adventure. Our children are strong and free. They have families and children to sustain them. They don't need anything else. *They* know I'm ready to die. They don't need to see it happen. I want to be alone with you and when I am gone, I want you to bury me where only you can find me. You found me over sixty years ago and gave me a life so rich. So rich I have never once regretted spending it with you. Now all I need is for you to give me my final rest."

Hinoch was silent a long time, then he began to sing their family song and she started with her part.

"Today I become a bird,
My life is renewed . . . "

She fell silent. Hinoch reached out with a shaking hand and closed her eyes, now glazed and lifeless. His soul felt her spirit that had sustained him these many years crying out for the loss of their days together. She was afraid. He sat motionless, letting the boat drift down the river, his eyes filled with tears.

Do not be afraid, my love. Your spirit is as safe with me, as you have been these many years.

Thank you, my love, but I will miss your touch.

As will I . . .

Time passed unnoticed, since it bore no significance in the events taking place in Hinoch's heart.

When she spoke to him again, she seemed much recovered. *Look, over there, that's where you took the spirit of Gaulaqut. Take me there. That's where I want to be.*

Hinoch turned the boat toward the shore and began to row.

Remember how furious I was with you? But you calmly took all my anger and patiently taught me that it was necessary to take chances in order to fill our life with truth, honesty and the only real wealth anyone needs. Thanks for that lesson, Hinoch; the risks we've taken have made us the happiest people in the world.

He found the site where he had taken the spirit of Gaulaqut and where she had rescued him. At the base of a large rock overlooking the bay, he dug a shallow grave and prepared to place her in the depression. As he arranged her clothing, he found a lump inside one pocket. He hesitated a moment, then reached inside. He touched a strange cylinder that crackled softly as he withdrew it. As he realized what he had found, he fell forward onto her body and allowed his grief to find voice. He cried aloud for her and for what she had given up to be with him. In his hand, he held a badly worn paper wrapper, the contents still untouched — her last chocolate bar.

After a time, he felt his strength returning, along with his will to complete his appointed task. He placed her body to rest in the soft sand of the riverbank. He ate well and set up his camp for the night. Next day, he woke grieving once more, after reaching for her, but not finding her at his side.

Hear me, Great Spirits. This day I rise from my sleep to add a finishing touch to the tapestry of my people. Now I summon the strength of the Great Spirit, Gaulaqut, to help me create a memorial to Joanna, my partner in life these many years. Come, Gaulaqut, help me lower this stone to make a monument for the love of my life.

Hinoch moved to the side of the immense stone. His stooped frame seemed to straighten and fill out, regaining a good deal of the vitality it possessed years ago. He turned and placed his back against the immense stone, flexed his legs and pushed it over onto the freshly dug grave. As it rolled over, it became apparent that the newly exposed surface bore a strong resemblance to a recumbent polar bear. It was so strong as to suggest it had been carved, perhaps millennia in the past.

He spoke to the stone in his mind, *You are now tasked with guarding her memory and with the honour of representing her strength of heart to all who find her here.* This said, he touched the stone with his shaman's walking stick. The stone began to emit a low, blue flame and shed the accretions of the centuries to reveal a pure white stone. As it shed the moss and dirt, it also resumed its original shape and condition — a masterful Yup'ik carving of Nanuk, the polar bear.

I will remain here now for six suns, to honour the six decades of joy you have given me. Your greatest source of concern in our time together, my battle with Gaulaqut, is represented by his image. I have charged him with the protection of your worldly remains. He paused, observing his vision of her spirit, *You are pleased. I see your spirit smiling.*

Yes, Hinoch, I am pleased. The life I have lived with you and our people has been so much more than the greatest thing I could have accomplished with my life as it was before I met you. Thank you for the lessons we have had together.

He looked down. *I have many things left that I wish to accomplish. I foresee that it will be many seasons before I join you.*

Even the spirits must wait until the time is right. I will be here when you are ready.

I note a change in your speech, my love. You are speaking to me as I speak to you.

She laughed. *It is my way of showing the complete union of our spirits.*

You honour me, my love. Hinoch smiled his broad innocent smile, turned and laid his sleeping skins against the monument. He built a small fire and lay back to sleep. He felt old and physically drained from his efforts at placing the memorial. As he slept, his sixth sense was aware of a strong presence nearby. His spirit rose from his body to seek the source. He floated through the low bush, a whisper on the shore breeze. Small animals were everywhere, going about their nocturnal activities, oblivious to the Great Spirit passing over them on the breeze.

Kapvik, Hinoch whispered to himself. *He senses my present state of mind and body and seeks an advantage over me. Look, he noses the air. He knows I have found him, yet he does not sense where I am. A little whirlwind should give him a clue.*

Hinoch turned sharply, creating an abrupt whirling breeze that picked up small debris from the ground and scattered it into Kapvik's pointed face and beady eyes.

Kapvik snorted and pawed his eyes. "Hinoch, you play tricks with me. That is dangerous, I have many tricks of my own."

"I am aware of your powers, Kapvik, and that is our problem. We are both old and wise, too wise to seek shedding blood as a means of resolving our rivalries."

"Shed blood! How can you shed blood when you are no more than a voice on the wind? If talk and vapor is all you will risk against me, you will never gain the opportunity to possess my spirits and my powers."

"So, you are challenging me now, on the night I mourn the loss of my mate of sixty years?"

Kapvik turned to face the moving voice, "I will choose the moment. Your talk will not influence when I act."

"You must be truly a coward. I am physically exhausted tonight and I am in mourning, which detracts from my focus to your intentions. You are passing up an ideal opportunity."

Kapvik sat back on his haunches, "You are not so exhausted as to be unable to summon one of your spirits to do battle for you. I have seen you cower from battle in past, resorting instead to trickery, taking the form of one of your spirits to protect your sorry hide. You speak of cowardice — look to yourself, Hinoch." Kapvik looked around, emphasizing the fact that he was speaking to an invisible opponent. "You are afraid to face me and I have an eternity of time. My nature is to wait until you are an easy kill. I will choose the time and when I attack, you will lose your powers to me." Kapvik raked the air with his long claws, "Your precious people will be left to starve and die, the cowards they truly are."

Hinoch swirled around Kapvik, ruffling his coat. The beast spun, expecting to see Hinoch appear behind him, fearing an attack. Realizing too late that he was revealing his nervousness over his invisible enemy, he began wandering toward the hills, hoping to force Hinoch to return to his visible self. Hinoch moved beside him and whispered, "You still roam the land with no home and no family. You have no successor. I know your young have all perished in the hard times." Kapvik looked away, trying to ignore this voice on the wind. Hinoch persisted, "I have young, strong successors, well trained in the ways of the spirits and ready to receive them. In a short time, if you do not act, you will face young, more powerful shamans than I. However, there is another way."

Kapvik sighed and sat down, resigned to the fact he was not going to force Hinoch to take a visible form. He directed his gaze in the direction of the sound. Hinoch continued, "If we were to set aside our rivalry and join forces, we could combine our ancient powers, making us the most complete spirit in existence. You would gain access to the wonders of community life and a history at least as old as your own. I would gain the last link in the powers that were scattered among all the beasts at the time of creation. Think about it. The rivalries could be set aside and we would be free to concentrate on rebuilding the world as nature intends it to be. We would be able to help nature recover, wisely choosing our prey, varying our sustenance as needed to restore the balance among the species."

Kapvik sat, attempting to preen his matted coat. "A pretty speech, Hinoch, but I am not so old that I cannot produce a litter. With your powers and mine, I would be the supreme hunter. My kind would dominate the world, killing anything we wished, when we wished — "

"Until there was nothing left," Hinoch interjected. Then you would perish and take all the spirits with you. Your nature is to kill for pleasure. If you gained my powers, your kind would indeed flourish for a time . . . until you destroyed everything. If you join me, we will never want for sustenance or companionship. We will survive forever."

"Forever?" Kapvik shook his head in disbelief, "What is that?"

"You view things only in terms of ending them. Consider them continuing with no end, in balance and harmony." As Hinoch spoke, he circled Kapvik.

Warily, Kapvik turned, following the voice. He was becoming unnerved by this situation and the words were no more reassuring. "There is no such thing. Everything must end."

"So long as you believe that, it will be so, but if you join me, we will be able to change that so-called fact of yours. If all species are kept in balance, nature will return to the original state. The weather will resume its normal patterns and each species will find sufficient food to sustain itself at the correct level."

"The way it did the last time your kind ruled the world. Remember, it was the humans that destroyed whatever balance existed."

"You are right, but they did not possess the wisdom of the ages. With no guiding spirit, the world's species will never achieve real balance, meaning we will continually cycle through feast and famine until our eventual demise."

"You argue well, but you are risking nothing and suggest that I just surrender my spirits. How do I know you will not eliminate my kind from the world?"

"Your kind are as necessary as any other species. You are one of the key predators, whose job is to harvest those species in overabundance."

"Tell, tell, tell! Show me!"

Slowly, the area filled with the beasts and humans in Hinoch's spirit. Kapvik became truly alarmed at the visions he found invading their council. He looked to one side, where hundreds of people were floating on the air toward him. The nearby waters came alive with all manner of fish, seals and whales bringing the surface to a boil as they rose from the depths and swam at the surface. The skies over his head filled with raven, eagle, owl, hawk and dove. To his further alarm, he looked behind to be confronted by Gaulaqut, the massive polar bear and deer, caribou, fox, wolf, lynx.

Kapvik summoned his courage, realizing this was not an attack, "I see something now that had never occurred to me. I share many of these spirits with you already, but none of the Great Spirits."

"Yes, and many times we have harmed each other's chances for survival by both hunting the same species, placing them in danger of falling below their proper numbers."

Kapvik flicked sand in the direction of the voice, "Your kind grows beyond the proper numbers and simply takes more to sustain them."

"In the past humans have done that, but they did so in ignorance, believing the bounty of the world to be endless. They were unaware of the spirits in themselves, or in others, so never learned to take counsel from them. My people have learned to do everything with respect to the spirits around them, including governing their own numbers. When an area is occupied to the extent that all species are in balance, we send our young people away on an adventure to find their new home. They will occupy an area that is capable of supporting them and bring it into balance."

"If they do not find such a place?"

"Then they will not survive."

"No, they will return and overpopulate their old home. That is in *your* nature!"

Hinoch sighed, "That is the risk we take when we leave our home to explore. We know full well that we cannot return to condemn the people who gave us life to starvation. We must find a new home capable of sustaining us, or perish."

"I understand the wisdom of what you say, but I doubt your resolve to carry out your lofty ideals. I maintain that nature operates through feast and famine. That is how the species are kept in check. Your species has caused the greatest dying off since mammals occupied the globe, after the demise of the dinosaur. Now it is *our* turn to dominate. No, I will await my opportunity and take you at my leisure."

"Your opportunity will not come. You are too old."

Kapvik snorted an insolent blast, then turned and shuffled off into the distance.

Earlier that day, at the village, Abel and Dianne looked at each other with tears in their eyes and sorrow in their hearts. They had both experienced dreams of their father and mother in the *umiak* many miles down the river. Joanna had passed into the spirit world. They gathered their families and the people and began a ceremony of mourning.

Seven days later, Hinoch returned alone and quietly assumed his customary routine.

"My people, it is seventy years since we came to this place. We have struggled and we have thrived in harmony with the fortunes of nature. Many of our elders are no longer with us, but in their place, we have a young, strong group of families to carry on our traditions. We have reached the stage in our residence here that our numbers begin to threaten the balance of the species. Today I am seeking two leaders to take groups to explore for new homes. We will divide our numbers into three groups. I will remain here with this group; the others will seek permanent homes far afield from this place. Who will lead our people to their new homes?"

"I will," Abel spoke as he stepped forward.

"And me," Dianne said, joining her brother.

A loud cheer rose up from the gathered people. It was clear the offer was popular.

Hinoch's heart sank as the realization came to him; his family would be leaving to begin their own lives. Other than in his visions, he would lose contact with them, their mates and their children, for extended periods. But he knew this was the way. He knew they must seek their own lives in freedom, just as he had done.

"So be it," he said, mustering his best voice. "Begin your preparations and select your people."

Hinoch turned and entered the lodge house, suddenly feeling every one of his one hundred and four years. He walked using his father's cane for support now, and his frame was lacking the supple muscles of his youth.

That night, Hinoch dreamed. His dream of creating a flourishing group of people had come to fruition; however, the conflict in his heart was deep. His dream was being realized at the cost of not having his own children with him in his final years.

Father, Abel spoke in his dream, *we will be with you always in spirit and we will come to you often in spiritual counsel, seeking your wisdom to help us guide our people.*

You are wise beyond your years, my son. I have had the joy of your presence, watching your children grow for nearly seventy years. Now I will share the joy of our dream. You are right. I am being a selfish old man to want you to remain here. Before you depart, we must complete your transitions into the lives of shamans.

Slowly, his eyes opened to the dim light of the lodge. Dianne and Abel were also awake and alert.

Come, my children. Let us perform the rite of the shaman.

They rose silently and went outdoors. The day would be fine, with light winds and sunshine. To the east, the sun had just risen above the Torngats.

Abel was a strongly built, tall man of seventy years, Dianne, nearing sixty years, was also tall, but more finely built than her mother. Hinoch was pleased to see his children in the prime of their lives. His legacy would thrive in their hands, he knew. He led them to an *umiak* and bade them launch it.

Where are we going, Father?

Your mother is a powerful spirit in my soul. I want to be near her earthly remains when you are initiated.

Abel responded immediately, *We will take you there. Come, Dianne, we have seen her resting place in our dreams. It is time to see it in reality.*

You know where it is? Hinoch asked in surprise.

Dianne smiled, enjoying her father's surprise. He often forgot the intimacy of their communication as he aged. *Yes, you think of it often. We can't help but know.*

Hinoch saw her smile and understood. *It is where I wish to be taken when I die.*

Abel gave him his assurance, *We'll tell our children. They'll see to it.*

Thank you, my children.

They rowed the *umiak* for a short time, then turned into the shoreline and assisted Hinoch as he struggled to step onto the beach. It had been years since Hinoch had come to this place. As beautiful as the shoreline was, opening its arms to the vast waters of the sea, it gave him a good deal of pain to be this close to Joanna's remains. He still missed her physical presence.

Abel and Dianne took his arms and helped him through the soft footing of the shoreline's sands. Hinoch was feeling his age today and was glad for the help his children gave. As they approached, Hinoch's eyes clouded with tears. He still missed her terribly, even though he spoke with her spirit at length every day. That communion seemed enough most days, but here . . . They stood for many moments in silence, absorbing the aura of Joanna's monument. The stone was indeed just stone, but so artfully carved as to seem alive, to be guarding its charge. "Here we are. The stone is returning to its natural state. We should clean it before we have the ceremony."

He watched with great pleasure as Abel and Dianne lovingly cleaned the monument to Joanna. They took sand and rubbed the smooth surfaces as one would a prized family pet. The details of the eyes, claws, even the carved textures of the animal's fur began again to emerge. Abel and Dianne became so absorbed in their work and their own feelings that they did not observe Hinoch sink to his knees and cover his eyes.

When they were finished, it had regained its original beauty.

Hinoch had gathered himself by now and was determined to begin the ceremony, "I will lie down near Nanuk and enter a dream. You will see a large white raven. Join hands and sing the shaman's song as I have taught you. The raven will alight on your joined arms and become one with your spirits. When it is done, leave me here to be with my Joanna for a time."

Hinoch lay down as he had said and within minutes, was in a deep trance. Abel and Dianne joined hands, looking around expectantly. In a nearby tree, a white glow began to take the promised form. A huge, resplendently white raven sat eyeing them carefully.

Abel whispered, "Let's sing together now, Dianne."

They sang a few moments, then Dianne stopped abruptly, *Look, he's flying to us. The light . . . it's blinding! I feel my senses becoming stronger. The inner vision. Now I understand what Father has been teaching us. It's beautiful!*

They stood, arms locked together, trying to absorb the enormity of their changed awareness. Hinoch's spirit rose from his trance and walked, much more confidently, as he had in his youth, to face them. He took their clenched hands into both of his, a smile of inner peace on his lips. *You are now full-fledged shamans, fully capable of leading your people. My children, you fill my heart with joy! Go now. Make your preparations. In three days return for me.*

Dianne reached up and tenderly touched her brother's face. "You have shaman's eyes now, Abel. Are mine the same?"

"They are, Dianne. We are shamans and you are the first woman to be initiated."

Hinoch's spirit returned to his body. He watched as they took the *umiak* and rowed upriver. The tiny vessel quickly outdistanced his faded vision. He waited until he was certain they had travelled beyond sight. He stood staring blankly into the haze of his weakened vision, then he looked down at the sand at his feet, something he could still see with a degree of clarity. Slowly, he shuffled back to Nanuk and crouched down against it. He began to allow his body to sleep. When he felt truly alone, he turned his attention to Joanna.

Our children are beginning their adventures. They are leading their people to new homes.

Your masterpiece is finished, Hinoch. Come to me now, I am anxious to be with you again.

I cannot. First, I must face Kapvik.

You have raised strong, capable children with healthy families of their own. Let them complete this quest for you.

Your counsel has merit, but I was given the task of gathering all the Great Spirits. It is something I must finish.

Joanna chuckled. *You always were stubborn and bull-headed about this. Some things never change. I will be here when you are ready.*

Thank you for your understanding, my love. It will not be long now.

Hinoch slept on, his memories providing him pleasure for his rest.

The following morning, he arose and began to wander in the surrounding hills, taking in the majesty of his home, which never ceased to please him. He climbed the rocks slowly, his body refusing him his previous vigor. Near the top, with laboured breathing, he paused to survey the view once again. He surveyed the valley, its waters sparkling in the morning light, then turned toward the sea, hoping to see some sign of a whale. As he turned, his foot slipped on the moist moss and he fell. Rolling and tumbling, he fell nearly one hundred feet where he became wedged in a cleft in the rocks, and where his head struck hard. As he began to lose consciousness, he looked over the edge to the rocks below.

Now, old man, you are mine. I can take you with no effort and be master of all nature!

Hinoch's sixth sense struggled into consciousness. He saw the emaciated body and ruffled, patchy fur of Kapvik.

You are barely alive yourself, Kapvik. You still have no young and very little prospect of producing them before your demise. If you take my spirits now, you will not survive to use them and you will have to face my children.

Your children? What have they to do with this?

I have passed on the shaman's powers to them. You will need to deal also with them.

You are that near death?

No, we are dividing our numbers. They are going out to find new homes.

You send your own children out to risk their lives?

They are the best equipped of my people to lead.

You fool. They will starve and die. Then I will be the only vessel of the spirits. I will rule all nature!

There is a chance of that, but if they survive you will always have a rival to your powers.

But I will be the more powerful, possessing all their spirits, plus my own! Now you die!

Kapvik threw himself on the inert body of Hinoch, clawing and tearing at him with all the ferocity he still possessed. He tore at his enemy's flesh, consumed by his killing frenzy, inflicting terrible wounds. He knew he had bested his opponent and was beginning to celebrate his victory. Suddenly, he felt a searing pain in his back. He was being lifted bodily from his prey and pulled up into the air. He turned to see Nektoralik.

"So, you use trickery again, Hinoch. Well, deal with this!" Kapvik began to take the form of a large caribou bull. Abel strained, using all of Nektoralik's powers of flight, but despite his efforts, the mass of the caribou bull pulled them downward. They began to sink to the ground.

Abel noticed his sister, who was on the shore below, preparing for her share of the battle. He spoke to Kapvik, "You are dealing with Abel, son of Hinoch. My sister, Dianne, awaits you below."

Kapvik looked down into the eyes of Gaulaqut, his massive paws flailing the air directly below. In a second, he returned to his original body.

"I concede. Let me go and I will promise never to seek your defeat again!"

Abel laughed in his heart and his eagle form screeched, "You joined the battle. Now you must pay the price."

Nektoralik flew out over the ledge, over the rocks on the beach below, then released him to crash helplessly into oblivion. He dove, landed, and shared the beast's spirit with Dianne as Kapvik died.

Later in camp, as his wounds healed, Hinoch could feel that his soul was anxious to pass into the spirit world. One question remained that Hinoch had to answer. It weighed heavily on his mind.

Over his entire life, he had cared for his people and worked for their survival in exile here in the north. He had brought them to the wilderness of northern Labrador, based on his conviction that the modern world had been in serious decline and would not survive.

The weather and changes in nature had been as extreme as he had seen in his early visions, yet he wondered whether his people would have fared better had they remained in Nain. Yes, he decided. He must see with his own eyes, justify his decision to flee to the far north. Although he had come to accept his guilt at not attempting to educate the people of the world, he still felt the need to vindicate himself. Had he been right? Had life ended for the millions he had seen perish in his visions? His son and daughter could oversee his people while he sought his answers.

"Abel, Dianne, please come to my side."

He watched as his children rose, strong, even though now also senior in years. He was pleased at how strongly they showed their mother's features, their long legs, blonde hair and height of stature. They moved assuredly to their father's side.

"We are here, Father."

"Soon you and Dianne will become the leaders of all our people. I am contented in my soul that you have been diligent in becoming persons worthy of leading and caring for them. I have one question remaining in my life that I must answer. I will take a journey to the south to see with the eyes of our spirits the world we left behind. I must learn whether my decision, taken so long ago, was truly wise. You must care for my body while I am away. I do not know how long I must travel, or how far I will roam, but do not despair, I will return."

Abel answered, "All is well in our villages, my father. Food is plentiful and we are strong in body and spirit. We will await your return."

Hinoch smiled. He felt his spirits rise from his body as they had done so many times before. There were so many more now. He was, he knew, the first of his line to prevail over all the warring spirits he had encountered. His last battle with Kapvik, the wolverine, had taken a terrible toll, but now he, too, lived with the other spirits and Hinoch, his son and daughter maintained peace among them. The world would be a better place for his people. As he passed through the roof of the lodge, he looked back at his wizened old body.

Yes, it is time old man. You have spanned one hundred and four years, the longest life of any of our people's shamans. It is time.

He looked around at his people going contentedly about their lives in the brilliant arctic sun. Preparations were underway for the fishing season at the mouth of the river. The snows had melted. The caribou moss and lichens were growing abundantly. Fish were teeming in the waters and the game was making a strong comeback in the interior. Yes, life would be good again for a number of years to come. His children would preside over a time of plenty. Hinoch spread Nektoralik's wings. It would be a long journey requiring great powers of sustained flight. He climbed with powerful beats of his wings to catch the winds aloft. Looking down with the magnified vision of a raptor, he could see the details of the landscape passing rapidly thousands of feet below.

He came upon Nain in a very short time. Nothing remained except the concrete pier, just now re-emerging from the waters. The buildings were in complete ruin and spirits of lost souls were everywhere. Using his raptor's vision, he scanned to the south as he turned again in that direction. He saw the towers of the cities. So, they remained. He must see them at close range. He flew onward, swiftly consuming the miles. As he penetrated the air, his body sensed a gradual increase in temperature and dryness, searing dryness. Below, the greenery of his home country was fading, becoming caked, cracked and lifeless earth. He soared over Montreal, where he had lived for a time as a young man.

The lifeless canyons between the buildings were cluttered and dirty. Soil sifted down the streets, carried on the howling winds, forming drifts like rivers of brown snow. It piled up on the abandoned vehicles, furniture and debris, burying some and grotesquely altering the appearance of others. He saw no one.

To the west, he sensed there was water . . . and life. He would search for signs. The St. Lawrence River stretched to the west below him, a bare, dry and barren valley. He followed it to its source, the former Great Lakes.

Toronto lay destroyed. He could tell many fierce battles had been fought here. The devastation was complete, yet plant life was beginning to return to the open areas, sprinkling tinges of green into the parklands. To the south, he saw water some fifteen miles away. And smoke. There was a wisp of smoke rising from a small area of greenery near the shore. Could this be where some people now lived? He flew to the south, maintaining his height to maximize the area he could survey. He began to circle as he approached the smoke. Yes, here were some people. They were gaunt and in poor health, with large sores on their naked bodies. They carried pointed wooden spears and knives, so perhaps they hunted for game. As he watched, the people were foraging in the bush for fruit and berries, eating whatever they found immediately.

Then, hiding behind the hulk of an old sunken ship, now high and dry on the land, he saw others lying in wait. They were using the huge propellers and rudder for cover as they surveyed the trees. They pointed and spoke softly among themselves. It was apparent they were trying to determine the numbers of the other group. The people in the bushes were moving in the general direction of the derelict ship and Hinoch sensed their meeting would not be friendly. He gave a mighty screech to warn them. One or two looked up, then the other three. They gathered together, completely enthralled at the sight of him soaring so high above.

Of course, he thought to himself, *they may have never seen a bird, let alone Nektoralik. If they remain distracted like this, they will be even more vulnerable to attack.* The other group had seen him as well, but had quickly refocused on their objective.

As he watched, the group from the ship attacked. The people in the trees responded quickly despite the distraction. Each group began mutilating the other with rocks, knives and spears. They were so weak and diseased they could hardly mount a fierce fight. Rather than dealing quick deathblows, they harried and bloodied each other until they succumbed from the slow, painful attrition of many small wounds. It reminded him of himself those many years ago when, starving, he had harpooned a small whale. He had barely mustered the strength to bring the source of his survival up through the ice. He had nearly died with his salvation in his hands.

The battle limped along for thirty minutes at most, ending when the two remaining survivors of the bush group fled. The intruders had killed three of their quarry at a loss of two of their own.

Immediately, they began to eat their prey and their own fallen, carving the flesh from the bones and skewering it on sticks to place over the fire. The spirits of the dead were floating around the scene, trying to find new hosts, but none of the survivors was aware of them. No one invited them into their soul. After a time, they drifted off, lost forever.

As dark settled over the scene, the victors began to dance around the fire, singing loudly. The food was giving them some energy, but it seemed unwise to him for them to expend such hard-won energy.

Celebrate when the times are good; conserve everything *when times are bad,* he thought to himself.

Hinoch recognized some of the songs drifting up to him. He had heard them on the radio when he lived in Montreal. They had been handed down among these people now for more than eighty years. The old memories of his school years still haunted him. He remembered Lucien, the one person who had helped him to cope with those foreign surroundings. He remembered talking at length with his song brother about his reactions to the people from the cities, their insensitivity to one another and their artificial priorities. He had told him of his belief that the corrupted state of this society would lead to its demise. Even at that young age, he had anticipated the collapse, but he had never imagined the complete devastation he was discovering today.

They tried to retain some of their traditions, he thought. *Unfortunately, they did not possess traditions that were useful for their survival as their environment fell apart so rapidly around them.*

He noted also that these people made no concerted attempt to foster their health. The diseased flesh they were eating had not been on the fire long enough and they made no attempt to clean or groom themselves.

Disease must take many from their numbers, he concluded.

Again, Hinoch turned to the west. The lakes below him were tiny, polluted remnants of their former oceanic proportions. He sensed and saw small bands of people and even smaller numbers of animals roaming the surface. He spoke with the spirits of these animals, finding that they were in poor health and living short lives filled with deprivation. The waters of the lakes were devoid of life.

Each city site he encountered was a barren hulk of concrete and asphalt. In each place he could see that plant life was beginning to take hold again. Nature was renewing itself, but the process would be long and uncertain. He questioned whether these small marauding bands of people would persist long enough to benefit from the improving conditions.

Yes, he had chosen the promised land well. The legends of his people would remember these times as the rescue of human beings. The Inuit, it appeared, stood a good chance to inherit Earth.

Across the barren mountains of the west he soared. No trees remained. The mountains were huge piles of bare rock. Only the valleys showed faint signs of greenery. Out over the vast Pacific he flew. Life in the waters was slowly returning, but many species were now extinct. For that reason, others would proliferate to excess, generating multiple cycles of plenty and devastation. Until the natural ratios of predator and prey were re-established, life would be a protracted series of feasts and famines.

He flew tirelessly, his powerful wings bearing him across the vast distances. He sought diligently over the entire planet, anywhere that showed any likelihood of supporting life, but found only small numbers of human beings scattered in small groups. The aborigines of Australia were the only group he discovered that appeared to have survived with only minor depletion in numbers. Even the remotely located natives of the Amazon valley had suffered greatly from the huge shifts in their ecology.

It seemed the environments that were the most lush before the changes began were the hardest hit. Strangely, the harsh climates of Australia and the polar regions had seen comparatively less deviation from their previous norms.

He turned north again. As he approached the polar regions, it was clear that here, wildlife was more abundant, but there were no people. Even the natives of this country had not prevailed. Hinoch surmised they had given up too many of their traditional ways, had been too dependent upon technology. As the industrial machinery of the south had fallen into hibernation, the regular shipments of supplies had dwindled, then ceased. The people had perished. He would tell his son, Abel, to move his people west across the Arctic as their numbers grew. Then they could move south, slowly re-populating the land.

The traditional wisdom of his people had served him well and the spirits of his predecessors had given him good counsel. The future would be bright for his people.

Hinoch set course for his home.

He attuned himself to his body and was led to Joanna's monument where he saw a new stone had been laid and carved in the form of the raven. Something else was here, something compelling and ominous. He circled, wanting to visit Joanna's monument, wanting to examine the magnificent white raven more closely, but his sixth sense was on full alert, warning him of a significant event about to unfold.

As he came to earth, he felt a presence that struck fear in his heart. The ground shook and a voice boomed in his ears. He closed his eyes and knelt in fear for his continued existence. "Hinoch, I am Torngassuk, lord of the Earth. My brother, Nekkavik, lord of the Seas and I have observed your progress and are well pleased with what you have accomplished. We wish to ensure that your people thrive and build a great new future. We possess knowledge, knowledge that, if properly used, can ensure their success."

After a few moments, he dared to open his eyes. The entire area was bathed in a blue fire. He was encircled by fire, yet he did not feel the heat. "I . . . I do not know what to say. I am accustomed to communing with the spirits of my people, sharing the knowledge we have gained over time."

"Their knowledge is impressive, but it is limited to the perfection of a subsistence way of living. Our knowledge of the sciences will permit you to enhance your lives beyond the greatest accomplishments Nuna has yet seen."

"But, what of nature?"

"If you use this knowledge as it is intended, nature will thrive under your governance. Be not afraid, Hinoch, you will be the bearer of good news."

It was now that it fully entered his awareness; he was about to evolve. He understood he was entirely of the spirit world now, but what was he about to become ... a supreme being, like those with whom he was conversing? Hinoch shivered uncontrollably at the energy coursing into his being as Torngassuk and Nekkavik filled his consciousness with knowledge.

When he opened his eyes again, the fire was subsiding to a glow and the earth merely trembled. Or was he the one trembling? He was uncertain. It became evident to him as he considered his lessons, and began to manipulate his new wisdom that with these skills, his people could achieve wonders never before seen on Nuna. He rested for a time after the customary quiet of the place returned, then sought counsel with his son and daughter to tell them of his adventures.

Joanna, love of my life, it is time for you to join with me again. Our people need us once more. I have been given great knowledge that I must share with you. Together, we can give it to our people.

I am here, my love. I have always been with you.

Her form appeared, a barely visible wisp of light, beside Hinoch. They embraced, their bodies taking new form, filled with light.

To their surprise, they did not need to adopt the form of a bird to fly, but rose of their own volition.

Hinoch's immediate impulse, upon receiving the gift of Torngassuk and Nekkavik, had been to reveal everything to his children, but as he floated over the land, he realized he would be bringing them out of the Stone Age; their entire lives had been lived in a primitive setting. The vast changes would necessitate their evolution, their manipulation of the new information in small stages, gradually leveraging the skills he had given them into the skills of their future. For them to comprehend the full scope of what he foresaw would take time. No, he and Joanna must pass the knowledge of the gods to his children incrementally, so they fully understood the responsibilities of each new power he gave them.

Now he understood. His masterpiece would never be finished; it would grow and flourish . . . forever.

C.J. BEUHLER was born in Saskatchewan and grew up in Regina. During his career with the Canadian Air Force, he saw North America from coast to coast and from the arctic to the Gulf of Mexico. In that time, he encountered a generous measure of life and death drama. Upon reflection, he wanted to share some of those experiences, while commenting upon how we perceive the world and our place in it. *We Are Still Here* reveals this unique combination of experience and social commentary. C.J. Beuhler lives in Climax, Saskatchewan.